ALSO BY DON MANN WITH RALPH PEZZULLO

SEAL Team Six: Hunt the Wolf

SEAL Team Six: Hunt the Scorpion

SEAL Team Six: Hunt the Falcon

*Inside SEAL Team Six: My Life and Missions
with America's Elite Warriors*

SEAL
TEAM SIX:

HUNT THE JACKAL

DON MANN
WITH RALPH PEZZULLO

MULHOLLAND
BOOKS

HODDER

First published in Great Britain in 2014 by Mulholland Books
An imprint of Hodder & Stoughton
An Hachette UK company

First published in paperback in 2014

1

A CIP catalogue record for this title is available from the British Library

Paperback ISBN 978 1 444 76910 4
eBook ISBN 978 1 444 76911 1

Printed and bound by Clays Ltd, St Ives plc

Hodder & Stoughton policy is to use papers that are natural, renewable
and recyclable products and made from wood grown in sustainable forests.
The logging and manufacturing processes are expected to conform
to the environmental regulations of the country of origin.

Hodder & Stoughton Ltd
338 Euston Road
London NW1 3BH

www.hodder.co.uk

"He who has a why to live for can bear almost any how."
—Friedrich Nietzsche

*To all the brave men and women who courageously
defend and nurture freedom and justice*

SEAL TEAM SIX: HUNT THE JACKAL

CHAPTER ONE

> *Reality is that which, when you stop believing in it, doesn't go away.*
>
> —Philip K. Dick

FORTY-TWO-YEAR-OLD Lisa Clark sat in the pearl-white Jacuzzi spa bath with the red monoliths of Sedona shining through the floor-to-ceiling window, reading *Fifty Shades of Grey*. Sandalwood candles burned on the rough slate border as she reached for the glass of La Crema Russian River Valley Chardonnay. A senator's wife and mother of two children who worked hard to maintain her long dancer's body, she was indulging in a rare moment of relaxation and guilty pleasure. Usually she wore her hair pulled back or tied in a French braid, but now she wore it loose to her shoulders.

As she read, real guilt started to spread through her body. The relationship between college student Ana and überbusinessman Christian Grey brought back memories of her own one-year affair with a worldly restaurant owner she met while working as a waitress in Washington, D.C.

Twenty-four years ago she was a tall, blond, fresh-faced

eighteen-year-old girl from the little town of Boykins, Virginia, perky in every way, taking courses at American U when she met Henri Gaudier. The world-famous chef-restaurateur represented everything she thought she wanted—worldliness, sophistication, and high-society status among a network of rich and powerful friends. Her sole claim to fame at the time was having placed as runner-up in the Miss Southampton High beauty pageant. Unlike the character of Ana in the book, Lisa wasn't a virgin when they met—but at least she was uninitiated to hard drugs, S&M, and group sex.

Henri quickly changed that. He also introduced her to senators, generals, cabinet members, sports stars, mobsters, movie stars, and other celebrities. Along the way she learned that sex and drugs formed a dark, illicit river that many famous and highly esteemed people in Washington waded into when they thought they were safe.

For the past twenty-three years, since the night she met Jesse Abrams Clark at a Bastille Day party at the French embassy in Washington, she had tried her best to erase the interlude with Henri from her memory. Clark was a young navy lieutenant working as an aide at the White House then. Now he was the senior Republican senator from Virginia, but still straightlaced, aggressive, self-confident, and solidly Christian.

She'd never told him about the wild, sexually adventurous year she'd spent with Henri, or her cocaine habit, or the night it ended. She had never fessed up to anyone, including herself, how her time with Henri had affected her and made her wary of losing control.

She considered that now as warm sandalwood-scented water churned around her, softening her skin and relaxing her muscles. The past was a burden, and being a senator's wife wasn't easy, despite its many rewards. Maybe that explained the weariness and ennui she'd been experiencing lately. In addition to the several weekly appearances she was required to make with her husband on the Washington social circuit, she had to attend political and charity events and run two households—one in Chevy Chase, Maryland, and one a farm outside Charlottesville, Virginia. She also served as her husband's cheerleader and political advisor.

Together they had two children, whose upbringing was primarily her responsibility. Fifteen-year-old Jesse Abrams Clark, Jr., was the apple of Lisa's eye. Jesse Jr. was not only handsome and athletic, with a magical smile, but he and she had had a natural rapport from the day he was born.

Seventeen-year-old Olivia was more like her father—strong-willed and reserved. She was tall and blond and had her father's strong jaw and steady blue eyes. Olivia was always respectful to her mother, but Lisa hadn't felt close to her since Olivia entered puberty and started directing most of her attention to horseback riding and the Presbyterian Church.

Lisa had planned this trip to Sedona, Arizona, as an opportunity for the two of them to spend time together before Olivia entered Duke University in the fall.

Now her daughter sat in the adjoining bedroom of the Enchantment Resort *casita* ostensibly studying the Bible, but really posting pictures on Facebook of herself and her mom standing outside the *casita* in their climbing apparel.

As Lisa read further, lascivious memories rose to the surface of her consciousness and burst like bubbles. One of them involved a cocaine-fueled night with Henri and an NFL star in Henri's suite at the Watergate Hotel. One moment they were laughing and drinking champagne with dinner, the next she was naked on Henri's king-sized bed with her ankles and wrists tied to the bedposts.

She quickly stopped and put down the book. Almost simultaneously, the chimes rang at the front door of the *casita*. Craning her long neck toward the iPhone on the counter, Lisa saw that it was 6:13 p.m. One of the maids had probably come to turn down the beds, or maybe Olivia had requested something from room service.

She thought about the dinner reservation she had made for seven thirty and what she wanted to wear. In the background she heard footsteps and muffled voices.

"Olivia," she called, her voice bouncing off the tile floor. "Darling."

Deciding to call the concierge to ask him to send someone to wash and blow out her hair, she stood and started to reach for the courtesy phone on the wall.

Just then the door opened and a young Hispanic woman appeared in the doorway.

She was dressed in black pants and a white polo and wore a silver crucifix around her neck. "Good evening, *Señora*," she said.

"I'm sorry," Lisa answered, covering her breasts with her left arm. "Did my daughter call you?"

"No, *Señora*," the girl responded, moving her right arm in front of her; it held a dark pistol equipped with a silencer. "But if you step out of there and come with me, there won't be a problem."

Coldness spread through Lisa's body. She couldn't imagine this was anything more than a routine robbery, or that the girl, who seemed to be no more than sixteen, was capable of real violence. She turned and started to reach again for the phone.

The girl stepped forward quickly, slapped Lisa's hand away, and aimed the pistol at her head. "You make one sound and I'll shoot you!"

Lisa nodded and swallowed hard. Blood burned her temples, and her knees shook. She remembered Olivia in the next room and hoped she'd run or called for help.

Two young men stepped inside the bathroom dressed in matching white polo shirts and black pants. They also looked like teenagers—smart and alert and with silver crucifixes around their necks.

One of them—a boy with black hair and a scar across his lip—held something over Lisa's nose and mouth. She inhaled the smell of chloroform as she heard the boy say, "We're here, *Señora*, in the name of La Santísima Muerte. She wants you to come with us."

Her legs started to melt. The two men held her naked body and lifted her out of the water. She felt a tingle between her legs, then lost consciousness.

SEAL Team Six (a.k.a. DEVGRU) Chief Warrant Officer Tom Crocker held on to the overhead bar that stretched between the twin side doors of the Black Hawk as the helicopter banked right over parched terrain in northwest Syria. The helo was hit by a headwind, which jerked it sharply right and kicked up a big cloud of dust.

"Hold on," he shouted to his teammates behind him. The darkening sky ahead turned eerie shades of orange and purple.

Like a bruise, he said to himself. The whole country was more like an open wound now, with over seventy thousand civilian dead and a strange alliance of Sunni rebels and terrorists, including the al-Qaeda–linked Al Nusrah, pitted against the repressive and stubborn Assad regime, supported by Iran, Russia, China, and Hezbollah.

Crocker didn't really give a shit about the regional politics, or the civil war in Syria. He was here with his team to complete a specific mission, which in this case involved a downed MQ-1B Predator drone. He was scanning the landscape for it now as his men—Cal, Ritchie, Mancini, Akil, and Davis—discussed Ritchie's upcoming bachelor party and wedding in the tilt-up seats as though they were back at ST-6 command or hanging at their favorite watering hole in Virginia Beach.

"I'm talking crazier than a Mötley Crüe binge," Ritchie shouted over the engines. "A final blowout tribute to the end of my bachelor days."

"I saw them perform in El Paso in '02. One of the wildest shows I've ever seen," Davis commented, which was somewhat surprising since he was the mildest, most soft-spoken guy on the team.

"You into Mötley Crüe?" Ritchie asked.

"I wouldn't say I'm into them," Davis replied, screaming over the engine and rotors. "I mean, I don't have any of their tunes on my iPod. I'm just saying they put on a hell of a show."

"Like we give a shit," Akil shouted back. He was the team's

8

muscular Egyptian American logistics expert, and the lone bachelor, except for the Asian American sniper, Cal, who almost never spoke. "Let's hear more about the bachelor party."

"What?" Ritchie asked as the helicopter passed over the ruins of a stone structure that looked like it was centuries old.

"The bachelor party!"

"It's gonna be so wild I'm gonna have you guys sign nondisclosure forms," Ritchie boasted.

"Me, I'm not signing shit," Akil growled.

Davis: "I might have to pass."

"Your loss," Ritchie replied, grinning from ear to ear and lighting up his roughly handsome face. Immediately likeable, with a big smile and high cheekbones, he resembled the ballplayer Johnny Damon. "Dude, I gotta swear you guys to secrecy," he continued, "because there's gonna be some wild shit going down, which I'm definitely partaking in. Monica can't find out."

Monica was his bride-to-be—a former swimsuit model and now a successful real estate developer with a killer body and expensive tastes. Crocker thought she might be out of Ritchie's league in terms of ambition and sophistication, but he kept that to himself.

"Rich, you might not want to hear this now, but as your friend I gotta tell you: Honesty is the bedrock of marriage," Davis shouted. He had young kids and a pretty wife and had put his wild motorcycle-riding past behind him.

"Thanks, Reverend Holier-Than-Thou Dickhead," Ritchie shot back. "I'll work on that...after I tie the knot."

"You gonna have strippers?" Cal asked, holding a PSG-1 sniper rifle across his lap.

Akil turned to him and said, "Look who's interested in strippers."

"With special skills, man. And that's just the start," Ritchie answered.

Akil: "When? Where? Count me in!"

Mancini wasn't interested in the bachelor party or the locker room banter. This was men's work, given that they were operating in someone else's country without permission and both Syrian Army and Hezbollah units had been spotted in the vicinity, neither of which were likely to greet them with handshakes and pats on the back. Searching the rough terrain with Steiner Commander military binoculars from the door opposite Crocker, he spotted something white against the black backdrop.

Leaning into the fuselage, he yelled, "I see something, boss. Target at nine o'clock!"

Crocker took a couple of steps toward Mancini, leaned out the door, and spotted the drone, which looked like a crumpled toy.

Cupping his hands together, he shouted at the pilot, then pointed. "The target's on our left!"

The 160th Special Operations Aviation Regiment (SOAR) pilot turned and nodded back, his wide face covered with reddish stubble. When he banked the helo over a parched wadi and some dried scrub, the MQ-1B Predator drone came into view, its wide nose pointing up like a sea lion lounging on a rock.

For some technical reason unclear to Crocker, it hadn't self-destructed on impact like it was programmed to do. Black Cell's job was to blow it up before the Syrian Army or their Hezbollah/Iranian partners got their dirty paws on it and purloined the advanced technical doodads and three AGM-114 Hellfire missiles.

Black Cell was a badass special compartmentalized cell at SEAL Team Six—designed to conduct the most dangerous, top secret counterterrorism missions on direct orders from the White House and CIA.

Minus the front antenna and intact, the drone measured twenty-seven feet long and had a wingspan over fifty-five feet. The whole thing weighed 1,130 pounds. Crocker had watched one being unloaded from a C-150 Hercules in a box called a coffin and assembled in three sections.

He didn't have the patience for highly detailed, tight little tasks like that and preferred roaming, canoeing, riding, or running in the outdoors in his spare time. Even putting together bookcases from IKEA drove him nuts.

The Black Hawk hovered about eighty feet over the site, which was the best the pilot could do, given the wind, sand, and dust. Not the ideal platform to launch from, but in their line of work conditions were rarely perfect.

Crocker gave the thumbs-up and pointed to the ground. The guys readied their gear and weapons, and Mancini and Akil dropped two special braided nylon ropes out the left door that were anchored to a hoist in the helo.

Davis and Akil fast-roped first, grabbing on to the rope with two leather-gloved hands, then stepping out of the helicopter and pinching the rope between their Salomon Quest boots to regulate their descending speed. It was like sliding down a fire pole, only a whole lot riskier. Black Cell had practiced fast-roping so many times it was as automatic as tying the laces on their shoes.

Light was right, in this case because they wanted to move quickly in and out, and a heavy load would make roping down from that height a hell of a lot more perilous than it was already, given the wind and dust. Which was why Crocker decided to stop Ritchie and Cal before they went out the door. Unlike the others, they wore big packs loaded with C-4, detonators, and other explosives gear.

"You guys wait on the bird," Crocker yelled. "We'll secure the site and help you unload once it lands."

"Piece of cake," Ritchie shouted back, pointing to the ground.

"No, Rich. You and Cal wait here!" Crocker commanded.

Ritchie nodded. Then Crocker grabbed hold of the rope and descended with Mancini beside him on the parallel rope. The SEALs were dressed in Crye Precision Desert Digital combat uniforms with Alta kneepads and duty belts packed with multiple Flyye pouches for MR141, MK18, and M67 grenades, canteens, and extra magazines. Additional Flyye pouches on their backs and chests accommodated MK124 flares, light sticks, Motorola Saber portable radios, VIP infrared strobes, energy gel, and SOG knives. On their heads, MICH 2000 helmets with SureFire strobe lights, quad-tube night-vision goggles, and bone phones, which sat on their cheekbones and allowed them to hear radio traffic through bone-conduction technology. Davis and Cal wore armored vests with ceramic plates. The others had chosen not to.

Crocker carried his favorite HK416 assault rifle with EOTech sight. Maneuverability, accuracy, and firepower all in one very deadly weapon. Others carried MP7s—German weapons chambered with 4.6x30mm rounds with a greater ability to defeat body armor. All were armed with standard SEAL-issue SIG Sauer P226 handguns. Akil and Davis also hauled single-shot, break-action M-79 grenade launchers, even though most guys on the team preferred the newer M203.

As soon as Crocker and Mancini hit the ground, Ritchie and Cal pulled the ropes back up into the helicopter body and the Black Hawk banked left over a two-hundred-yard hill. Akil, Davis, Mancini, and Crocker took cover behind rocks and established a perimeter. As Crocker surveyed the darkening landscape through his NVGs, Mancini ventured out to inspect the drone.

No one appeared in their vicinity, but a warm wind blew across the hills and through the scrub, creating an eerie hiss.

Through the headset built into his helmet, Crocker heard Mancini say, "Pred looks untouched. Must have been a technical problem, because I see no evidence of enemy fire."

"Good," Crocker said back into the mike.

"The Hellfires are intact. So are the multispectrum targeting system, infrared sensor, and TV camera." Technology, food, and history were Mancini's three big passions.

"All we're taking are the Hellfires," Crocker growled back in a low voice. "The rest we're going to blow up."

"Damn shame."

"Orders."

"It's a sweet piece of technology," Mancini continued in a low, gruff voice. "Each one of these babies runs about twenty mill without the bells and whistles." He loved technological doodads and was the guy on the team who coordinated with DARPA, which was the branch of the Pentagon that developed new military equipment.

"Not our call," Crocker said back, continuing to eyeball the stark landscape.

"What do you mean, not our call? Who pays for this stuff?"

Mancini often complained about government waste and profligate spending. Crocker jibed back: "Since when do you pay taxes?"

"Very funny. Actually—"

Crocker cut him off. "Not now." This wasn't the time for a personal anecdote, or any other kind of distraction. They were in Assad territory with a job to do. The wind started blowing harder.

Akil, twenty yards to Crocker's right, watched a little twister climb the hills to the east through a long-distance night scope. "All clear," he said over the radio.

Crocker: "Good. Let's get this over quick."

Mancini: "You want me to try to disassemble the satellite dish and communication component?"

"No time. Just detach the Hellfires from the missile pylons."

"Roger."

Crocker looked up at the darkening sky and realized that the helicopter hadn't returned yet. "Where the fuck is the helo?" he asked.

"Maybe they found a falafel stand and stopped," Akil wisecracked back. All he seemed to think about was food and willing young women, and he had an unquenchable appetite for both.

Crocker turned to the commo man, Davis, to his left and said, "Contact the pilot and tell him he's clear to land."

"Roger, boss."

"Might want to set it on that patch over there past that clump of scrub," he added, pointing to the spot. "Remind him to keep the engines running."

"Will do."

Akil: "Tell him we plan to be out of here faster than a knife fight in a shithouse."

Their job was to retrieve the Hellfires, then destroy the wreckage, which they'd do as soon as Ritchie (the explosives guy) landed with the C-4. Northern Syria wasn't a location Crocker felt like hanging in. Major cities had been turned into rubble by the Assad army as the rest of the world watched. Lately, Assad had attacked his own people with chemical weapons. Still the UN had done nothing but talk. Like Somalia and Rwanda all over again, which would probably yield another anarchic state that the United States would have to deal with one way or another. Global politics made him sick.

This mission had been a last-minute emergency call as they were packing their gear and getting ready to leave the secret base in Israel for home. Lately he and his team had been spending a lot of time launching ops against Hezbollah and the Quds Force—both controlled by Iran. Dangerous, seat-of-their-pants ops in unfriendly territory.

Here they were again; friggin' Syria this time. Crocker heard a high whining sound past the hills, followed by a loud metallic noise that echoed and faded.

"What the fuck was that?" he asked, sweat forming under his helmet from the dry desert heat.

"Didn't sound good," Mancini said.

An understatement, to say the least.

Akil: "Maybe it was a camel fart."

"Or an explosion."

Crocker asked, "Where's the Black Hawk? Anyone see it?"

"Fuck, no. Don't hear it, either."

"What happened? Somebody tell me something," he said, growing anxious.

Mancini: "No flash of light, no flames."

Davis shouted urgently, "No response from the pilot, either."

"You try the copilot? Cal? Ritchie?" Crocker asked, hoping it wasn't what he thought it was.

"I did, yeah. Tried all three."

"And?"

Davis shook his head.

Crocker's stomach sank. Grimacing, he glanced at his watch. The time-on-target (TOT) was already approaching ten minutes, which was too damn long, especially with enemy in proximity. Also, the explosion, or whatever it was, was sure to attract attention. He'd operated practically everywhere in the Middle East before, with the exception of Syria. Given the Assad regime's longstanding support of Palestinian terrorists and friendship with Russia, it was never a place he wanted to go.

"You sure that piece-of-shit radio is working and you're getting no signal from the helo?" Crocker asked.

"Positive, boss," Davis answered.

"Try again!"

Davis did with a frown and shook his blond head.

Crocker groaned. "All right, you stay here with Mancini. Akil, come with me."

CHAPTER TWO

We meet our destiny on the road we take to avoid it.
—Carl Jung

THE LANDSCAPE had turned a thick, almost furry dark. And the moon hadn't risen yet. All they had to navigate by was their NVGs, which proved awkward because the two SEALs were moving fast over rocky, uncertain terrain around the crest of a hill. They weren't following a path, just picking their way over loose rock, sand, and gravel at a thirty-five-degree angle, carrying their packs and weapons.

Crocker hoped they'd find the helo intact with maybe some minor mechanical problem, or hear over the radio that for one reason or another, the pilot had had to turn the helo around and had returned to Israel.

Even if that meant he and the other four SEALs were marooned in Syria for the time being, he'd take that outcome over the more ominous alternative. He was already planning how they could hunker down and defend themselves until relief arrived.

"You see anything?" he whispered back at Akil.

"No, but I smell fuel."

Not a good sign, but Crocker saw nothing burning. And no lights.

He sniffed the air. "Fuel?" he asked. "You sure you're not smelling your cheap-ass Egyptian cologne?"

"I'm a Ralph Lauren man all the way. Classy shit."

"Shit is right," Crocker said. "Your big nose must be better than mine. Which way is the smell coming from?"

Akil licked his index finger and held it up to determine the direction of the wind. He pointed up the far side of hill. "This way."

"That's west."

The next gust of desert wind carried the unmistakable scent, which sickened Crocker even further. Richie and Cal had recently healed from injuries sustained chasing some Quds Force operatives in South America. Ritchie, in particular, had suffered a nasty bullet wound to his jaw, which required extensive plastic surgery. He was scheduled to get married at the end of the month. All the guys on Crocker's team were like brothers. He didn't have the stomach for more wounds and broken bones.

The higher they climbed, the stronger the stench of fuel.

He slapped his headset and addressed Davis. "Alpha Two, Alpha One here. You hear anything from the guys on the helo?"

"Negative, Alpha One."

Squelching the fears running through his brain, he focused on the uneven ground ahead. Then he heard Davis's voice through the headset, more urgent this time: "Alpha One, looks like we've got something approaching."

Another unwelcome complication. "What's that?"

"Vehicles," Davis reported from near the Predator. "Still too far away to ID them. All we see are headlights. What's your status?"

"We smell fuel but haven't established visuals."

"Helo fuel?"

"Possibly," Crocker answered. "You got anything in terms of number of vehicles or whether they're armed or not?"

"Negative. But I'll update you when we have more info. Over and out."

Crocker stepped around Akil, who had paused to take a swig of Powerade. Akil was a beast and a former marine sergeant who spoke multiple Middle Eastern languages. If Mancini was Crocker's right arm, he used Akil like his right leg. In fact, he depended on them all, completely, which was why they made an especially lethal and useful team. Six of the best warriors on the planet acting as one.

JSOC, SOCOM, the CIA, and the White House requested the services of Black Cell so often, they had them operating overseas up to three hundred days out of the year. Not that Crocker was complaining. It was good to be appreciated, and to be doing the work you were born to do with men you admired and respected.

He climbed another three yards, stopped, held on to a gnarled branch poking through some slatelike rock, looked back at Akil, and asked, "You coming?"

"It's that friggin' plantar fasciitis acting up again," Akil said, holding his right foot. He'd injured it during an op inside Iran.

"Stop whining."

Crocker turned and in his right periphery spotted the tail rotor of the UH-60M Black Hawk slowly turning against the backdrop of a shade-lighter sky. His heart clutched in his chest. He took a deep breath, pointed to the location, and grunted, "Akil, look!"

Together the two men ran the approximately thirty yards, Akil's plantar fasciitis be damned. The stench of fuel grew stronger with each step. So did their sense of despair.

The scene was eerily quiet. No moaning, or screams for help; only the wind rattling the dry leaves around them and the creak of the damaged tail rotor. The Black Hawk lay on its side like an elephant taking a nap. The moment Crocker saw the smashed cockpit and the dark outlines of two bodies by the side door, his medical training kicked in.

He wasn't a team leader or friend anymore, he was a SEAL corpsman doing his job. Ignoring the spilled fuel and the danger of the whole damn thing igniting any second, he removed his NVGs and illuminated the red lens flashlight that he kept on his belt. Then he hurried from one man to the other, checking for vital signs, starting with the pilot, who lay across the seat with his forehead and the top of his head smashed in. Purple-gray brain matter spilled across the sides of his head like a Halloween wig.

Still, Crocker checked for a pulse. Negative.

He moved to the copilot, who lay on his stomach. Gently turning him over, Crocker saw a big dark wound below the copilot's armored vest and the place near his groin where he'd been blown open. Tendons, bone, and flesh all in shades of red and pink. He had no pulse, either.

As surreal as the scene was, it was the strange serene smile on the copilot's face that really struck him—as though he had seen something pleasant, or had actually welcomed death.

Moving to the middle of the wreck, Crocker saw Ritchie, and the tragedy hit him fully. For several seconds he had trouble breathing, because his buddy and teammate of eight years had literally been cut in half at the waist by a piece of the top rotor. His stomach, liver, and intestines spilled over the ground, and his dark eyes were wide open and protruding out of his head like exclamation points.

Crocker reached down and started to push Ritchie's guts back inside him. When he heard Akil gasp behind him, he stopped, muttered a silent prayer, and closed Ritchie's eyes.

Then he stood and backed away, taking care not to step in the big circle of blood, as though that might constitute some form of desecration. Looking over his shoulder, he saw tears streaming down Akil's rough face.

Crocker muttered, "Oh, fuck." Then, remembering that there had been four men on the helo, asked, "Where's Cal?"

As combat-hardened and mentally tough as they were, they had hearts, consciences, and feelings. Akil's mouth hung open, forming a big O, but no sound came out.

"Cal? Where is he?" Crocker asked, momentarily dissociated from his body.

Akil pointed to Ritchie. "You forgot to...to cover him."

Crocker reached into his backpack for his E&E kit, in which he usually carried a tightly folded space blanket, then remembered that he hadn't packed one this time.

"Where the fuck is Cal?"

He was about to climb into the fuselage when he saw Akil pointing to a body lying facedown under one of the wrecked T700-GE-701D engines. Crocker got on his hands and knees, ducked under the still-hot engine, leaned close to Cal's ear, and whispered, "Cal."

No answer.

Louder, he asked, "Cal, can you hear me?"

He carefully reached around to the front of Cal's neck, located the carotid artery, and felt a faint pulse. A sign of hope.

Turning back to Akil, he said urgently, "Call Davis, tell him we found the helo. Three dead, one seriously wounded and in need of immediate medevac. We're gonna need to evacuate the bodies. We're also gonna need additional C-4 to destroy the Black Hawk."

Akil choked back the contents of his stomach. "Boss..."

Crocker carefully ran his hands along the front of Cal's body. He felt warm blood coming from a wound near his stomach and stopped.

"Akil, I need your help."

When he looked back he saw Monica's face where Akil's used to be. The vision was so real and unexpected that he said, "I'm sorry, Monica. But...unexpected stuff happens."

She opened her mouth like she was about to start shouting.

Instead he heard Akil ask, "Boss, who you talking to?"

Crocker blinked and, seeing Akil where Monica had been a second ago, said, "Come closer. I need you to help me turn him over."

Akil wiped tears away with the back of his hand and said, "Yeah."

"Hold him under the shoulder. On the count of three. Slow and careful."

"Right."

"One, two, three."

The wound was higher than he thought. Feeling air being sucked into it, he said, "Reach in my med kit. Give me a blowout patch, QuikClot, and the plastic wrapper the QuikClot comes in."

Crocker did a quick primary survey of Cal's ABCs. Airway first. Cal was unconscious but breathing, which meant his airway was clear. Crocker cleared Cal's mouth of blood and sand, then turned Cal's head up in the sniffing position to facilitate breathing and made sure his tongue would not obstruct the airway.

Breathing: somewhat labored, although full and bilateral. Circulation: weak and thready.

Having completed the primary survey of life-threatening injuries, Crocker moved on to the secondary survey, including a full head-to-toe check.

Disability: Crocker saw no obvious trauma to the head or face. Cal's pupils appeared equal in size and were reactive to light, and there was no indication of fluid oozing from his ears or nose. Next, Crocker felt gently along Cal's neck and back and found no abnormalities in his spinal column.

Exposure: Crocker checked for an exit wound. But found none. He removed the clothing from Cal's chest to get a good visual on skin color and feel for other problems.

With QuikClot and blowout patch in hand, he focused on the wound, ripping Cal's uniform open, holding the jagged two-inch incision open, applying the QuikClot, then covering the wound with a blowout patch and applying pressure.

It didn't look like a high-velocity wound, and hopefully hadn't done too much damage, like puncturing an internal organ or the stomach and releasing poisonous digestive enzymes. Crocker knew that lung tissue was less dense and had more elasticity than, say, the liver, spleen, or adipose tissue, which have little elasticity and are easily injured.

All this information was burning through his head as he held the bandage down with one hand and applied pressure to the femoral artery with the other.

He looked up at Akil and said, "We've got to get him out of here, in case the helo catches fire."

Akil nodded, but he still didn't seem focused.

Crocker made sure the blowout patch and the plastic he had taped over the wound were secure, then rolled Cal toward him until he was on his side, positioned his top leg so that his hip and knee were at right angles, tipped his head back to keep the airway open, and with Akil's help slid him clear of the helo engine. They carried him by holding him under the legs, hips, shoulders, and head to a relatively flat spot about two hundred yards away, and laid him down.

"He'll be okay if we get help fast, his vitals remain stable, and he doesn't go into shock," Crocker whispered.

Akil removed his helmet and shook his head. "How the fuck did this happen?" he asked.

"What?"

"To the helo. Was it hit by enemy fire?"

"I'm not an air crash forensics expert," Crocker answered. "Put your helmet back on. Make the call."

"What call?"

"I told you to call Davis. We need medevac. We need to remove the bodies and destroy the helo."

"Check."

"Do it now!"

Crocker's right hand shaking, he climbed into the helo and held on to the bar along the ceiling, using the red lens flashlight on his belt. He found no bullet holes or evidence of enemy fire. But that wasn't what he was looking for.

Past twisted seats, under a couple of rolled-up blankets, he saw Ritchie's backpack, which he recognized by the Shooter Jennings patch on top. The badass country singer's version of "Walk of Life" had been one of Ritchie's favorite songs. In his head Crocker heard Ritchie singing it in the shower at the base east of Tel Aviv like a drunken cowboy.

"He got the action, he got the motion..."

Hanging from the bar with one arm, Crocker hooked his boot under one of the straps and pulled it high enough to rest it on the side of the crushed seat. Then he reached down and grabbed it with his right hand.

The singing continued: *"Oh, yeah, the boy can play..."*

Outside on the ground, he checked to make sure that the C-4 and detonators were intact. They were. Seeing a smiling photo of Rich and Monica taped to the inside flap, Crocker bit his tongue.

Some things never get started. Some people die before they should. A cavalcade of images passed through his head—his high school girlfriend, Molly, who was killed in a car accident, his cousin Willie...

The taste of blood in his mouth, he climbed back inside to get the blankets and a tarp, which he used to cover the dead bodies.

Part of him wanted to hide under a blanket himself. War

sucked. Life made no goddamn sense. You worked hard, struggled, did the best you could, then died.

As they dragged Ritchie in two pieces away from the helicopter, Akil threw up over his hands.

Next thing Crocker remembered was reaching into the cockpit and slinging the pilot over his shoulder and feeling his dead weight, and warm blood dripping down his back.

Akil knelt next to the bodies, then lowered his head to the ground. When Crocker gently slapped the side of his helmet, he looked up with red-rimmed eyes and growled, "I'm praying, goddammit!"

All Crocker could say was "Finish."

Akil bowed again, stayed with his forehead to the dirt for twenty seconds, then mumbled some kind of salutation to God and got up.

"Okay."

Crocker asked, "You feel better?"

"Not really."

"Either way, I need you to stay alert," Crocker said.

"I'm trying!" Akil spat the words at him, raw and angry.

"What did Davis say?"

"Davis?"

Crocker said, "I asked you to call him, remember?"

"He said the Israelis have dispatched two helicopters. They're coming, okay? They're coming! Leave me the fuck alone."

Crocker grabbed the front of Akil's uniform. "We're both upset," he growled. "But this mission isn't over, and we need to think clearly!"

Akil partially snapped out of his funk and said, "You're right, boss. I know."

Crocker managed to keep his own emotions in check by focusing like a laser on the tasks ahead. First, he knelt down next to Cal and checked his pulse and vital signs again. They were steady, but weak.

Next, he got up and grabbed his weapon. "You've got light sticks and flares on you, correct?" he asked.

Akil felt the Flyye pouch on his chest and located them. "Yes. Yes."

He wouldn't let his mind wander back to Ritchie and the consequences of his death. Instead, he said, "All right. Wait here and continue to monitor Cal. I'm gonna place the C-4 on the Predator so we can blow it first. When you hear from me, you're gonna crack the light sticks and activate your strobe so the rescue pilot can locate you. Leave 'em around here, so he lands near the bodies."

"Leave what here?" Akil asked.

"The flares and strobe. I want the Israeli helo to land on this exact spot. He gets too close to the Black Hawk, a spark flies, and the whole thing blows. You understand me?"

Akil nodded his big head. "Yes."

"And stay near the radio. Listen and be alert."

"Got it."

"Make sure they load the bodies on board, and take care of Cal. Promise me you'll do that!"

"I will."

"Then have the pilot fly over the wreck and drop some flares. Make sure it catches on fire. Then get the fuck out of the area!"

"Got it!"

"You understand all that?"

"Yes. I said, I got it."

"You have a question, or a problem, you call me."

"Understood."

Crocker slapped Akil on the shoulder and said, "I'll see you in a few."

CHAPTER THREE

When you come to the end of your rope, tie a knot and hang on.

—Franklin D. Roosevelt

HE RAN in the direction of the Predator as fast as his legs could take him, fell, pulled himself up, lost his footing again, and put his arms out fast enough to keep his face from smashing into a boulder. But he let go of his HK416 in the process. So he recovered it, and wiped the dirt off the barrel by squeezing his thighs together and pulling it through.

He took a couple of deep breaths and told himself he had to calm down. The combination of adrenaline coursing through his body and the anger over the deaths filled him with a rage-like, I-don't-give-a-fuck-anymore kind of energy.

By the time he had counted to four, he became aware of guns discharging on the other side of the hill. Then Davis shouted anxiously over the headset. Crocker was too crazed to distinguish the words. But when he ran and peered past the edge of the hill, he saw what was going on.

There were two pickups between him and the Predator,

which was approximately a hundred yards away from where he stood. A fighter in the bed of one of the trucks was firing a nasty fifty-caliber machine gun, which made a loud clanging noise and resulted in Davis and Mancini being pinned behind boulders about twenty yards above and to the north of the downed drone.

In addition to the guy firing the fifty cal, Crocker spotted three others inching toward the Predator with AK-47s, and another two with AKs to the left trying to circle around behind Davis and Mancini.

Crocker took it all in, and thinking *No more dead*, bolted into action, running to within fifteen yards of the trucks. He stopped, breathed hard three times, and grabbed two of the four M67 grenades from the pouch on his chest. With the HK416 clutched in his left, he pulled the pins with his right hand and flung one after the other.

Someone near the pickup shouted in Farsi, and a second later a big explosion lifted the truck in the air. Crocker watched it hit the ground grill first, explode in flames, and turn over. It reminded him of a bucking bronco. He swung left around the truck, firing his HK416. *Phit-phit-phit*. One enemy cut down. *Phit-phit*. Two. *Phit-phit-phit*. Three.

The second truck caught fire and exploded to his right, knocking his feet out from under him. Crocker rolled over, assuming a prone position, reloaded, and continued to fire. When he couldn't see any more of the enemy through the smoke and flames, he stopped and inhaled fumes and dust.

His mouth and nostrils were clogged and his ears were numb. That didn't stop him from loading another cartridge into the HK416 and watching the light dance on the side of the Predator, which was strangely beautiful and reminded him of a Navajo rite he'd witnessed in the Arizona desert.

Hot air churned around him. He half-wished it would pick him up and pull him into the sky. Looking up, he saw a bright light approach and readied his weapon.

Through the sight, he saw a grinning Mancini hurry toward him, cradling an M4. "You okay, boss?" he shouted.

Crocker didn't hear him at first, but saw the tribal tattoo on his neck and his smile. "Stop grinning," he snarled.

Mancini said, "I like the way you took care of business."

"There's nothing to fucking smile about," Crocker said. "Ritchie, the pilot, and the copilot are dead."

He watched the expression change on Mancini's face.

"Cal's badly injured."

"No..."

Next thing he remembered was sitting in the rear door of the Israeli helicopter watching the Predator burn in the distance. A warm wind slapped his face and tore at the little hair he still had on the top of his head. He'd let God take all of it and his right arm, if he promised to bring Ritchie back.

He was trying to remember where they had come from and where they were going when he heard Akil's voice over the headset radio.

"Help! Taking fire from two directions! Need backup a-sap!"

"Hold on, Akil. We're on our way!"

The Israeli Yas'ur 2000 helicopter (a variant of a Sikorsky CH-53 Sea Stallion) was banking right, away from Akil and the downed Black Hawk, which was on the other side of the hill. Crocker looked back into the helo, spotted Davis by the door, and shouted urgently, "What the fuck is going on?"

"What do you mean?"

"We're going in the wrong direction."

"The medevac helo had to pull back. They were taking fire. The Israelis have called in another assault team to clear the area around the Black Hawk first."

"Where is it?"

"Don't know."

Crocker was already on his feet, climbing over the gear in the cargo bay. He squeezed between the fold-up seats, one of which was occupied by Mancini, then held on to the bar in front of the center console with his right and grabbed the pilot with his left. The pilot, who wore a green helmet, matching green flight suit with an Israeli patch on the shoulder, and goggles, vigorously signaled to Crocker to move back.

The helo was about 150 yards off the ground, flying blacked out.

Crocker didn't move. This time he slapped the pilot on the helmet. "Where's the assault team?" he asked.

"It's deploying now. Move back!"

"We left some men back there!" Crocker shouted, pointing behind him. "We've got to go back and get them!"

The pilot turned to his right, shouted something to the copilot in Hebrew, then placed a hand on Crocker's chest and shoved him. "Sit down!"

Crocker stumbled, caught himself on the back of Mancini's chair, then pushed forward aggressively. All the while, Akil screamed through the headset in his helmet, "I've got five minutes max! Soon I'll either run out of ammo or be overrun!"

"Listen—"

"Get back. That's an order!" the pilot shouted.

When Crocker didn't move, the copilot got out of his seat and met him in a half-crouch. "You heard him," he shouted in accented English, his face splashed with red instrument light. "The flying here is dangerous. We can't talk now! Sit down!"

Crocker grabbed him by the front of his flight suit and shouted into his blue eyes, "You don't understand. I've got a man trapped down there. We've got to turn this goddamn thing around."

"We don't take orders from you."

"Fuck that!"

He was about to lean past the copilot and grab the pilot when he felt something hit him in the throat and lost consciousness for several seconds. When he came to, he felt big bodies grappling around him.

Davis had the copilot pinned against the seat while Mancini pounded him in the stomach as the helo rocked from side to side.

Crocker heard the pilot scream something in Hebrew, then saw him raise a pistol and point it at Mancini's head. Not waiting to see if he was going to pull the trigger or not, Crocker grabbed the pilot's wrist and slammed it against the forward console. The pistol sprang loose, flipped in the air, crashed against the reinforced-glass forward window, and hit the floor.

The bird banked sharply right, throwing Mancini, Davis, and the copilot into a jumble of bodies against the cockpit side panel.

Crocker held on to the pilot bar, pulled his SIG Sauer P226

from its holster, and pressed it against the side of the pilot's face. "You either turn this fucking thing around and land it, or I'll put a bullet in your head!"

"Go to hell!"

"I'll take you with me."

When the copilot lunged for his arm, he clocked him with his elbow and then smashed him in the nose. Blood flew throughout the tight space.

Crocker pushed the pistol up to the pilot's cheekbone again. "I'm not fucking around!" he shouted. "Turn this thing around, now!"

The pilot swore up and down in Hebrew as he glanced at his wounded colleague, then up at Crocker. "You're out of control!"

With his free hand, Crocker grabbed hold of the flight director. "I'll do it myself if I have to."

The pilot tried to push his hand away. "No."

"Then turn this fucking thing around!"

"Okay."

Crocker kept the pistol pointed at the pilot's head as he slowed the helo and made a sweeping left turn. Within seconds, he spotted the burning flares on the hill ahead and tracers like little angry fireflies buzzing around the downed U.S. Black Hawk, reminding him of a bonfire on a beach.

"There it is!" he shouted.

"I see it."

"Akil, you still there?" he shouted into his headset.

"Yeah, boss! But I'm surrounded!"

"Hold on! We're coming!"

"Quick!"

Turning to Davis, Crocker shouted, "Strap the copilot in one of the fold-up chairs and zip-tie his wrists and ankles together! Then keep an eye on the pilot and give him directions. Mancini, come with me."

Together they readied the twin 7.62 machine guns mounted on the side windows and started directing fire at the enemy, kneeling around the downed U.S. Black Hawk. Through his NVGs Crocker saw Akil pinned down behind some boulders about twenty yards above where they had placed the flares.

Ducking inside the cabin and shouting at Davis, Crocker said, "Tell the pilot to circle around once, so we can lay down fire. Then I want him to land this baby on the patch of land near where the flares are burning."

"Got it!"

Yellow-and-white tracers flew up at them, and several bullets slammed into the reinforced metal fuselage. One glanced off the barrel of the machine gun Crocker was holding, making a screeching sound and sending up long white sparks, one of which burned his lip.

He kept shooting, picking out targets around the downed Black Hawk until the barrel of the weapon was red hot. From the cockpit, Davis launched the Hellfire missiles mounted on the sides of the Yas'ur. They slammed into the Black Hawk and exploded. Within seconds the wreckage was engulfed in orange flames.

"Excellent!" Crocker shouted.

"Fuck 'em."

"Now let's hit the enemy position near the top of the hill."

Relentless fire from the twin 7.62s and more Hellfire missiles silenced the enemy there. The helo circled once more; then Crocker instructed the pilot to set it down.

The heavy rotors turning and stirring up an enormous cloud of dust, Crocker and Davis jumped out. First, they found Cal, then loaded the bodies. Finally, they helped Akil aboard; he had been wounded in the arm by a piece of shrapnel from an enemy frag grenade.

They didn't pause to recon the scene, ID the enemy, or count enemy dead. Instead, Crocker checked Cal's vitals while the Israeli helicopter lifted off and a last enemy round zinged off his Kevlar helmet and crashed into the ceiling.

"Good thing you keep your bonnet on," commented Mancini.

The bleeding from Cal's wounded stomach seemed to have stopped, but his pulse was even weaker than before.

"Tell the pilot to radio ahead and have a medical team and ambulance ready," Crocker said.

"Roger," Davis responded.

Akil, seated with his back against the fuselage, his face covered with dirt and soot, his hands caked with dried blood, muttered, "Thanks."

Crocker sat beside him and started to roll up his sleeve to see where he'd been nicked. "Good work," he whispered.

But the big SEAL's eyes were already shut, and he started snoring.

Crocker's arms were weary and shaking from firing the big machine gun. He took a swig of Gatorade as the pilot announced that they had entered Israeli airspace.

No one responded.

To his right, Crocker saw Mancini looking down at

Ritchie's tarp-covered body on the floor. The recovered Hellfires were strapped to the floor beside him. Mancini's lips moved as though he was saying a prayer, or a goodbye.

Feeling tears gather in his eyes, Crocker turned to the window and stared deep into the night sky. He was looking for a place to put his grief, which clung to him like a second skin. It wasn't ready to be shed and wouldn't be for a long time.

CHAPTER FOUR

Facing it, always facing it, that's the way to get through.
—Joseph Conrad

SHE FELT like she was moving and imagined her body spinning across a dance floor. Strong, sure hands guided her. And in her mind's eye she saw men's faces with dark hair slicked back and the color orange.

Lisa realized that she was sitting. But her head kept spinning, reminding her of all the things she had to do to prepare for her husband's forty-fifth birthday, which was only six weeks away. Besides hiring the caterer and planning the meal, she had to order flowers and put together a guest list, which was always the hardest part of organizing any political gathering. Family and friends were easy. It was determining the people Clark couldn't afford to offend that made the guest list difficult and required study and input from Clark's legislative and administrative assistants.

Clark himself might spend more time considering who to

invite or not to invite to his birthday party than how to vote on an upcoming military appropriation bill.

Politics were personal. And the longer Lisa lived in Washington, the more she appreciated that. Who got along with whom, which senators played poker together, or golf, or had an interest in antique cars. She reminded herself that friendships, feuds, rivalries, slights, prejudices, and dislikes defined everything from what bills could pass through the Senate, to which individuals were likely to be appointed to fill certain seats in the president's cabinet.

It wasn't ideal, or the way politics were described in textbooks. But it was the way they worked.

Realities were realities, she said to herself. One had to make tough compromises in order to lead a successful life. In the case of planning a successful birthday party for her husband, that meant drafting a guest list and e-mailing it to Clark's legislative assistant. But when she tried to reach for her iPhone, she couldn't move her arms. And when she tried to look at what was binding them, she couldn't see, even though her eyes were open.

That was when the cold reality of her situation hit her and she remembered Sedona and the armed young men in her room. Instinctively, the muscles in her neck and her sphincter tightened, and she realized that she wasn't coming out of a normal sleep, or even a dream. She'd been drugged and was being transported somewhere. Ripped away from her complex life.

She'd read a story recently about the hundreds of thousands of women who were captured every year and sold into sexual slavery. Was it possible that they had mistaken her for a much younger woman?

Struggling not to panic, she willed her mind to focus and slowly became aware that she was bound to a seat, and that a blindfold of some sort covered her eyes. When she turned her head to the right, an orange light filtered through.

The vehicle she was in was moving very fast, a seeming reflection of the rate at which Lisa felt herself losing control of her life.

Minutes later she was jolted by the wheels of the plane hitting a tarmac and the jet's engines slamming into reverse. Her mind snapped back to the interrupted bath, the young woman pointing the pistol. And in that instant, she remembered the dark eyes and warm-colored skin and started to panic, because she realized that this was her reality and there was no escaping it.

Remembering her daughter and wondering what had happened to her, she attempted to rip herself out of the seat. She tried to open her mouth to scream and get someone's attention, but her mouth was taped shut.

Crocker lay on the mattress on the cement floor of the six-by-eight cell looking up at the Israeli guard's bald head and thinking back on how he had been arrested the night before, led away by armed Israel Defense Forces (IDF) soldiers while Mancini, Davis, and Akil were held back by more armed soldiers. With his wrists and ankles chained together, he had watched from the back of a truck as Cal was moved from the desert-camouflage-painted Yas'ur helicopter to a white-and-blue ambulance, and the bodies of Ritchie and the SOAR Black Hawk pilot and copilot were carried to a coroner's black van. Even though he was angry and the muscles in his arms and legs were sore, it was a heavy sadness that dominated and wore him down.

Part of him seemed lifeless, switched off, even as he performed multiple sets of push-ups and sit-ups and picked through the gray, tasteless meat and couscous that were delivered on a tray through a slot at the bottom of the gray door. He drank the metallic-tasting water, stretched, and remembered the charges that had been read to him by the IDF officer the night before—disobeying orders, aggravated assault, attempted murder, and assault with a deadly weapon.

He had no argument with any of them. What had happened, had happened. Looking back, he wouldn't have changed any of it. But if he could, he would alter the order he had given Ritchie and Cal to stay on the Black Hawk. He'd had his reasons then, which he repeated to himself now. But they seemed hollow and stupid in light of what had transpired. And he knew the decision would haunt him the rest of his life.

He pictured his teammate's wide, smiling face with the wise-ass look he got just before he made some smart remark. It seemed impossible that Ritchie was dead, because the memory of him seemed so real.

Crocker sensed Ritchie's presence in the cell with him and heard him comment on the shitty accommodations and tell Crocker that one of these days he had to learn how to treat himself better.

He thought he felt a hand on his shoulder, which caused the little hairs on his neck to stand at attention.

A key rattled in the door; then the door swung open. In the stark fluorescent light stood three men—an IDF officer in uniform, an American navy commander, and an American civilian in a beige suit.

"You okay, warrant?" the navy commander asked.

"Sir?"

Crocker blinked. Realizing he was standing naked, he covered his privates with his hands.

"You acted recklessly last night."

"I wouldn't characterize it that way, sir."

The pale U.S. commander stepped forward, handed him a khaki uniform, and said, "We're going to ask you to listen to the charges and sign a statement. After that you'll be released."

The civilian moved out of the stark light so his face became visible. "Sometime within the next six weeks you'll have to return to face charges," he said. "We don't know exactly when that will be."

Crocker nodded. "Understood."

He showered, dressed, and stood at attention in a hot little room as the charges were read. Then he made a statement into a digital tape recorder in which he recounted the incident with the Israeli pilot and copilot moment by moment. He sensed Ritchie's presence with him the whole time.

An hour later, he was escorted onto a military jet bound for Andrews Air Force Base just outside D.C. Another short flight, and nineteen hours after he'd departed from Tel Aviv, he walked into his house in Virginia Beach. Holly was sitting with her legs curled under her watching *Late Night* when he entered and set down his gear.

"Tom, you okay?" she asked as she hugged him.

"I'm back," he answered, noticing the red around her eyes. "How about you?"

"I spent the last two hours on the phone with Monica."

"Bad?" he asked, leaning over and kissing her.

"She just can't accept it."

"Neither can I," Crocker said.

They sat on the sofa and held hands as he talked about the irony of Ritchie's death—the apparent result of a simple mechanical problem, even though they had been operating in dangerous enemy territory. In a low voice, he confessed that he had ordered Cal and Ritchie to stay on the doomed helo.

"But you had good reasons for doing that, didn't you, Tom?"

"They feel real stupid now."

"Don't blame yourself."

He couldn't help it, because part of him demanded an explanation. Which was why he needed two Ambiens and a couple of glasses of bourbon to fall asleep.

The next morning, feeling tired and numb, he put on his navy dress blues, which he had grown to hate, drove to a local funeral parlor, and entered with Holly by his side. He moved among mourners like a ghost. They were talking in hushed tones.

"Glad you could make it," Mancini whispered as they took seats next to him and his wife, Teresa.

"Me, too."

"I'm still pissed at those fucking Israelis."

Crocker nodded. He looked at the SEALs and their wives sitting around them, all thinking that one day this could happen to them. It was something they lived with and that bound them together into a tight community. Death, injury, mental breakdown, and divorce were always present, even as they raised their kids and tried to plan for the future.

Friends and family took turns getting to their feet and walking to the front of the room, where a dark wooden coffin sat against a backdrop of thousands of white and red roses. To the right, resting on an easel, sat a large framed picture of Ritchie smiling in his navy dress uniform, looking full of mischief like he always did.

The whole scene felt sad and unreal, like a strange pantomime or a bad dream.

Crocker knew Ritchie wouldn't approve. He hated ceremonies, particularly funerals. He'd always been a casual, fun-loving guy with an unquenchable appetite for action and danger who understood the risks he was taking.

His death's coming two weeks before he was to be married seemed wrong.

Crocker shifted his weight on the cushioned seat and said to himself: *If only I had let Cal and Ritchie fast-rope with us, all of this could have been avoided.*

In his head, for the umpteenth time, he repeated the reasons he'd told them to stay on the helo. The packs Ritchie and Cal were carrying were too heavy. It was safer to land the helo first.

Safer. *Yeah, right.* The guilt and irony hit hard.

"How's Cal?" he whispered to Mancini, trying to change the subject in his own head.

"He was moved out of the ICU in Tel Aviv last night."

"Good," Crocker said, nodding.

He spotted Monica across the aisle, looking like someone

had kicked her repeatedly in the head. Her eyes were swollen and her mouth twisted into a painful grimace.

Holly leaned into him and whispered, "They're going to close the casket now. We should pay our last respects."

"Last respects?"

"Yes."

That phrase didn't make sense. First of all, Ritchie wasn't there, either physically or spiritually. Secondly, Crocker had always respected him, and forever would. Thirdly, the bond between them transcended respect or even friendship, which was something most people couldn't understand. They had picked up girls together, gotten drunk and into bar fights, hazed each other mercilessly on birthdays, fought, bled, cried, and laughed together. They had even spent two full days together in a little water-filled hole on a beach in Somalia.

Your experience of someone was your experience. There was no way to sum it up in a few words, explain it, or fit it into a pretty little Hallmark homily. It was what it was—the laughs, misunderstandings, highs, lows, annoyances, pleasures, and all.

Crocker felt Holly pulling him up. "Come with me," she whispered.

They walked stiffly arm in arm to the front of the room. He saw people turn to them and nod solemnly—including Ritchie's half brother, Mitch, his ex-girlfriend Tiffany, his mother.

When they passed Monica sitting on the aisle, Crocker leaned over to her and whispered, "Ritchie loved you very much."

She squeezed his hand and whispered back, "Thank you."

They knelt before the open coffin, and a strange chemical-masked-with-perfume smell oozed out, tickling Crocker's nostrils and making him want to sneeze. Holly squeezed his forearm. The thing lying in the coffin looked like a ceramic doll dressed in a black suit.

Holly whispered, "They did a good job, didn't they?"

Crocker almost said, "No, not at all!" But bit his tongue instead.

She was trying. They all were. And the discomfort they felt only seemed to make it worse.

He wanted badly to get out of there, take off the uncomfortable uniform, and go for a run in the woods. Maybe he'd stop at Stumpy Lake, where he and Ritchie sometimes went kayaking together. He'd sit and remember his friend, whom he now saw in his mind's eye riding his Indian Chief, wearing sunglasses and with the sun highlighting his proud Cherokee cheekbones and the wind blowing his shiny black hair back.

If he sensed him there, amid the buttonbush and cordgrass, Crocker would tell him that he admired him and missed him, and that would never change.

Lisa Clark sat on a veranda overlooking a garden and pool feeling like she was trapped in a strange dream and didn't know how to make it end. There wasn't much to see—a high ocher-colored wall, semitropical flowers and foliage like hibiscus, orchids, and bougainvillea, an Olympic-sized pool with a dolphin statue spitting water into it at the far end, the yellow-and-white-striped awning she sat under, high cumulus clouds and a light-blue sky in the distance.

Everything seemed oddly still and ordinary, except for

the young man with the automatic weapon who watched her and the other armed men in khaki who patrolled the grounds.

She stared at a salad of grilled tuna, tomatoes, and avocado, and the glass of iced tea, but didn't want to eat or drink because she suspected her captors were drugging her.

What she wanted most from herself was to think clearly so she could ascertain where she was, who was holding her, and what she could do. But she was finding that hard because of the fear, drugs, and sense of dislocation. In her sleep she was haunted by dreams of being chased by animals and strangers. And when awake, her mind seemed to fixate on strange things like her husband's schedule, or household budgets, or unpleasant experiences from her past.

Despite her hunger, she pushed the salad away. Then, glancing up at the good-looking young man with the nasty-looking submachine gun and a silver crucifix around his neck, she said politely, "Excuse me, but I need to use the bathroom."

There was no reason not to maintain her dignity and appear polite.

"Of course, *Señora*," the young man answered. "You are not hungry today?"

"No. My stomach is bothering me."

"It's upset, *Señora?* I will call someone."

"Thank you."

She had to wait for a female guard to accompany her. As the young, oval-faced woman looked on, Lisa did her business, washed her hands, and drank heartily from the bathroom tap. Somewhere she had read that a person could live for two weeks or more without food, but only a couple of days without water.

The last day and a half had been weird, disorienting, and frightening, but not unpleasant as far as her physical comfort was concerned. Aside from the fact that she was being held prisoner; had been drugged; wasn't allowed access to a phone or computer, books, newspapers, or news of any sort; and was watched 24/7 (even by a female guard as she took a shower), she had been treated relatively well.

Her current surroundings reminded her of a very upscale resort, not unlike the one in Sedona, which felt like it was a million miles and many years removed.

She had her own beautifully appointed room and bath with sixty-four-inch plasma TV equipped with Netflix, the finest bath and spa products, and a closetful of resort attire and shoes in her size. Anytime she wanted anything from the kitchen, all she had to do was ask one of the young guards—all of whom were well groomed and polite—and it was served to her by a servant dressed in white.

Her primary worry had been her daughter, whom she loved more deeply than she had even realized. But as the hours and days passed and she didn't see or hear her, she became more and more convinced that Olivia had managed to escape or had been spared.

She held on to that belief because the alternative was too awful.

Every time she asked why she was being held and who was in charge, she was told that the *jefe* would arrive soon and explain. But she was given no indication who the *jefe* was.

Since *jefe* was a Spanish word that meant "boss" and the

people guarding and attending to her spoke Spanish, Lisa concluded that she was somewhere south of the border—maybe Mexico or Costa Rica, two places she had visited in the past.

Turning to the young woman who was sitting with her now, she asked again politely in English, "Can you please tell me when this is likely to end?"

The young woman shook her head. "I'm sorry, *Señora*. I don't know."

"Does the *jefe* want something specifically?"

The young woman smiled. "We all want something, *Señora*."

"Do you know the *jefe* personally?"

"Of course. He's like my father."

Lisa tried not to reveal anything about herself, or what she was feeling, or to offend her captors. The room was elegant, with ornate Moorish-style plaster flourishes in the cornices and on the walls, but didn't say much about the people who owned it, or ran it, because there were no personal or unusual items in it, except for a large framed picture of a skeleton in black nun's robes holding a scythe on the wall beside the bed.

She thought it looked vaguely Mexican and might have something to do with a Catholic sect or cult.

"Who's that?" she asked, pointing at the picture and feeling relatively clearheaded for the first time since her abduction.

"La Santísima Muerte," the woman answered.

"La Santísima Muerte."

"Yes."

"Doesn't *muerte* mean death?"

"Yes."

Lisa, who had been raised Catholic but had rarely gone to church before she was married, had never heard of La Santísima Muerte. Her husband studied and regularly quoted the Bible, but she had never heard him mention anything like this.

"Who is she?" she asked.

"La Santa is a very powerful force," the young woman answered. "Some say she's an incarnation of the Aztec goddess Mictecacíhuatl, who is the wife of the death god Mictlantecuhtli."

Lisa wasn't familiar with Mictecacíhuatl and knew very little about Aztec culture and worship, except that the Aztecs had devised an elaborate sun calendar and believed in human sacrifice.

"Others say she is the spirit of the Virgin Mother, who still haunts the earth."

Lisa shivered, then asked, "What does she represent?"

"I don't know what you mean."

"What does she do?"

"She's very powerful and grants special favors to people in need," the guard answered. "If you pray to her, she can protect you from all kinds of violence."

"Violence?" The word frightened her.

"Yes, *Señora*. For the magic to work for you, you have to give up your conscience first. Because the black arts demand this."

"I don't understand."

"La Santísima Muerte knows the reality," the young woman explained. "This is a dark world, *Señora*. We didn't create this world of violence, obstacles, and enemies, but we are not naive. We know that love and kindness don't work."

"Who are *we?*" Lisa asked.

"The people, *Señora.* The ones who understand the power."

Pushed by the same wild, relentless energy he'd had since he was a kid, Crocker rode his Harley south, winding through country roads, not really aware of where he was going or why, just enjoying the rural scenery, the sunshine, smells of nature, and fresh air. There was something liberating about being on the open road with no real destination. Edenton, Tarboro, Rocky Mount, Smithfield, Clinton, Whiteville, Marion, Lake City. Towns flew by, schools, churches, golf courses, junk-yards filled with rusting cars and buses, lakes.

He was searching for an answer or direction. Was it time to retire, leave the teams, and start something new? Had his string of narrow escapes from tragedy run out?

As he rode, he thought about his mother and father, and the cycle of life and death.

His mother had died of emphysema several years ago, but his father was still alive and living in Fairfax, Virginia. Lately, he'd befriended a thirty-five-year-old Gulf War vet named Carla and her nine-year-old son. According to Crocker's sister, their dad had been giving Carla money—possibly as much as twenty thousand dollars so far.

Maybe the old man was lonely and she was taking advantage. Or maybe Carla was a good person and meant to pay him back.

When Crocker was eighteen and constantly in trouble with the police, his father had told him a Cherokee story about a man and his grandson.

The grandfather, seeing that his grandson was being self-destructive, said, "My son, there's a battle between two wolves inside us. One is evil. It's jealousy, greed, resentment, inferiority, lies, and ego. The other is good. It's joy, hope, humility, kindness, and truth."

The boy thought about it and asked, "Grandfather, which wolf wins?"

The old man replied quietly, "The one you feed."

For the past twenty-some years, since joining the navy, Crocker had fed the good wolf. But now he could sense the bad wolf's hunger. It was a big hole at the bottom of his soul carved out by the people he'd killed in the line of duty, and his anger at life's injustices, and the wrongs that had been visited on the people he loved.

Last night he had stopped in Santee, South Carolina, and eaten blackened catfish for dinner, washed down with several Skull Coast Ales. Later he'd parked near the state park, watched the stars, and reminded himself that even they weren't immortal. Everything in nature came and went. Stars died and broke up into asteroids. Trees felled in lightning storms rotted into mulch. People died and were consumed by worms. Maybe there was such a thing as reincarnation. He didn't know.

What he understood was that life went on, mysteriously, hurtling toward something new, like he was now.

He parked his bike outside C J's Sports Bar & Grill in Ellabell, Georgia, a few miles west of Savannah. He was minding his own business, sitting at the bar, which was lit by strings of little red-and-white lights. He threw back a shot of Jack Daniel's with a St. Pauli Girl chaser and considered asking for a menu. The Atlanta Hawks were losing to the Heat on the big TV, which didn't interest him. The little one to his right was tuned to CNN. Something about another budget deadline in Congress.

A poster past the bartender's head listed the Ten Steps to Self-Esteem. They were (1) know yourself, (2) understand what makes you feel great, (3) recognize things that get you down, (4) set goals to achieve what you want, (5) develop trusting friendships that make you feel good, (6) don't be afraid to ask for help, (7) stand up for your beliefs and values, (8) take responsibility for your own actions, (9) take good care of yourself, (10) help someone else.

It interested him enough to read it twice and stop at number eight.

An older, potbellied guy with a long gray beard seated to his right turned to him and asked about his Harley parked outside. The man had gray eyes, badly stained teeth, and a drinker's nose, and reminded him of some of the old bikers he'd known growing up.

Crocker found it easy to talk with him about Harley models, engines, and close calls both of them had experienced riding. Crocker's last had been one night on his way home when he was hit smack in the face by a buzzard.

He laughed and said, "I don't know how he didn't break my neck. I literally got a mouthful of wet feathers and could taste that bastard for days."

The old man drained his glass, pulled at his beard, and chuckled. "I remember one Sunday night riding down a deserted country road thinking about the ol' lady," he said. "I rolled off the throttle as I crested a hill and sensed someone warning me even though I was all alone. I look up and see this big-ass truck has swung into my lane to pass some guy in a sedan. I had no time to stop. Had to pull my left shoulder back to avoid clipping the truck's side mirror. Barely squeezed past, and shit my pants."

"You're lucky."

"You know what I saw painted on the side of that truck?"

"No idea," Crocker answered.

"Dana Mills. My girlfriend was named Dana. Her mom's maiden name was Mills. She dumped me two days later. Broke my heart."

Sounded like the lyrics to a Waylon Jennings song, Crocker thought.

The old biker bought another round and shifted the conversation to biker movies. Crocker listed his favorites. "*Mad Max* was good. *Knightriders*, *The Great Escape*. I liked *The Wild One* with Marlon Brando."

"You ever see a movie from the seventies called *Werewolves on Wheels*?" the bearded man asked as though he was a connoisseur.

"No."

"It wasn't no blockbuster," he said, "but damn if it don't have its own sleazy charm. I'm talkin' female bikers, one of whom is possessed by the Devil and changes into a real sexy werewolf at night. And black-robed monks who worship Satan."

Crocker's interest started to wander. The man moved his stool closer and signaled to the bartender to refill their glasses.

"You running away from something?" the old man asked.

"I don't think so."

"You had much experience with Satan?"

Crocker stared at the amber Jack as it entered the clear glass, considering that maybe the bad wolf and Satan were the same.

"You hear what I asked ya?" the man repeated, the little lights behind the bar reflected in his gray eyes.

Crocker downed the drink and nodded as he searched for an answer—one that dodged the question but was respectful. "I'm not sure I know what you're talking about," he said.

"I think you do," the man answered, his eyes boring into Crocker. "Matter of fact, I got a notion you're struggling with him right now."

Crocker knocked back the beer and looked up at the TV. Anderson Cooper was talking. His face looked gray and pinched.

"Maybe," Crocker said. "Maybe not." It hurt to look inside himself, because every time he did, he remembered Ritchie lying on the ground with his guts spilled out, which opened a Pandora's box of his own issues having to do with death, the meaning of life, his will to continue living the way he had.

What had seemed so clear and easy a week ago was now a murky mess.

He signaled to the bartender to bring him the check.

"You feel like talkin' about it?" the man on his right asked.

"Not tonight."

"You see this face? You think I haven't done my share of wrestling with the Devil?"

Crocker looked over his shoulder at the exit.

"You ever hear the Proverb: 'Avoid it, pass not by it, turn from it, and pass away'?" the bearded man asked.

Crocker reached for his wallet and shook his head. "No."

"It means that if you're fighting an opponent with sword and shield, and that fellow is about to strike the first blow, what do you do?"

Crocker checked the tab, which read $26.00. He tossed his Amex card on top of it and pushed both toward the bartender.

"Do you walk into the blow hoping that your shield will protect you, or do you move out of the way?" the man asked.

Crocker was about to say, "If he attacked me, I'd wrestle the goddamn sword away from him and slice his throat," but instead looked at the poster behind the bar. The first of the Ten Steps to Self-Esteem was *know yourself*. He grinned, turned to his right, and saw a familiar face on CNN. It was a former SEAL Team One member, now senator, Jesse Abrams Clark, standing on the steps of the Capitol facing a group of reporters.

Crocker waved to the bartender and asked him to turn up the sound.

Clark, who usually appeared confident, looked anxious and worn out. His distress communicated clearly and stirred something in Crocker's chest.

The man beside him said, "You never answered my question."

"I'm listening," Crocker said, pointing to the TV.

Reporters asked Clark if he thought the event in Sedona was related to the strong position he had taken against the Mexican drug cartels and his repeated calls for more aggressive U.S. action and stiffer sanctions.

"I hope not," Clark answered, "and have no reason to believe that's true at this time."

Crocker knew Clark. The two men had gone on a mission together when Clark was a SEAL.

He'd also been Ritchie's platoon leader at Team One. He was the guy who came to Ritchie's defense more than a decade ago when he was arrested for murdering a biker in a bar and the navy wanted to kick him out. Clark not only stood up for Ritchie, he also helped pay for the lawyer who got him exonerated by claiming self-defense. Ritchie was forever grateful and had spoken of him often.

The man beside him repeated the Proverb: "'Avoid it, pass not by it, turn from it, and pass away.'"

Crocker reread number ten on the chart of Ten Steps to Self-Esteem—*help someone else*. He wasn't a thinker or a religious man, but he had his answer.

Knowing what he had to do, he signed the credit card receipt and bade good night to the man with the beard.

"Remember that without the shield of faith to protect us, the Devil can easily strike us down," the old man said. "But when we stand in faith we can quench all the fiery darts of the wicked."

"I will."

CHAPTER FIVE

Act as if it were impossible to fail.

—Dorothea Brande

LISA CLARK sat watching an old episode of *Mad Men*, thinking that the character Roger Sterling reminded her of her old friend Henri Gaudier. They had the same kind of hair and shared the same jaded sense of entitlement and need to bend people to their will. The latter was a skill she'd been learning from her husband—the ability to get people to project their power onto you. It involved creating a perception that you were smarter, more attractive, and more in control of yourself than they were, and could make things happen.

If she'd ever needed to marshal her abilities and influence people, it was now, she thought as vehicles stopped in the driveway below and car doors slammed, making her jump from her seat and rush to the window. From her second-story room, Lisa couldn't see who had arrived, but her fear spiked dramatically.

She paced the room trying to harness her emotions, reminding herself that she had a sophisticated understanding of people and was intelligent. An armed male guard entered, followed by the maid with the long black braid and the flat oval face of a Mayan madonna, who proceeded to light candles and turn off the lamps and TV.

"What's going on?" Lisa asked the guard.

He left without answering.

She turned to the maid and asked in broken Spanish, "*¿Porque paga la luz?*"

"The *jefe* doesn't like electric light," the young woman answered in English.

"Why not?"

"He believes it disturbs the spirits."

"What spirits?" Lisa asked, glancing at the picture of La Santísima Muerte to her right.

"The spirits of the dead, *Señora*."

"So the *jefe* is here in this residence, now?"

The maid nodded. "He is, *Señora*."

"Does he have a name?" Lisa asked politely as the young woman straightened the cover on the bed.

"People call him El Chacal."

Lisa stopped. "El Chacal?"

"Yes, *Señora*."

"Is that his real name?"

"In English, you would say the Jackal," the young woman answered.

"The Jackal?" The name conjured images of nasty, leering beasts sinking their teeth into wounded prey.

"Yes, *Señora*."

Clark had told his wife stories about the vicious, out-of-control Mexican and Colombian drug lords with strange aliases who corrupted local officials and acted as though they were above the law. Men like Joaquín Guzmán (a.k.a. El Chapo) of the Sinaloa cartel, who had once escaped from a high-security prison in a shopping cart and started bloody turf wars all over Mexico, and Ismael Zambada-García (a.k.a. El Mayo), who worked as a furniture deliveryman before becoming a gangster; Heriberto Lazcano (a.k.a. El Bronce) of Los Zetas, and Vicente Carrillo Fuentes (a.k.a. El Viceroy) of the Juárez cartel. But she had never heard of anyone called the Jackal.

In the flickering candlelight, with the full moon rising past the high back wall, she considered what attitude to take when she met him. Outrage? Defiance? Zenlike acceptance?

She felt it was important to project an aura of confidence to let him know she wasn't afraid of whatever cult or criminal organization he was part of, because her husband was a highly influential man in the most powerful country on earth.

But her kidnapper had to understand that already. Aside from the fact that she was a senator's wife, what did the Jackal know about her?

If he'd seen her photo, he knew she was tall, thin, blond, and attractive. But what else? Did he know she had fallen out of a school bus when she was six years old and the back wheels had run over her little body, crushing her pelvis? Did he understand that the resulting nerve damage and dozen operations had left her with an unusual ability to endure pain?

Did he know she had killed someone?

Lisa almost jumped out of her skin at the sharp knock on the door. The maid answered and someone in the hallway handed her a gray business suit on a hanger, a white silk blouse, and black high-heeled shoes.

She laid the clothes on the bed and said, "*Señora*, please put these on."

"Why?"

"Because *El Jefe* wants you to join him for dinner."

"Where?" Lisa asked.

"Downstairs in the dining room."

The label in the suit read ARMANI and the fabric was a supple silk-wool blend with pinstripes. Skirt, jacket, and white silk blouse. The shoes were patent leather, designed by Jimmy Choo.

"The Jackal has good taste," Lisa said.

The maid nodded.

Lisa stood in a dark corner of the candlelit room and undressed while the young woman watched. The skirt and blouse fit perfectly.

"How did you know my size?" Lisa asked.

"*El Chacal* finds out," the young woman replied.

"How?"

"I don't have that information, *Señora*."

An older, heavier woman entered and did Lisa's makeup and combed her hair as thoughts and worries flooded Lisa's brain.

Whoever the Jackal was, he had an appreciation of style and beauty, which should have given her hope. But instead it unnerved her, and brought back memories of another sensitive, twisted man she had known—someone who understood how to manipulate people far better than she did.

She heard another sharp knock on the door.

The maid said, "It's time, *Señora*."

As Lisa stood, she steeled herself for what lay ahead and reminded herself that she wasn't an innocent girl anymore. She'd learned a tremendous amount in the past twenty years about power, influence, and determination.

She'd fight tooth and nail if she had to. Whatever happened, she'd do what she had to in order to survive.

I've gotten this far on guts, drive, and instinct, and I'm not gonna change now, Crocker reminded himself as he parked his Harley in the SEAL Team Six compound. The changeable April weather had turned cold, so he wore an old brown leather jacket over his habitual black T-shirt and pants, and a black wool cap on his head. Since he'd driven all night and was dirty and tired, he stopped in the bathroom near his cage to wash up. Ritchie used to call the team room the testosterone pit of America.

He wasn't wrong. The guys on Team Six were the elite of the elite—highly motivated individuals constantly trying to improve themselves and give themselves an edge. As much as they trusted and respected one another, the competition between them to be the best shooter, jumper, diver, or boat crew leader was intense.

Outside he passed a young African American operative from Blue Team, who offered him a big purple jar of Iso Mass nutrition powder, which he said was packed with free-flowing glutamine and BCAAs for building muscle mass. Crocker thanked him for the offer but turned it down. He lifted and worked out as hard as anyone on the teams but preferred to keep his body lean.

Someone had written a quote from soccer player Mia Hamm on the blackboard: "I am a member of a team, and I rely on the team, I defer to it and sacrifice for it, because the team, not the individual, is the ultimate champion."

Last time he was here, he had joined Cal and Ritchie at the shooting range as they tested a new variant of the Heckler & Koch MP7A1. When he passed Ritchie's cage, he noticed that his gear had already been cleared out.

It was almost two weeks since his death, and the tenacity of Crocker's grief surprised him. He carried it with him as he crossed the concrete grinder where Green Team was doing push-ups with loaded packs on their backs.

Still burdened with guilt over the decision he'd made in the helicopter, he climbed the concrete stairs to HQ and heard his footsteps echo down the hall to the CO's office. Captain Sutter sat behind his desk studying plans for a new team mess with a young lieutenant from the Special Operations command.

Crocker knocked on the doorframe, then ran a hand over his stubble-covered chin, removed his hat, cleared his throat, and said, "Excuse me, sir. Can I have a minute?"

Sutter glanced up at him and turned to look at the digital clock on the wall. "I'll give you five," he said, nodding at the lieutenant, who saluted and left.

It was a big room done up in a quasinautical theme. Crocker settled into one of the brown leather chairs and laid his jacket across his lap. "Thanks, sir," he started. "What's the latest on Cal?"

"Cal's better. How are you?" Sutter's Kentucky drawl filled the space between them.

"Fine."

The CO always cut to the chase. "What's bugging you, Ritchie or the incident with the Israelis?"

"Both," Crocker answered. "Ritchie and I were close. We had history."

"I know."

"I miss him."

"I do, too. It's perfectly natural."

Crocker nodded, then cleared his throat. "I know you're busy, so I'm gonna make this quick. It relates to Ritchie. I'm sure you've been keeping tabs on the situation with Senator Jesse Clark and the kidnapping."

"Yes, I have."

"You know Ritchie always looked up to Clark as a leader and mentor, which he was, sir. In terms of the teams, he's one of us. So I've been thinking—"

Sutter held up his hand and said, "You can stop right there."

"Why?"

"I know what you're gonna ask."

"Sir."

Sutter leaned forward over his desk. "I know and respect Clark at least as well as you do, Crocker. And Ritchie was one of the finest, bravest men I've ever had the pleasure to work with."

"Yes."

"And I appreciate your coming here and volunteering," Sutter continued. "But as you know, I take orders just like you do. And the answer I got, and the one I'm now passing on to you, is no."

"Sir, I haven't even told you what I'm volunteering for."

"You want to rescue the hostages and punish the kidnappers." Sutter slapped his hands together. "So do I, Crocker. So do I. But it's not as simple as us wanting to do something. Is it?"

Crocker objected. "Sir, Clark's one of us. We can't sit here with our fingers up our butts while—"

Sutter's face started to turn red. "When did I ever give you the impression that I'm a coldhearted commander who doesn't give a shit about the men under him? Didn't I let you remain in Tripoli after your wife went missing? Haven't I defended you and your men countless times when you did things without prior authorization or pissed somebody off?"

"You have, sir. I'm sorry."

"I'm trying to clean up more of your shit now with the fucking Israelis."

"You're the best, most supportive CO we've ever had, sir. All the men feel that way." Crocker meant it.

This time Sutter waved his hand in front of his face and looked embarrassed. "I appreciate that, Crocker. I'm not some teenage girl fishing for compliments about her looks. The point is that I did take the Clark request higher up command. And you know what they told me?"

"No, sir."

"The FBI and DEA are handling it and don't want our help."

Crocker cleared his throat into his fist. "Do they know where the hostages are being held?"

"Somewhere in Mexico. That's all I've been told."

Crocker had worked with the FBI and DEA before and knew their training, skill levels, and expertise. Finding and taking out kidnappers and terrorists in a foreign country wasn't among those.

He said, "No disrespect to the FBI, but they aren't going to move as fast and hit as hard as we are."

Sutter leaned back in his chair with his hands behind his head. "I know that, Crocker. But there are political considerations. For one thing, the Mexicans recently elected a new president, and he doesn't want us kicking up a fuss in his backyard."

Crocker had read about Enrique Peña Nieto and knew that he was a young, baby-faced guy from the Institutional Revolutionary Party (PRI). He also knew that he'd had three children with his wife, who died in 2007 of an epileptic seizure, and a fourth child, a daughter, with a mistress two years before his wife's death.

"So what's he doing about the situation?"

Sutter shook his head. "All I know is, he doesn't want American military personnel operating in his country."

"But under the circumstances—"

Sutter cut him off. "Those are the circumstances. If they change, I'll let you know."

Crocker grabbed his jacket off his lap, stood, and said, "I appreciate that, Captain."

Sutter stood, too. "I don't mean to be short with you, Crocker," he said. "I'm sure you can tell that I'm frustrated, too."

"We're in the big boys' club, sir."

It was Crocker's way of saying *Message received, no hard feelings, move on.* But it wasn't completely honest, because he knew he had no intention of letting it go.

* * *

Every nerve in Lisa Clark's body tingled as she sat at the long table covered with a white linen tablecloth, ivory-and-gold Lenox china, cut-crystal stemware, and large silver candelabras filled with burning candles. A half dozen male and female servers dressed in white waited with their hands behind their backs. One stepped forward and refilled Lisa's long-stemmed glass with ice water.

"Wine, *Señora?*" he asked.

"Not now, thank you," she answered, her back straight and her chin held high.

Looking over the water glass as she drank, she noticed that the big table was set for three and the room had two doors. One set of doors, to her left behind the head of the table, stood between large windows covered with white gauze curtains; the second door was behind her.

The significance of the three settings didn't register, even though she was trying to be hyperalert to every tick of the clock in the corner, every movement and expression of the servers, every scent from the kitchen, every change in her own mood.

She immediately regretted drinking the water, because a strange feeling of detachment came over her, as though she was perceiving the world from inside a cotton-lined box.

She looked around again slowly in a last effort to take everything in before whatever they had given her had its full effect—the rich texture of the air, the subtle light, the glowing, eager faces of the servers, the sepia-colored walls.

A strange stillness pervaded everything, except for the candles that flickered gently.

She waited, counting her breaths, silently praying for sympathy and deliverance. Then, without warning, a current of excitement stirred the languid air, and she turned to the French doors seconds before they opened. Three very large men entered. One wore a Pancho Villa–type mustache. They all had dark, shiny hair and brought with them the musky smell of outdoors. The three were dressed in white guayabera-style shirts over black pants and cowboy boots, and looked like they meant business.

Behind them limped a shorter man with a cane, dressed entirely in white linen. He was thin with muscular legs and long straight hair that fell to his shoulders and hid his face. An aura of power and menace hung around him.

One of the bodyguards pulled back the high-backed chair at the head of the table and helped the man into his seat. He placed the carved ivory cane on the back of the chair with a long, dark, sinewy hand, then turned to face Lisa.

She held back a gasp. On first impression, she felt as if she was looking at Johnny Depp's older brother. He had the same straight dark hair, high cheekbones, thin nose, and square chin. As in some recent photos of Depp she'd seen, he also favored aviator sunglasses with blue lenses.

But as she studied him more closely, she realized that the resemblance ended there. Whereas the actor's skin was uniformly smooth, this man's skin was rough, twisted, and scarred, especially along the right side of his face, but oddly regular along his forehead and under his eyes.

Botox, Lisa concluded. And extensive plastic surgery, maybe the result of an injury.

When he removed the sunglasses, she saw that it was his eyes that really distinguished him. They were wide-set, mesmerizing, and fierce.

They seemed to pull her in like magnets and communicate some intangible dark knowledge. And in that moment, she sensed that there was something wrong with him physically. She found evidence in the yellowish tinge of his scleras and the unhealthy grayish pallor of his long lips.

It reminded her of a story Clark had told some dinner guests about Abraham Lincoln. When Lincoln was advised to include a certain man in his cabinet and refused, he was asked why he would not accept the man. The president answered, "I don't like his face." To which the man's advocate responded, "But the poor man isn't responsible for his face."

"Every man over forty is responsible for his face," countered Lincoln.

The face of the man at the head of the table spoke volumes—of big appetites, struggles, paranoid fears, self-hate, vendettas, and monumental ambition.

Turning to Lisa, he said, "Welcome," in a deep, confident voice with a slight accent.

She couldn't say "Thank you." Her heartbeat quickened. Sweat appeared on her palms and coated the insides of her thighs.

The man she assumed was the Jackal frowned, then whispered something to the men who stood guard behind him. Two of them walked to the door behind her and exited.

He smiled at something the third man said, revealing white, even teeth that looked as though they had been capped. He wore a silver crucifix, along with other amulets and bracelets, and a white linen shirt unbuttoned to his muscular chest, which had a dark tattoo on it. She made out the outline of a skull.

Despite his fine clothes and the care he had taken to re-shape his face and control his surroundings, there was something coarse and rough about him. She intuited that he'd come from a hardscrabble background and had ruthlessly clawed his way to the top of whatever this organization or gang was under his command.

The click of high heels registered in her head, and out of the corner of her eye she saw the two bodyguards reentering. Instead of turning to look at whoever the high heels belonged to, she focused instead on the intense, admiring, and almost ravenous expression on the face of the man at the head of the table as his eyes followed the person behind her.

"Are you the Jackal?" Lisa asked, trying to hide her fear behind a cold formality.

"Yes, but you can call me Ivan."

"Ivan what?"

"Just Ivan."

She had a speech prepared in her head. In it she offered to cooperate as long as he continued to treat her with respect.

The click of high heels continued to the seat across the table. Through her unfocused eyes she caught a glimpse of the suit, which was identical to the one she was wearing. But Lisa felt far away, and receding. She thought that if she tried to say something, she'd have to shout to be heard.

It was hard to see the face beyond the glow of candles. As the woman bent to sit, Lisa registered that she was young and wore her blond hair pulled back like her own.

Unexpectedly and for an instant her perceptions sharpened, and she recognized her daughter. Lisa blinked and looked again to make sure she wasn't hallucinating, then gasped as though she'd been punched hard in the chest. "Olivia!"

"Mother. You're here?"

"Yes." Her hands reached for her heart. Despite the admirable restraint her daughter was showing, the complex and powerful emotions she felt were impossible to hold back.

Lisa started to tremble and angry tears poured from her eyes. She rose unsteadily to her feet and shouted, "No! No! I won't accept this! It's wrong. So very wrong. Please, stop!"

Crocker looked down at the crab cakes on his plate, then up at his father. As the old man ate, he talked about goings-on at the local VFW he commanded. Funds were tight, and the chapter was divided between those who wanted to spend money on chapter activities like meetings and dinners and those who wanted to focus on helping disabled vets. His father led the latter camp and complained about the self-centeredness of some members. Takers, he called them.

He mentioned that Senator Clark's wife had served as the hostess of the chapter's fund-raising picnic at Harpers Ferry two years ago.

"Great gal," he said. "Cares about vets. Her father served with the Special Forces in Vietnam."

"Yes." Crocker had met her once at the SEAL Team One reunion that she attended with her husband in Coronado. He remembered a friendly woman with the face and build of a model.

"It's awful about her being kidnapped. I hope she makes out okay," his father said.

"Me, too."

Crocker's immediate concern was Carla and the fact that she hadn't come. This was the second time she had wiggled out of an invitation to meet.

When he brought her up, his father defended her, saying she was a busy, hardworking woman with a son to take care of and little support from the army, which had denied her benefits despite the fact that she was a Gulf War vet suffering from PTSD.

Crocker's father was the kindest, most honest man he'd ever met. So it pained him to ask, "Dad, is it true you've been helping Carla out financially?"

His father ran a hand through his gray hair and groaned, "I don't know why that's anyone else's business."

Crocker had learned to confront problems quickly and head-on even if it meant pissing people off. "Because Karen and I care about you and don't want anyone taking advantage." Karen was his younger sister—a ball-buster and CPA, with an alcoholic husband and three kids.

"Let's change the subject," his dad said, reaching for the iced tea.

"How much is she into you for?"

"I'm not telling."

"How much?"

"Around thirty."

"Thirty thousand?"

His dad nodded. He wore a checked cotton shirt open at the collar and a pair of the same black pants he'd used when he sold insurance.

Crocker looked at his dad and considered that thirty grand was roughly half his savings and a hell of a lot of money to a seventy-eight-year-old man living on Social Security.

"Shit, Dad," he said. "She planning to pay you back?"

"Sure." His father nodded, but even in that gesture there was more than a hint of doubt, which made Crocker feel sad.

"The older you get, the lonelier you become," his dad said. Crocker noticed that he still had on the thick gold wedding band he'd worn since he was married to Crocker's mother fifty-five years ago in a little Protestant church in South Boston. "A woman, even if it's only to listen, brings a kind of tenderness that a male friend can't."

Crocker couldn't argue with that.

His dad explained that Carla was using the last ten thousand he'd given her to enter a private rehab facility where she would kick the dependence she'd developed to prescription drugs like Vicodin, and cover her bills while she took time off from work. Once she got clean, he was confident that she'd pull her life together and find a better-paying job.

"When does she start the rehab?" Crocker asked.

"She started already, Monday morning. That's why she couldn't join us tonight."

73

CHAPTER SIX

Sanity is madness put to good use.

—George Santayana

THE FOOD looked and smelled fantastic—grilled lamb and fish, black beans, rice, fried plantains, asparagus, fresh tomatoes, a heart of palm salad, mango mousse—but Lisa refused to eat. She wanted to be as focused as possible, strong, and ready. A dull ache throbbed from the pit of her stomach and a sick numbness filled her head.

All she could do was sit stiffly, watch, and marvel at the poise of her daughter, who picked at her food and acted like nothing was wrong.

Lisa wanted to whisper some words of encouragement, tell Olivia how proud she was, or how much she loved her. But her daughter was completely focused on the man at the head of the table, nodding and listening intently.

He'd been speaking nonstop for the last forty minutes. It was part sermon, part political diatribe, part history lesson delivered with table-pounding, arm-waving, snarling passion. The general theme: the exploitation of Latin America.

He started with a description of the Aztec, Incan, and Mayan civilizations, and explained how everything had changed with the arrival of the Europeans, who killed hundreds of thousands of Indians, forced the survivors to work as slaves in silver and gold mines, and spread infectious diseases like small pox that decimated entire tribes.

He talked about the aggressive paternal energy that came from Europe and how it had joined forces with the Church to form a lethal, compassionless river of fire that burned through indigenous cultures that had worshipped and respected Mother Earth. And how this pattern of exploitation had extended for hundreds of years and still continued.

The dynamic had always been about filling the huge appetites of the aggressive Europeans. Their unending greed and lust for blood and money had taken many forms—plundering natural resources; demanding cheap labor to toil in their mines, on their farms, and in their factories and assembly plants; consuming vast quantities of oil to run their cars and heat their homes; and procuring beautiful young women and narcotics to quiet the unease in their souls.

He explained that people from Europe and the United States were spiritually empty and, therefore, compelled to surround themselves with riches and symbols of power. When material things didn't fill the spiritual void, they turned to drugs to try to escape their existential reality.

"But you people can't be honest," he said with fire in his eyes. "We dutifully fill your demand for drugs like marijuana, cocaine, and heroin, and you turn around and blame the problem on us. We give you our people to clean up your shit, pick your crops, and work in your kitchens, but you refuse to give them citizenship and self-respect. Instead, you hunt us down like dogs when we try to cross the border and throw us in jail."

Lisa's lower back ached and she felt exhausted and dizzy. The Jackal continued to pile on the guilt with the zeal of a latter-day Che Guevara.

He seemed to be gathering speed and intensity, shifting from one topic to another—the sex trade, the selling of stolen babies, the indiscriminate spraying of crops, the rising incidence of cancer in Central America and Mexico, the dwindling monarch butterfly migration to Michoacán, Mexico.

And the more he spoke, the more keenly her daughter seemed to listen. Olivia leaned toward him, taking it all in, even nodding sometimes as though she agreed.

What the Jackal had said so far left Lisa with more questions than answers. Was he a drug cartel leader or a revolutionary? Was he explaining why he was going to have to kill them, or trying to win them over?

His speech, the situation, even her daughter's composure left her feeling naked and vulnerable. When she couldn't take any more, when she thought she was going to faint and fall from her chair, she said, "Please, stop."

The Jackal's blazing eyes turned to her, and she felt ashamed. This wasn't what she expected from herself.

Hiding her face behind the cloth napkin, she said, "I'm sorry. I'm not feeling well."

The Jackal didn't appear annoyed. Instead, a kind, knowing smile stretched across his face.

"It's my fault, *Señora*," he said. "I speak too much. But I feel things strongly and get carried away."

"No, no, not at all," she said awkwardly as she stood. "I think I'd better say good night."

"Not yet, please." He stood, too, with the help of his body-guards. When he grabbed Lisa's wrist, she felt a dark, violent, primal energy course through her body.

He said, "Allow me a minute to show you ladies something before you leave."

The Jackal escorted them out the French doors and down some steps to a patio.

He stopped under an arbor and switched on a light, which illuminated a large cage built into the foundation of the house. In it were about a dozen golden-and-brown animals that looked like a cross between dogs and wolves. Seeing their owner, they rose and started to pace expectantly in front of the thick iron bars.

"Magnificent, aren't they?" the Jackal asked with the expression of an eager teenage boy.

Lisa nodded. The hypnotic movement of the animals and the look in their eyes filled her with a strange, exotic energy.

"The one on the right, she is Chantico, named after the Aztec goddess of fire," he explained. "And the big one with the stripe on his back is Tlaloc, after the god of fertility."

The Jackal pushed his head between the bars, and the animals gathered around and started to lick him feverishly. Throwing his head back, he produced an eerie high-pitched whine that sounded like a baby crying. The animals in the cage whined back, as though they understood and were responding.

The exchange between animals and human continued for several minutes. Then the Jackal leaned close to Lisa and whispered, "You're an animal, too, *Señora*. We're all animals underneath, living with the law of the jungle. The strong prey on the weak. The weak wait for a moment to strike back."

Some impulse in her caused her to shake her head and say, "No. There's more to us humans. You should know that."

He grabbed her by the shoulders and pulled her tight to his chest. So tight that her breasts were smashed against him and she could feel the beating of his heart.

"Of course you're right, *Señora*," he whispered so that his hot breath brushed her lips. "You're a sophisticated woman. Which is why I can see in your eyes that we understand each other. Maybe I'm a black plague to you, something you look on with disgust, but we've met before on the plains of Analocha and the altars of Teoni. I might seem insane to you, but even my disease has a purpose, which your body and blood will cure."

Lyrics to the Buck Owens classic echoed in his head as Crocker parked his bike near the curb and moved closer past some maple trees to try to peer through one of the windows of the ground-floor apartment just east of Wilson Boulevard in Arlington.

"There's no fool like an old fool, that's loved and lost at least a hundred times."

He didn't want to interfere in his dad's life, but he couldn't allow him to be played, either.

Through a sheer pale-yellow curtain he saw a dim light

inside beyond the kitchen but couldn't make out anyone inside. So he circled the block. Light rain fell as he walked and remembered all the people he'd known who'd fallen victims to drugs—numerous friends growing up, a girlfriend, his brother, and his stepson, Carl (Holly's son), who got involved with drugs as a teenager and was gunned down on the street by a drug dealer.

Crocker hated what drugs did to people—destroying their wills and draining their self-respect. His brother was the only person he knew who had escaped more or less intact.

The third time he passed the window, the kitchen light was on. Moving closer, he saw a dark-haired woman standing with her back to him. A tall man entered the room behind her. Crocker saw her reach into a drawer and tear off a piece of aluminum foil. The man pulled something out of his pocket and squeezed her butt.

When she turned, Crocker recognized Carla from the photo his dad had shown him. She looked harder and more haggard in the stark kitchen light, but still attractive, with straight bangs and big brown eyes.

So much for her being in rehab, he said to himself.

Standing in the rain, his muscular body buzzing, he considered his options.

First he thought of circling to the front and ringing her buzzer. Then he saw the two of them exit the kitchen and noticed that the window was partially open.

He scanned the yard and parking lot behind him to make sure no one was watching, then climbed up to the sill, pushed the window open, and pulled out the screen. He set it down gently on the kitchen counter and climbed in over the aluminum sink, taking care not to touch the bowls and plates piled inside.

It resembled other post–World War II brick apartments he'd been in. A galley kitchen with gray linoleum floor.

Marvin Gaye asked, *"What's going on?"* from a stereo inside as Crocker squeezed his body around the corner into the living room. Opposite a sloppy brown leather couch, the TV was tuned to Fox News, but the sound was off. A little Christmas tree with white lights sat in the corner, even though it was the second week of April.

He heard a man's gruff voice in a room to his right off a narrow hallway. The door stood partially opened and a light burned inside.

"Mother, mother; there's too many of you cryin'…"

He stood in the strange, sour-smelling space and waited. Water dripped from a sink in the bathroom behind him. He sniffed something that reminded him of a burning plastic shower curtain, pushed the bedroom door open, and entered.

Carla sat on the edge of the bed, sucking crystal meth vapor through a three-inch glass pipe. The man knelt beside her, cooking it with a lighter on a piece of aluminum foil.

He had a sharp profile and coarse straw-colored hair that stood up straight. He turned, saw Crocker, and asked, "Where the fuck did you come from?"

Crocker let the situation sink in and the anger settle inside him.

"Who the fuck are you?" the man demanded.

"A friend of a friend," Crocker answered, his arms at his sides.

"How'd you get in?" the man asked. He had hard blue eyes and a rough confidence.

"I slid down the chimney."

This guy didn't appear to be the sharpest knife in the set, or maybe his perception was warped by the meth. Blinking several times in succession, he asked, "What'd you say?"

Carla sat with her head craned back and her eyes closed, enjoying the buzz. So she didn't witness any of this. Nor did she notice when the man beside her set the cooked meth on the floor and stood to confront Crocker.

"You a friend of Carla's?" the tall man asked.

"No."

"You work in the building?"

The scene struck Crocker as absurd, so he said with a straight face, "Santa Claus sent me. I came to tell both of you that Christmas is over."

"What?"

"Hi, Carla," Crocker said.

Her eyelids fluttered but didn't fully open.

The man stepped closer and reached into his back pocket for his wallet. He was taller and bigger than Crocker, with steroid-enhanced biceps that bulged from under a gray Georgia Tech T-shirt. He pushed a Fairfax County Police Department badge toward Crocker and snarled, "I'm a cop, so get the fuck out."

"I came to talk to Carla," Crocker countered, the tension between them growing.

"Well, she's busy now. So either turn around and get out the way you came, or I arrest you for breaking and entering!"

"I don't think so."

They were practically nose to nose. So close that Crocker could smell the mildew on the man's clothes and the cheap vanilla-scented cologne.

"All right, asshole," the man growled, his eyes shining with crazy meth energy and belligerence. As relaxed as Crocker appeared, he was completely alert to what was coming. So when the tall man cocked his fist back to clock him, he grabbed the man by the collar and used his momentum to throw him into the lamp on a corner table near the wall. The small table fell over, the lamp shattered, glass went flying, and the man crashed to the floor.

Carla looked up. She wore a red tank top with no bra. Lank hair hung over her bleary eyes.

Crocker said, "I guess you're not in rehab, are you?"

"What? I mean…what did you…?" She pointed to the man groaning in the corner.

"Don't worry about him."

"You…you from the center?" she asked.

"I came here to tell you to stop taking money from my father," Crocker said.

She squinted up at him. "Who are you?"

The man behind him was trying to pull himself up as blood dripped from a cut on his forehead.

"My dad's Jim Crocker."

He saw the recognition reach her eyes, then watched her make the decision to reach back across the bed toward the dark brown nightstand. He didn't know if she was going for the phone or something else. But when he saw her slide open the drawer, he sprang forward and slapped her hand away.

She shouted, "Hey! That hurt!"

He saw the silver pistol inside the drawer and grabbed it.

She pushed the pipe and foil with the meth under the bed and said, "I know who you are. I'm calling the police."

"I thought your friend was a cop."

The man behind Crocker had managed to get to his feet and was leaning against the wall for support. Crocker walked over and kicked his feet out from under him, then turned back in time to fend off the blow from a charging Carla. He twisted her arm behind her, spun her around, and threw her onto the bed.

"You're asking for it, fuckhead!" she shouted. "You're messing with the wrong people!"

He leaned on the bed with one knee, clamped a hand over her mouth, and pointed the pistol at her head. "You want me to end your miserable life right now, Carla? Do you?"

Part of him wanted to rid the world of a useless parasite. But another reminded him that she had a nine-year-old son who was probably somewhere in the apartment. Carla shook her head vigorously from side to side. "No. No, please!"

"You take another penny from my dad, and I'll break every bone in your body. You understand?"

She nodded. "Yes."

"Good."

He let go of her and started to back out the door, stopping to give the tall man on the floor another kick in the ribs.

From the doorway, he said, "Easter is past, Carla. So it's time to take down your Christmas tree. And get yourself to rehab. You need it."

Lisa Clark dreamt that she was at the beach and the sun was in her eyes. Squinting into the bright light, she saw chubby two-year-old Olivia playing happily in the sand like an angel. She wore a pink bathing suit and held a little green shovel in her right hand. Her face shone with pure delight, and her hair was so blond it looked almost white.

"Look, Mommy," she squealed as she threw a shovelful of sand in the air. A gust of sea air pulled the sand and tossed it back, so that most of it landed on top of Olivia's head and got into her mouth and eyes.

In an instant, the little girl's expression changed from happiness to distress. She scrunched up her mouth as though she was about to cry.

Lisa lunged forward to pick her up. But when she tried to locate Olivia, the sun blinded her. So she reached out across the hot sand.

A stern voice said, "Don't move, *Señora!*" Firm hands held her.

"What?" She squinted into the bright light and saw a man with gray hair looking down at her.

"This will just take a minute," he said gently.

She saw that she was lying on a beige sheet and a heavyset woman was holding her right arm. When a needle entered her finger, she tried to pull away.

"Who are you? What are you doing?"

Her head felt swollen, like a big balloon, and her mouth and tongue were dry.

"Where am I?"

She watched the glass vial fill with red blood. Then felt another needle enter her arm.

"Close your eyes, *Señora*. In another minute we will be finished."

She was trying to remember where she was and the last thing she had experienced. But all she could think of was Olivia in her pink bathing suit.

"Where's my daughter?" she asked.

"Your daughter is resting, *Señora*. Close your eyes."

The man's soothing voice entered her ears and swirled through her brain like a dancer holding a pink veil. She smelled alcohol and knew there was a reason why she was thinking of Olivia, and that it was important, but she couldn't focus enough to determine what it was.

Crocker sat in the dining room of his two-story house in Virginia Beach with his dog, Brando, by his side. Crocker was eating pasta primavera with his wife; his daughter, Jenny; and Jenny's red-haired friend, Leslie, listening to Leslie talk about the volunteer work she was doing for the Red Cross, when the phone rang in the kitchen. He got up, thinking that he liked Leslie and the positive influence she had on his daughter, turned down the stereo, which was playing Gato Barbieri's "Europa," and picked up the phone.

He heard his XO's voice on the other end say, "The CO needs to see you."

"I'll be there in fifteen minutes," he answered.

"Thanks."

Returning to the table, he announced, "Sorry, but I've got to go in."

"Dad," Jenny said. "I thought we were going to talk about colleges." She was in the final semester of her junior year at First Colonial High School and had developed an interest in medicine and biology.

"We will, sweetheart, when I get back."

Holly sighed and reached for his plate. "I'll save the rest of your dinner."

He'd planned to spend the weekend with the two most important women in his life. Maybe take them to the movies tomorrow and do some work around the house.

"See you later," he said, pushing the chair back under the table and shifting his attention from home to work.

He turned and walked quickly downstairs to his pickup parked in the garage, removed the HUKI surf ski from the back, set it in its rack, and drove directly to SEAL Team Six compound, passing the spot where he'd hit the buzzard roughly two years earlier.

He entered the CO's office with the bitter taste of buzzard feathers in his mouth. Captain Sutter sat in khakis reading something on his desk, with Jim Anders from CIA looking over his shoulder.

Seeing the look on Crocker's face, the CO removed his reading glasses and cleared his throat. "You okay, Crocker?"

"Yes, sir."

Sutter pointed to one of the four high-backed leather chairs that formed a semicircle in front of his desk and said, "Then have a seat."

Crocker and the deputy chief of CIA operations shook hands. Anders stood about five foot ten and had the build of an NFL linebacker. His brown hair was neatly parted on the side and Brylcreemed back.

Sutter drank coffee from his blue DEVGRU mug and said, "I understand that you spoke to Senator Clark."

Crocker nodded. "Yes, I called to express my concern and support."

"Good," Sutter said, settling back in his chair.

The truth was that he had told Clark he wanted Black Cell

to be tasked with the recovery of Clark's wife and daughter, but that the only way he imagined that would happen was if Clark made that request directly to the White House.

"What do you think of Tino Suárez?" Sutter asked.

"Tino Suárez?" It took Crocker's mind a few seconds to shift gears and summon the image of the young SEAL.

Suárez was a tough young operative from Team Two who had been selected into Team Six three years ago. He'd grown up in the Bronx, the son of a Mexican immigrant mother and Salvadoran father, worked hard, seemed to handle all the challenges that were thrown at him, and didn't take shit from anyone. Like Ritchie, he was a breacher and explosives expert. And like all the SEALs on Six, he excelled in all aspects of maritime counterterrorism and small-unit tactics. He also spoke Spanish.

"I like Tino a lot," Crocker answered. "Why?"

"Because I'm sending him with you to Mexico," Sutter answered.

Crocker sat up. *Excellent*, he said to himself.

"I should have asked this first," Sutter said, adjusting the collar on his shirt. "Are your men ready?"

Cal certainly wasn't. Crocker didn't need to tell his CO that he was in nearby Portsmouth Naval Medical Center recovering from two broken vertebrae and trauma to his liver, stomach, and spleen. It would be a month at least before he was back on his feet.

That left Davis, Akil, and Mancini, all of whom were technically on standby, which meant they had to remain close to the compound and be ready to deploy in as little as four hours.

"Yes, sir," Crocker answered.

"How many are you?"

"Five, sir, including Suárez"

"That works."

Sutter grabbed a paper off his desk and handed it to Crocker. "This e-mail arrived today at Senator Clark's Capitol Hill office."

It read: "You started this war, now we're taking it into your backyard. Your wife will die in three days if the United States doesn't release the following people, who are being held in U.S. jails." Following was a list of forty Spanish names that meant nothing to Crocker. At the end it read, "Your enemy, Z-13. P.S. We will send you her head after we cut it off so you will have something to remember."

Crocker handed the e-mail back to Sutter and asked. "What's Z-13?"

Anders shook his head. "We think it's a cell of one of the major Mexican drug cartels."

"Who are the individuals listed at the bottom?"

"Drug dealers and hit men," Anders answered. "Mexicans, mostly. Two or three Colombians. The majority of them are associated with the Mexican drug cartel Los Zetas."

Crocker had heard of Los Zetas and their brutal reputation. They and the Sinaloa cartel were considered the most powerful in Mexico.

"Why'd they target Mrs. Clark?" he asked.

Sutter: "We don't know the specifics."

"If you look at it from their perspective, she's ideal," Anders interjected. "I mean, there's no one in the Senate who is a stronger and more vocal supporter of the war on drugs than her husband. Senator Clark's also a hard-liner on immigration and has lobbied hard for a heavily guarded border and the arrest and deportation of all illegal immigrants."

Crocker was already thinking ahead. He hadn't spoken to Davis, Akil, and Mancini in a week and a half and had no idea where their heads were at. Nor did he know what they thought of Tino Suárez or how he was likely to blend into the team.

He asked, "Where do you want us to deploy?"

Anders reached into his briefcase and handed him an envelope filled with papers. "Guadalajara, Mexico. You'll use the same cover you used earlier this year in Venezuela, namely that you're Canadian adventurers working for Balzac Expeditions and you're planning a trek into the Yucatán jungle."

Crocker nodded and said, "Okay."

"The FBI and DEA have set up a field office there, in Guadalajara."

"Why Guadalajara?"

"Because someone from the Yavapai County sheriff's office picked up something that, combined with tips phoned into Crime Stoppers and NSA intercepts, has made the FBI conclude that the kidnappers are operating in and around Guadalajara."

"Got it."

"You'll work with the joint FBI/DEA task force but report to me," stated Anders.

"What does that mean exactly?" Crocker asked, knowing how sensitive both the FBI and DEA were to anyone stepping on their operational toes.

"We're hoping everyone can cooperate, given the gravity of the situation," Sutter offered.

"And lack of time," Anders added.

It was a nice idea, but in Crocker's experience interagency ops rarely worked smoothly under any circumstances.

"What about gear and weapons?" he asked.

Anders turned to Sutter, who said, "You're going in as civilian adventurers, so take anything you think is appropriate. But no weapons. Whatever you need will be provided by the FBI field office in Mexico."

That was disappointing.

"Because of Clark's prominence in the Senate, and the fact that his wife is a personal friend of the First Lady, and because we're looking at a ticking clock, the White House will be wanting hourly updates," added Anders. "In other words, they're highly involved and want quick results. Which means no infighting or pussying around. If Mrs. Clark's head comes back in a box, the president knows he'll be facing major political problems."

Crocker nodded. "Understood."

"So follow whatever leads the joint FBI/DEA task force gives you, but move quickly. And don't trust the Mexicans. Consider anything involving them a nonstarter. I don't know what the FBI will tell you, but hear it from me: The whole damn country is corrupt from the president's office on down."

Crocker crossed his arms in front of him and said, "That's screwed up."

"The new Mexican president, Enrique Peña Nieto, is talking about scaling back the violence, and U.S. involvement," Anders continued. "He's made it clear that he doesn't want us there but is making an exception in this case."

"What Jim is saying is that the situation is a god-awful,

hopeless mess, which is why we're sending you," Sutter added.

"Thanks," Crocker said, anticipating the challenge.

Anders said, "You're booked on an eight a.m. flight to Dallas–Fort Worth. From there it's a short hop to Guadalajara."

"Okay."

"Obviously, we need quick results."

"You'll get 'em."

Sutter warned, "Don't start a war in the process."

Crocker was up and halfway to the door. "We'll try not to."

"I'm serious."

"So am I."

CHAPTER SEVEN

The past is never dead. It's not even past.
—William Faulkner

LISA AWOKE in the middle of the night, her stomach burning and her body damp with sweat. Reaching for the light switch, she saw the white bandages on her index finger and forearm and remembered the gray-haired man drawing blood.

The lamp cast a hideous shadow on the wall to her left, made by a young man slumped in the chair facing her bed with an automatic pistol tucked in the waistband of his pants.

Unlike on other occasions when Lisa had awakened from drug-induced sleep, this time she immediately understood her situation. Her alert mind darted from subject to subject, image to image. The white grip of the pistol, the slight mustache above the young man's upper lip, her own throbbing finger, the gnawing feeling in her empty stomach, her husband and son, Olivia, the Jackal, Johnny Depp, the cage filled with jackals, the fact that there were no clocks anywhere so it was almost impossible to keep track of time.

She sat up and focused on the pistol, which leered at her like a challenge as a sliver of moon peeked through the window and a lone bird called plaintively outside.

Do I dare take the pistol, free Olivia, and try to escape? Or should I wait for someone to rescue us?

She knew that Clark would do everything in his power to secure their freedom. He might not be creative and exciting, but he was steadfast and reliable, and she needed him now.

As the guard snored gently, Lisa remembered something Henri Gaudier had told her many years ago: Cowardice is the only sin.

Am I being a coward now for not grabbing the pistol and taking action myself?

She wasn't sure.

What if I screw up and get us both killed?

Sitting up in bed and chewing the inside of her mouth, Lisa started to argue with herself.

What constituted cowardice, and was it really a sin? Was it, as Henri had said, the only sin that mattered? Or the most important one? What about gluttony, lust, and pride, all of which she had been guilty of, too?

Hadn't he meant: Don't be afraid to acknowledge the truth. And when you find the truth, don't shrink from taking appropriate action.

Part of her reasoned that the reality as far as her husband was concerned was that he couldn't handle the truth about her past, which was why she hadn't told him. So why was it wrong to hide things from him in the interest of preserving their marriage and keeping their family together?

A second, deeper part of her said no. The truth wasn't something you could remodel or change according to the person you were talking to, or the circumstances.

She looked at the rumpled gray sheets, the guard with the pistol, the shadows on the wall, saw her own gaunt face reflected in the glass over the picture of La Santísima Muerte, and came to the conclusion that in some karmic way she had brought this current dilemma on herself.

In her mind's eye she pictured the Jackal's strange, scarred, rebuilt face, the fever in his eyes, the potent, almost violent energy he gave off, and its effect on her. And as she did, she recalled a September night more than twenty years ago.

But she didn't want to go there. Not now. Not ever.

Trying to force her brain to change the subject, Lisa closed her eyes and recalled gentle summer days growing up with her parents and older brother in Virginia—making peach ice cream with her friend Samantha, swimming in Crystal Lake in the summer, and meeting her boyfriend, Adam, after baseball practice. The freckles on his upturned nose, his long legs as he glided across the green field, the way he played guitar and sang to her, then kissed her on the lips.

But even those sweet memories circled back to Henri and the hot, humid night in September she had tried all these years to forget. It was a Sunday, shortly after 9 p.m. The streets of Georgetown were quiet. They had eaten fresh crabs and oysters for dinner at an outdoor table covered with newspaper. She could taste the salty brininess and the German beer.

Afterward they drove in Henri's white Mercedes to a two-story brick apartment building off MacArthur Boulevard, not far from Georgetown University. She was there to settle a debt she owed to a young drug dealer named Raj.

They parked in the lot behind the building. Henri, who was in a good mood, having won money in a recent backgammon tournament, offered to lend her the five thousand dollars she owed. She said, "No, that's very generous, but I'll handle this myself." She went in alone.

The elevator smelled of dirty laundry. The apartment stank of rotten food and BO. Raj sat on the couch playing Nintendo with one hand and holding a cordless phone with the other. Between phone calls and through the thick brown hair that hung over one side of his dark-skinned face, they negotiated.

He said he would cut the amount owed to two thousand dollars if she agreed to clean his apartment one day a week for the next six months. When she turned that down, he offered to forgive the debt entirely in exchange for Lisa's performing on him a certain lewd act that he would record with his camcorder.

She was outraged at first. But five thousand dollars was a lot of money. She agreed, with certain stipulations. She'd perform the act three times over the next week but wouldn't let him record it.

Sex was sex, she told herself. It wasn't love. She'd get it over with, clear the debt, learn never to get in that situation again, and move on.

But when gaunt, sweaty Raj lowered his pants and grabbed her, she pulled away and ran out the door. She jumped into the Mercedes, telling herself that she was a fool to get hooked on cocaine and an idiot to agree to Raj's offer.

She shouted at Henri to gun the engine and leave fast.

He turned to her and asked what had happened.

Looking past his shoulder, she saw Raj running toward them, pulling at his gray sweatpants. She thought he looked pathetic, then realized he was running into the path of the car. "Watch out!" she shouted.

In a moment of panic, she grabbed hold of the steering wheel with her left hand and turned it sharply to avoid hitting Raj head-on. The front right fender grazed his left hip and knocked him off his feet and into the side of the building. In the headlights, she saw his head hit the brick wall and shatter.

Two days later, she read in the *Washington Post* that Raj Malik Gupta had been found dead—"the victim of a suspected drug-related hit-and-run." The D.C. police never questioned her or Henri and, as far as she knew, never traced the Mercedes.

Henri dismissed it as an accident. But the truth was that they had left Raj bleeding to death in the parking lot and fled the scene. Had they called an ambulance immediately, he might have been saved.

Now she pictured Raj's bulbous nose and big limpid eyes. He had been young, greedy, and stupid, but he hadn't deserved to die.

Remembering his sour stench, her stomach clenched like she was going to be sick. She had thought over the years that somehow the past might come back to haunt her. But she had never imagined that it would happen like this.

Even if I deserve this, my daughter doesn't. I've got to save Olivia. She needs me. I've got to be strong!

Crocker had suffered pangs of conscience, too. But they weren't as deep, or as active. Part of that had to do with the role he played, defending his country, and his training.

He worked hard to be an honest man. And during quiet moments like this, he sensed that the lives he had taken in the line of duty had left a dark spot on his soul. When he thought about the young men he had trained and led, and all the young men and women in the armed forces who had killed others in combat, he knew that the emotional scars would stay with them forever.

There was a spiritual price a warrior had to pay, and Crocker saw honor in that, not shame. You had to be brave enough to look the horror of war in the face and acknowledge the shortcomings of mankind. Then suck it up and move on.

He faced forward and straightened his seat as the American Airlines pilot announced that the three-and-a-half-hour flight from Norfolk was about to end at Dallas–Fort Worth airport. After a two-hour layover, he and the other four SEALs would catch another two-and-a-half-hour flight to Guadalajara. They'd arrive around 1900 hours local, less than two days from the kidnappers' deadline.

Maybe because this was their first mission without Ritchie, the guys on the team seemed uncharacteristically quiet and lost in their own thoughts. Mancini sat behind Crocker reading a book titled *What the Dog Saw* by Malcolm Gladwell. Davis beside him watched *Braveheart* on his laptop.

Suárez and Akil, across the aisle, were the only ones talking.

Crocker heard Suárez ask Akil if he was Muslim and heard Akil answer, "Yeah. So what?"

"You don't have a problem fighting the war on terror against Muslim extremists?" Suárez asked.

"No," Akil answered. "Just like you're part Mexican, and we're on our way to that country now to kick the asses of some nasty mofos there."

"What I'm talking about is different," Suárez explained.

His skin was browner than Akil's, and he had brilliant black eyes and a wide face with a scar that ran from his cheekbone to his chin—the result of a diving accident during training.

"You're talking about nationality," Suárez said. "I'm talking about religious beliefs."

"You Christian?" the taller, broader Akil asked.

From across the aisle, Crocker watched Suárez make the sign of the cross. "Yes," he answered, "the Lord Jesus Christ is my savior."

"Then how can you be in the business of annihilating our enemies when Jesus told his followers to turn the other cheek?"

It was a good question, Crocker thought. Suárez responded by reciting Matthew 5:39: "'But I tell you, do not resist an evil person. If anyone slaps you on the right cheek, turn to them the other cheek also.'"

"That's exactly what I'm talking about," argued Akil.

"The Scripture also says in Exodus 22:2, 'If a thief be found breaking up, and be smitten that he die, there shall no blood be shed for him.'"

"So..."

"To me that means one has the right to defend his home,

his family, and his country," Suárez explained. "Because aren't the terrorists we fight against the same as thieves who are trying to steal our freedoms and liberties?"

Akil grinned. "Maybe."

"Or maybe not," Suárez mused out loud. "I ask myself those questions all the time and pray for an answer."

"Do you get one?"

"Sometimes."

Crocker liked Suárez more already. He wanted strong men with consciences who understood the personal and spiritual sacrifices they were making, not stone-cold killers and sociopaths.

And he hoped that Suárez and Akil were getting off on the right foot but wasn't sure when he exited the plane beside Akil, who described the new team member as "a nice guy with shit for brains."

Crocker said, "Don't be so judgmental, and cut the new guy some slack."

"I'll try."

After the dull sameness of the plane cabin and the stale air, the sights and sounds of the Dallas–Fort Worth airport terminal woke him up. Tall, buxom blondes; an old couple holding hands while being pushed in matching wheelchairs; an overweight family sitting around a huge bucket of fries; anxious young men in business suits selling stuff over cell phones; a group of smiling young recruits in camouflage fatigues boarding a flight to North Carolina; a couple of college guys in shorts and flip-flops carrying Mexican sombreros; women in power suits and patent-leather shoes pulling black carry-ons; kids dressed all in black covered with tattoos.

These are the people we're defending, he said to himself with a smile.

Carrying his Starbucks double espresso and Greek yogurt, he approached Suárez, Davis, and Akil. The last two were sitting near the gate howling with laughter.

"What are you two baboons laughing about?" Crocker asked.

Davis: "Suárez was just telling us that his ex-wife used to ask him to piss on her in the shower."

"What for?"

"I'm not kidding, chief. She used to wipe it all over her face and body like this. She said it was good for her skin."

"Where is she now?" Akil asked.

"She's living outside Albuquerque making jewelry."

Akil: "Next time I pass through, I'll look her up."

Their banter was interrupted by a PA announcement informing them that their flight's gate was being moved from concourse A to C, which meant gathering their stuff and taking the Skylink. They walked in a group, dressed casually in jeans, polo shirts, and hoodies, looking like athletes.

Aside from Mancini, with his perpetual scowl and numerous tattoos, they seemed like a genial group of guys. Only if you looked carefully would you notice the confidence with which they carried themselves and the intensity in their eyes.

Approximately three hours later, the Boeing 767-200 they rode in cut through the smog and low-lying clouds and landed at Don Miguel Hidalgo y Castilla International Airport in Guadalajara.

As they stood in line at Immigration, Mancini explained that the modern steel-and-glass structure they stood in had been named in honor of Miguel Gregorio Antonio Ignacio Hidalgo y Castilla Gallaga Mandarte Villaseñor, who was a priest born of pure Spanish blood. Father Hidalgo was so shocked by the poverty he saw in his rural Mexican town of Dolores in the early 1800s that he marched throughout the territory preaching revolt against the Spanish and eventually raising an army of a hundred thousand *campesinos* armed with sticks, stones, and machetes.

When his peasant army ran into a force of six thousand trained and armed Spanish troops, they were slaughtered, and Father Hidalgo was executed by a firing squad. His last words were "Though I may die, I shall be remembered forever."

His head was cut off in Guanajuato City, east of Guadalajara, where it was displayed for ten years. It was finally taken down and buried when Father Hidalgo's goal of Mexican independence was achieved in 1821.

"Mexicans seem to have a thing about cutting people's heads off," remarked Akil, referring to a recent spate of Ciudad Juárez drug vendettas that had been reported in the U.S. press.

Suárez, whose mother's family hailed from the colonial city of Puebla, east of Mexico City, turned to Mancini and asked, "Where did you learn all that?"

"I guess nobody told you that Manny's really an oral encyclopedia," Davis answered.

"More like a freak who reads constantly and never sleeps," Akil added.

"But don't cross him. 'Cause he's crazy strong. Bench

presses three seventy-five like it's nothing, even though he looks like a puss."

They had passed through Immigration and were retrieving their bags.

Grabbing Suárez by the shoulder, Mancini said, "You probably know that Mexican independence is celebrated on September sixteenth, which is the day in 1810 when Father Hidalgo gave a speech called the *Grito de Dolores* during Mass, which was essentially a battle cry for independence. I can quote a few lines from it, if you like."

"Are you part Mexican?" Suárez asked.

Davis answered before Mancini got a chance. "Joey Mancini. He's as Italian as meatballs and spaghetti."

Akil whispered into Suárez's ear, "Don't tell anyone, but Mancini's our secret weapon. We use him to bore people to death."

Suárez choked back a laugh.

"Akil thinks it's cool to be ignorant," Mancini responded. "He believes that his boyish insouciance makes him more attractive to the random chicks he picks up in bars and hotel lounges."

Akil: "What the fuck does 'insouciance' even mean?"

"Look it up, Akil. Any good psychologist can tell you that you're compensating for your small dick and latent homosexuality."

"You wish, Manny."

Crocker always enjoyed Mexico and had visited almost a dozen times. The last was a cave-diving trip that he had taken with Holly to the Yucatán. Not only were the underground air and cave water restorative, but as they swam and looked up at patches of sky through holes in the caves, Crocker felt that they were in the presence of spirits that were thousands of years old.

There was something deep and mysterious about the country. He wasn't a big reader, but his interest in military campaigns had drawn him to the incredible *True History of the Conquest of New Spain* by Bernal Díaz del Castillo—an eyewitness account of the Spanish conquest of Mexico. Crocker had marveled at how the relatively small group of six hundred soldiers, with fifteen horses and fifteen cannons, had prevailed against an Aztec army numbering in the hundreds of thousands.

Especially interesting was the pivotal role played by La Malinche, the Nahua Indian woman from the Gulf Coast of Mexico who served as Cortés's guide and interpreter and later bore him a son. Nearly six hundred years later, she was still a controversial figure in Mexico. Crocker had heard that to call someone a *malinchista* was to accuse that person of being a traitor to their people, or someone who hated Mexicans.

As they approached the exit, his thoughts were interrupted by a large Hispanic-looking man who stepped into his path. "Tom Crocker?" the man asked.

"Who wants to know?"

"Carlos Nieves, FBI. I've got a colleague and two SUVs waiting on the curb. You want a lift?"

"How much?"

"A round of beer and a plate of nachos."

Crocker checked Nieves's ID and indicated to his men to follow. He'd been told that the man running the joint

FBI/DEA task force was named David Lane, so he asked, "Where's Lane?"

"He's waiting at headquarters, which is actually in a compound in the Zapopan part of town," Nieves answered as he helped load the SEALs' gear into the back of one of the SUVs. "You'll be bunking in the same compound, in a separate structure. It's pretty damn posh, with a barbecue, nice patio, even a pool. You bring a suit?"

Crocker shook his head. He wasn't interested in pools or amenities. The little time they had left was ticking past. As they rode into the city, he pictured Lisa Clark's face and tried to imagine the stress she and her daughter were under. He considered pulling innocent women and children into conflicts and using them as barter to be the lowest form of cowardice.

Nieves slowed the black Honda Pilot. Looking ahead, Crocker saw a sea of red brake lights covering all four lanes of the expressway.

"What's going on?" he asked. The sky was dark purple and charcoal gray.

"Looks like a roadblock," Nieves explained, steering the vehicle onto the shoulder and passing a long line of cars and trucks. He was broad with a big square head, stood six foot three, and must have weighed 260 pounds. Like a lot of really big men Crocker had met, there was a gentleness about him.

"What kind of roadblock?" Crocker asked, looking back to check that the second SUV with Davis and Mancini aboard was behind them.

"I don't know what you've been told about Guadalajara," answered Nieves. "It's always been a sophisticated city. Big parks; universities; lots of history, culture, and art; and a real vital tech industry that some people say is a close second to Silicon Valley. Even though it's the second-largest city in Mexico, it's been pretty much untouched by the usual drug cartel violence, until last year. Since then the shooting, bombings, and other acts of violence have been virtually nonstop."

"How do you explain that?" Crocker asked. A billboard to their right advertised *The Hangover Part III*, showing Ken Jeong parachuting into Las Vegas. The Spanish translation of the title was *¿Qué Pasó Ayer? Parte III* (*What Happened Yesterday?*)

"A war's raging between the two major cartels for control of the city," Nieves answered. "The Sinaloans have quietly owned this area for years, buying judges and cops, absorbing local groups, and plying their dirty trade. Their main business, by the way, is crystal meth."

"Really?" Crocker interjected. "I'm no expert, but I thought it was coke and pot."

"Crystal meth has the highest profit margin," Nieves explained, "and the cartels can make it themselves. They don't have to worry about growing marijuana and poppies, which requires cropland, rainfall, and harvesting. And in terms of cocaine, they don't have to hassle with producers in Colombia, Ecuador, and Peru, or middlemen in Central America and Haiti."

"I hadn't thought of that."

"Meth is not only relatively easy to produce, it's also cheap and highly addictive, whether smoked, snorted, injected, or swallowed in a pill. Which explains why worldwide consumption has skyrocketed."

Crocker flashed back to the image of Carla smoking meth on the edge of her bed and wondered if it had been imported from Mexico. Ahead, flashing blue lights marked the roadblock.

"If it's the military, they'll probably wave us through," Nieves offered. "But if it's the police, we might be stuck here for hours."

"How come?"

"Because almost all the police in this country, whether they're local, municipal, state, or PFM, are corrupt up to their fucking eyeballs. Locals will tell you they fear them even more than the narcos. The army, on the other hand, conducts raids of labs and warehouses, then disappears back into their barracks. They're all about seizing drugs and burning them in a big bonfire show. But they rarely make arrests."

"Doesn't sound like a winning strategy."

"It isn't. Not by a long shot."

Crocker had a practical question: "How do you tell the difference between the police and the army?"

"The army guys look like soldiers."

"Meaning?"

"They dress in uniforms, act more professional, and generally don't stick their hands out asking for bribes."

Crocker nodded. "Good to know."

As they inched up to the roadblock, Nieves continued. "The Sinaloa cartel is a family-based enterprise run by a guy named Chapo Guzmán. You might have heard of him. He's also known as Shorty. The little bastard's in his late fifties and grew up poor on a little cattle ranch near the U.S. border. Today he's considered the most powerful drug trafficker on the planet, with a net worth of over a billion. *Forbes* magazine has him at forty-one in their list of the most powerful people in the world."

Soldiers armed with automatic weapons and wearing black masks over their faces signaled Carlos to stop and roll down the window. He obliged with an easy smile, flashed an FBI badge, then engaged two of the soldiers in conversation. Though Crocker spoke some Spanish, the men talked too fast for him to understand.

After the soldiers waved them through, he turned to Nieves and asked, "What was that about?"

"It's a bad situation. Something like forty people were gunned down by guys with AKs this afternoon."

"Where?" Crocker asked.

"Downtown."

"Downtown Guadalajara?"

"Yeah."

"Who did they attack?" Crocker asked.

"According to the soldiers, a bunch of random people—shopkeepers, a couple tourists, a retired professor feeding the pigeons in the park, students. My guess is it's part of the Los Zetas campaign to scare the living shit out of everyone and gain respect."

Crocker had read somewhere that Mexican officials estimated there had been as many as thirteen hundred beheadings and public hangings, and tens of thousands of other drug-related killings, in the past year.

Nieves veered off the highway at high speed and drove down modern tree-lined avenues with office buildings that displayed familiar names—Citibank, HSBC, American Express, IBM, General Motors, etc. The handsome city appeared prosperous and offered a few elegant vestiges of its colonial past.

"Usually these streets are crowded," Nieves remarked. "People are staying inside."

They passed a large country club and entered an upscale residential area filled with green parks and squares. Many of the houses were hidden behind high concrete walls. At the gates stood armed guards.

Nieves pointed at a newly constructed house and remarked, "The newer ones with palm trees belong to drug traffickers."

"How do you know?" Crocker asked.

"Apparently, they've got a thing for palm trees," he answered with a shrug. "Palm trees and diamonds. Diamonds around their necks, diamonds in their teeth, big diamonds in their girlfriends' belly buttons. Beats the shit out of me. You ever try to make love to a babe with a diamond in her belly button?"

"Can't say I have," Crocker answered.

"Me, either. But it's got to be uncomfortable, right?"

They stopped at a red light in a little commercial area with shops. Through the passenger window Crocker watched a group of young people sitting at an outdoor café laughing and acting like happy, normal—if somewhat privileged—teenagers.

He heard an approaching siren. Seconds later a black Ford pickup filled with men wearing black helmets and uniforms skidded through the intersection. Two of the men stood holding on to the roll bar with one hand and AR15 automatic rifles with the other.

"Who are they?" Crocker asked.

"The Federales," Nieves answered. "Federal police."

"They looked scared," Crocker remarked.

Several blocks later, Nieves turned into a driveway with a tall blue gate, stopped, and honked. A very thin, weathered Mexican man with short gray hair and a crooked smile opened it from inside and nodded.

"That's our man Ramón. He takes care of the pool and grounds."

CHAPTER EIGHT

In Mexico, you have death very close.
—Gael García Bernal

THE ACCOMMODATIONS were a couple of notches higher than acceptable—an older-looking two-story structure with a garage built into it that sat under lush laurel trees. It reminded Crocker of the kind of vacation house you'd find on a lake in New Hampshire, with living room, dining room, and kitchen downstairs and three bedrooms and a bathroom upstairs.

Crocker tossed his kit on one of the beds and hurried downstairs to do a quick survey of the house—access through two doors, one at the front of the house, another side door that led to the garage. The lock on the garage door was broken. All of the windows had simple latches and were easy to punch in.

Security sucked, but they weren't planning to stay long. The refrigerator was stocked with beer, sodas, milk, and eggs. He popped open a bottle of Bohemía, gulped it down, and looked out the front window to the more modern house that sat on the other side of an Olympic-sized swimming pool.

They'd only been there ten minutes and he was already feeling antsy.

"What do we do now?" Mancini asked as he plopped down on the sofa, picked up a copy of *Esquire* someone had left behind, and opened it to a photo of a half-naked Lena Headey—one of the stars of *Game of Thrones*.

"Nieves said he'd come get us," Crocker responded, understanding that as long as they lacked their own transportation and had no weapons, they were totally dependent on their FBI/DEA hosts.

"I guess that means we wait."

Sitting at a desk across the room, Davis slipped a CD into his laptop. The theme from *The Outer Limits* played, followed by the deep voice of a narrator who said, "Through all legends of ancient peoples, Assyrian, Babylonian, Sumerian, Semitic, runs the saga of the Eternal Man, one who never dies, called by various names....The hero who strides through the centuries."

Crocker waved at Davis to turn down the sound. The SEAL science fiction aficionado complied.

Glancing at his Suunto watch, which had adjusted automatically, Crocker saw that the local time was 1944. He opened the large envelope Nieves had given him and started to leaf through the classified FBI and CIA reports. On the first page of one, he read the highlighted sentences: "Mexican drug cartels have been in operation without much interruption from the Mexican and U.S. government for decades. **Their net-**

works are more extensive than any intelligence network in the world."

The last sentence startled him, so he read it again. Then he saw that the wholesale value of illegal drugs from Mexico sold in the United States was estimated to be about $40 billion.

Crocker was about to repeat this staggering number to Mancini when he heard a knock at the door. Seconds later Nieves entered, carrying a yellow menu. "We're ordering in," he announced as if they were a bunch of guys about to watch a football game on TV. "If you've never had Oaxacan food, I recommend the chicken mole, which is a rich, spicy chocolate sauce."

"Screw the mole," Crocker groaned. "When are we gonna get moving?"

"Relax, dude. Lane's working on something for you guys now."

"Don't call me dude," Crocker responded, thinking that the best strategy might be to strike fast before the bad guys knew they were in the country. "We didn't come here to fuck around."

"I know that. I didn't mean any disrespect."

Crocker's head was already spinning. Forty billion was more than eight times the entire CIA budget. Returning to the reports, he read about cartel attacks on parties and drug rehabilitation centers, the firebombing of a Monterrey casino that burned fifty-two people to death, the targeted killings of journalists and media workers, the shootings, kidnappings, and mass graves—seventy-two in Tamaulipas on the southern border, forty-nine in Monterrey, another forty in Nuevo Laredo.

He threw down the reports and started to pace from one end of the room to the other as the rest of the team drank beer and snacked on chips and salsa.

Nieves picked up his exegesis on the drug cartel war where he'd left off. "Some say Chapo Guzmán and the Sinaloans have grown fat and happy. I don't know about that. Maybe he's gotten so big and powerful he doesn't care about what happens in Guadalajara. It's rumored that about half the ministers in the government are on his payroll. All I know is that about a year ago, Los Zetas, which has traditionally operated along the Gulf Coast, started moving in, and things got ugly. I'm talking gunfights, kidnappings, decapitations, full-scale terror."

"What's the difference between the Sinaloa cartel and Los Zetas?" Davis asked.

"Sinaloa is basically a family-run organization that has grown by leaps and bounds and now employs something like two hundred thousand people. Generally they go about their business of dealing drugs and making money and leave other people alone. El Chapo is like a character out of a popular *telenovela*—a common man with a third-grade education who has built a global empire and continues to evade capture by the government and the U.S. Songs are written about him; journalists are constantly spreading gossip about which beautiful woman he's been seen with."

Nieves cleared his throat and sang the verse of a song in Spanish. "That one's called *'El Regreso del Chapo.'* Translated, it says: 'Short guys are always fierce.' That's how the saying goes. It's been proved with Chapo Guzmán."

"Short guys, Suárez," Akil cracked. "He's talking about you."

At five eleven, Suárez was now the shortest guy on the team. Based on the confused expression on his face, he still wasn't up to speed in terms of the group's give-and-take humor.

"Nice song," Davis offered, "but I still prefer Black Crowes or U2."

Akil: "Why don't you just say 'I'm vanilla'?"

"Black Crowes aren't vanilla."

"Bullshit."

"Tell us about the Zetas," Crocker said, steering the conversation back to business.

"Los Zetas are a whole different story. Their founders are deserters from Mexico's elite special forces. They're brutal, efficient, highly organized, and well armed. They don't care about their popularity. They're all about power, influence, and money."

"What does this have to do with the kidnapping of the Clarks?" Crocker asked.

As Nieves opened his mouth to answer, his phone rang to the theme from *The Godfather*. He held up a hand to Crocker and nodded as he listened to the person on the other end. Putting down the phone and rubbing his big hands together, he said, "That was Lane. He's ready to see you."

Crocker slapped the side of the sofa where Mancini, Akil, and Suárez were sitting and said, "Good. Let's go."

David Lane was younger than Crocker expected—mid-to-late thirties, medium height, short dark thinning hair, a long face. He wasn't anyone who would stand out in a crowd, but he projected commitment and intelligence. He also looked harried and tired.

The FBI agent in charge sat at a dining room table covered with papers, the sleeves of his blue-check oxford shirt rolled up to his elbows. He was typing furiously on a laptop and sipping a Diet Coke when Crocker approached.

"Welcome," Lane said. "I'm finishing a report on the violence today."

"I hear you have a plan."

Lane finished typing, leaned forward and reread what he had just written, and pressed Send. Turning to Crocker, he said, "The violence here is shocking to our sensibilities but not unusual for them."

"I just read a bunch of news reports Nieves gave me. Gruesome stuff."

"A Mexican academic I know explained that it goes back to the Aztec view of the world, which was frightening, and ruled by gods who were dangerous and demanding. Our God isn't so demanding, is he, Crocker?"

"I don't know."

"Our God wants us to be fair and considerate, but he doesn't demand our blood in return for simple things like the sun rising in the morning or rainfall," Lane said, nodding toward a redheaded woman who entered in tight blue pants with a pistol in a holster on her hip.

She smiled back at Lane as if they had made some secret communication.

"No, he doesn't," Crocker remarked.

"The Aztecs believed that the gods gave nothing without demanding something in return," Lane continued. "In the case of the Aztec god of rain, Tlaloc, he required the blood of children ages six and seven to ensure the end of the dry season and a sufficient period of rain. Boys and girls were chosen who had double cowlicks in their hair, which was considered an auspicious sign. He preferred the children of nobles. After they were selected, they were dressed in colorful paper costumes and carried from the city to seven ceremonial sites. Their mothers followed them. If they cried a lot, that was considered a good omen. The quantity of tears the children shed before they were sacrificed was considered a direct correlation to the rain that could be expected in the coming year."

Lane was obviously thoughtful and well read. But Crocker hadn't come to hear a lecture on comparative religions, or on the cultural connection between the Aztecs and the modern cartels. "Interesting," he said. "Now let's talk about the mission."

"The more time I spend in this country, the more I appreciate the difference in cultures," Lane continued, maintaining a composed demeanor. "I don't think we fully understand the cultural and historical context we're dealing with here."

"I'm sure you're right."

"You're nodding your head like you agree," Lane said, "but you're looking at me like I'm full of shit."

"I was told that a senator's wife and daughter are scheduled to be executed less than thirty-six hours from now."

"We're well aware of that, Crocker," Lane replied.

"For your information, we've been operating without sleep for more than two days, with little in the way of resources," the redhead announced as she pulled a document out of a printer.

"You'll be moving soon enough," said Lane. "We're planning a raid for early tomorrow morning. Isn't that correct, Karen?"

"Right."

Crocker quickly glanced at his watch. "You're talking six to eight hours from now?"

"Yes, Crocker. Is that soon enough for you?"

He didn't care about their attitude, or whether or not they'd slept. He wanted to make sure that what he had just heard was right. "So you've established where Lisa Clark and her daughter are being held?" he asked.

Both Lane and Karen nodded. "That's correct."

Crocker's sense of urgency shot up. "Where are they?"

"Nearby."

"How'd you find them?"

Lane stood and indicated to Crocker to follow him outside through the double glass doors. Karen grimaced and shot him the middle finger.

Crocker didn't waste a second worrying about the impression he had made on her, or on Lane, for that matter. He stood facing Lane as a warm breeze blew through the compound, stirring the full trees, and Lane lit a Marlboro. From a distance the lights of the city conveyed only promise and beauty.

Lane's eyes narrowed as he exhaled a long stream of white smoke through the amber porch light.

"I understand that you and your men are the best at what you do, which is why you're here. And I totally respect that," he said in a measured tone of voice. "But I want you to know that my people are incredibly capable and dedicated, too.

Karen, Nieves, Marion, Higgins, the others. They've worked their butts off and risked their lives to bring us to this point."

Crocker said, "I don't mean any disrespect."

Lane exhaled again. "Not a problem." He tossed the partially smoked cigarette and crushed it with the heel of his shoe. "This is my operation. My team has spent many hours piecing together shards of information from a myriad of human and electronic sources, analyzing them, and drawing up a plan. In a little while, some people are going to arrive, and we're going to brief you on everything A to Z."

"That's not necessary," Crocker said. "We trust you."

"No. You and your men are about to undertake a very dangerous operation and I think we owe you that."

"All we need to know are the logistics of the operation. How many people we're going up against, how they're armed, where the hostages are being held; details like that. How good is your intel?"

Lane pulled an NEC Terrain out of his back pocket and scrolled through his messages. "I've been working the border area for years, assisting local police departments, ICE, border patrol, and the DEA. It's a losing battle. The only way we can be effective is to get inside the cartels and close to the guys calling the shots. And that involves enormous risks."

"You know someone close to the people who executed the kidnapping?" Crocker asked, stretching the muscles in his lower back.

"Yes, we have a source," Lane whispered back.

Crocker got excited. This was what he wanted to hear. "Who are they, the kidnappers?"

"Members of a very dangerous narcoterrorist group called Los Zetas."

"Nieves told me about them. But…why?"

"Why did they kidnap Lisa and Olivia Clark?" Lane asked back.

Crocker nodded. "Yeah."

"It has to do with a power struggle they're involved in with the Sinaloa cartel," Lane answered. "We don't know if all the Zetas are behind it. But according to our source, this particular leader, the guy who executed this, is trying to show the power and range of his particular cell, while also earning brownie points with the Mexican people by giving the United States a black eye. Senator Clark isn't a very popular figure here, because of his pronouncements on drug trafficking and immigration."

"I get that. Where specifically are they being held?"

"Specifically, a house, or estate, two miles northeast."

Someone was tapping on the glass door behind them. They turned in unison and saw Nieves pointing at his open mouth and waving them inside.

"I think he's trying to tell us that dinner has arrived," Lane said.

"Then what?" Crocker asked.

"Then we wait for our asset. She's scheduled to arrive soon," Lane said, sliding open the door and waiting for Crocker to enter first. "She knows the entire layout of the estate, numbers of guards, the location of the rooms where the women are being held, everything."

Crocker stopped halfway. "She?" he asked. "Your source is a woman?"

"That's correct," Lane answered. "You have a problem with that?"

Crocker shook his head. "Not at all."

The truth was that he worried throughout dinner. He'd been burned by a female source several years ago in Algeria, when he was sent to intercept a shipment of weapons to a group of Islamic terrorists. Instead of expressing his concerns, he decided to wait until he could pull Lane aside and ask him if he had other information—like electronic intercepts—that could back up what his source was telling him.

Five minutes into the chicken mole, black beans, and rice, Lane was summoned upstairs by Karen.

Crocker watched Akil admire her as she climbed the stairs.

"I like the way she wears that pistol," cracked Akil.

"She can probably kick your ass," Davis responded.

"She will, too, if you piss her off," said Nieves as he licked spicy chocolate sauce from the side of his mouth. "Karen's a black belt in karate and a former female motocross champ."

Crocker had raced motorcycles as a teenager and had thought about turning pro before he joined the navy.

"Bring it on," Akil said, washing down the beef tacos he had ordered with bottled water.

Nieves: "She's not into guys."

Akil: "She will be when she meets me."

Nieves laughed loudly.

The flat-screen TV on the wall to the left of where they were seated was tuned to CNN International. When a picture of Lisa Clark appeared on the screen, Mancini grabbed the remote and turned up the sound.

The men grew quiet. A Mexican female correspondent named Carmen Aristegui was being interviewed by Christiane Amanpour. She said the kidnapping was a huge embarrassment to newly elected president Enrique Peña Nieto. One of the Mexican president's campaign promises had been to prioritize the reduction of violence. He also pledged that he did not support the involvement of armed U.S. agents in Mexico—a practice encouraged by the previous Felipe Calderón administration, which had waged a much-publicized and maligned war on drug traffickers.

"Dumb," Akil groaned.

Artistegui, who spoke as though she was an expert on Mexico, said that many Mexican political watchers theorized that the kidnapping was the work of President Peña Nieto's political rivals. She reported that the president was personally heading an all-out effort to locate the kidnappers and their victims. According to an unnamed source close to the president, his security advisors believed that Lisa and Olivia Clark were being held somewhere in the state of Chihuahua, which bordered the United States.

The city of Chihuahua was something like six hundred miles northeast of where they were now.

"Is that correct?" Mancini asked.

Crocker: "No. Her information is wrong."

"How come journalists never get it right?" Davis asked, lifting a bottle of Dos Equis.

"Because they listen to the experts, and the experts never know what the fuck they're talking about," Akil answered.

"And the people who do know generally keep their mouths shut," Nieves added.

A harried Senator Clark appeared on the screen. He was being interviewed in a Capitol Hill corridor and looked like he hadn't slept soundly in days. When he was asked about the kidnapper's demands to release the forty drug cartel associates from U.S. jails, Clark said, "I love my wife and daughter immensely and ask the people holding them to please let them go. They are good, loving people. As far as the kidnapper's demands, I support our government's policy."

It was U.S. policy never to negotiate with or give in to the demands of criminals or terrorists.

Crocker put his plate down on the glass coffee table and pulled Nieves into the kitchen.

"We need to get moving," he said, looking at his watch, which showed that it was 2100 hours and approximately twenty-seven hours from the kidnappers' deadline.

Nieves finished chewing and swallowed. "What did Lane tell you?"

"He said we're going to launch before dawn, and we're waiting for this Mexican woman who knows where the Clarks are being held. She's their source, which is fine, but in the meantime, we have some things to take care of, like getting armed."

Nieves knitted his thick black eyebrows together and said, "I don't know anything about her. I believe she's being run by that redhead you met, Karen Steele, and this other guy named Bob Marion. You'll have to ask Lane about that."

"You've never met her?" Crocker asked.

"The asset? No. It's not that they don't trust me. But it's FBI SOP in a situation like this to keep the circle small."

"What about gear and weapons?" Crocker continued. "Lane said we're supposed to move later tonight."

"I've got a shitload of stuff stored in the garage," Nieves answered. "SIG Sauers, HK45CTs, MP7s, HK416s, M79s, Teflon vests, explosives."

"All right, listen," Crocker said, thinking ahead. "I want you to show what you've got to my ordnance guy, Mancini. So he can get a sense of what's available. While you're doing that, I'll go upstairs to find out what's going on."

Nieves, who was so big and wide he filled a third of the narrow galley kitchen, warned, "No one except for us agents is allowed up there."

"I have a Level-Seven security clearance," Crocker said.

"I've got to check with Lane first."

"Screw that."

CHAPTER NINE

If everything seems under control, you're not going fast enough.

—Mario Andretti

CROCKER CLIMBED the wooden steps two at a time up to the second floor, entered the open door to his right, and saw Lane standing with his back to him speaking on an encrypted phone—which he indentified immediately from the configuration of the instrument and the key on top.

Lane, seeing Crocker, waved him away and snapped his fingers at Karen Steele, who was leaning on the edge of a metal desk talking to a guy with buzz-cut dark hair, who Crocker assumed was Bob Marion.

"Sorry, guy," she said, hurrying over to Crocker and holding up a hand to push him back, "you're not allowed in here."

"The hell I'm not. I need to talk to Lane," Crocker answered, shoving her hand off his chest.

"You can't!"

Crocker quickly glanced at the clock on the wall. Another

fifteen minutes had passed. He said, "Lane, if we're going to launch this mission tonight, we need to start making plans."

Lane covered the receiver and shouted, "I know that. Don't you think I fucking know that?"

"Then hurry up. I want to rescue these women while they're still alive."

He knew enough not to take it personally. Tempers frayed sometimes when type A personalities were keyed up and on edge. The important thing was that they were all fighting for the same cause and had a lot at stake.

Fight in people was a positive, not a negative, Crocker reminded himself. It produced good results when directed intelligently, which was what he hoped was going to happen now, as they all sat in the living room—he, Davis, Mancini, Akil, Suárez, Lane, Nieves, Karen Steele, and the wiry guy with the smirk on his face and buzz cut whom he still hadn't been introduced to but assumed was Bob Marion—listening to the sheriff of Yavapai County, Arizona, describe how a tip phoned into Crime Stoppers led them to an airstrip outside Flagstaff and a flight piloted by a man named Joss Clemson that terminated in Guadalajara.

Karen Steele explained that from the beginning she and other cartel specialists had suspected Los Zetas, in part because of the group's global ambitions and diversity. Los Zetas, unlike the other leading cartels, were involved in satellite businesses, including the theft of petroleum from the state-owned oil company, PEMEX, software and product piracy, prostitution, human smuggling, extortion, money laundering, assassination for hire, auto theft, and robbery. A July 25, 2011, White House executive order named them a transnational crime threat to U.S. national security.

Sheriff Higgins cut in to add that the cartel had become a major crime threat in over a thousand cities and towns in the United States. He related how a colleague of his, who was the police chief of Champaign, Illinois, had recently arrested three Zetas members in connection with a murder in a downtown garage. Subsequent to that, the chief started receiving calls on his cell and home phones warning him to release the men and threatening his wife and children.

"They knew the address of his wife's place of work and where his boys went to school," said Sheriff Higgins. "They're scared of no one."

Next, Steele explained that Los Zetas had evolved from a local Mafia to a quasipolitical organization with international ambitions. They had created alliances with other national criminal groups like Los Kaibiles in Guatemala, as well as the governments of Venezuela, Bolivia, and Cuba, and were known to cooperate with terrorists like Hezbollah.

"If they're such a threat, why haven't we been more aggressive in going after them?" Mancini asked.

"They make a lot of money," Lane answered.

"What does that mean?"

"Their money-laundering activities provide a huge stream of income for major U.S. banks."

Crocker's stomach started to turn. The unethical activities of U.S. financial companies and banks, and the fact that they often operated against the interests of the U.S. government and the American people, formed a subject that he didn't understand that well, but he knew enough to know it stank. Massive greed of that sort disgusted him.

Steele introduced the man with the short black hair. He was Bob Marion, a former CIA analyst who now worked as a high-level security consultant for several large multinational companies. His specialty, he said, was the Mexican cartels and their financial activities.

As coffee was served, Marion explained that since a number of Zetas leaders had been killed and arrested in 2011 and 2012, including two of its founders, Heriberto Lazcano, a.k.a. El Bronce, and Miguel Ángel Treviño Morales, a.k.a. Z-40, some individual cell leaders had become more ambitious and started to advance their own agendas.

One of these, a man named Ivan Jouma, was particularly pernicious, and even articulated a pseudoideological and quasimythical justification for his group's existence. "He orders extreme, symbolic violence to deal with his enemies," Marion remarked. "And projects a Robin Hood–type image to the poor by donating food and medical care and funding and building schools."

"In other words, he's building a popular following," Lane interjected.

"He's extremely active right now," Bob Marion continued, "and looking for ways to add to his growing legend. He's also the man who we believe kidnapped Lisa and Olivia Clark and is holding them hostage."

"Why?"

"To bolster his image as a Mexican nationalist and folk figure with a quality that's known as *duende*."

"What's *duende*?" Crocker asked.

"The ability to attract people through personal magnetism."

Crocker didn't give a shit about his charm. "Tell me about his background."

"His father was a Syrian immigrant and small landowner. His mother, a Sonoran Indian from the west coast. He was raised by his mother's family and recruited into the Mexican Army's elite Grupo Aeromóvil de Fuerzas Especiales—GAFE—at the age of nineteen. We know that he was a member of a GAFE unit that received urban warfare training from our Special Forces. He deserted with Lieutenant Osiel Cárdenas Guillén in 1999 to provide security for the Gulf cartel. And split from the Gulf cartel in 2010 to join Los Zetas. For the last three years, he's been running his own cell within that organization, and is considered aggressive and ambitious."

Crocker had helped train a group of Mexican paratroopers at Fort Bragg in the mid-nineties. "You have a photo?" he asked.

"Here are two, before and after he was shot in the face during a shootout with the Gulf cartel in late 2010," Marion answered, sliding them in front of him. "As you can see, he underwent some extensive plastic surgery."

Crocker first studied the newer picture, which reminded him of a Mexican Mickey Rourke because of the wise-guy sneer and long, stringy hair. The contrast between it and the older photo was considerable. The hungry expression in the eyes and mouth struck him. "Ivan, right?"

"Ivan Jouma, known to most people as El Chacal."

"I think I might have trained this guy in a fast-roping, rappelling, and climbing course at Fort Bragg, around 1996."

"That's possible."

"Where is he now?" Crocker asked, remembering a charming, hard-charging young man who seemed much more alert than the others, played the guitar and sang, and told stories about his uncle, who he claimed was a sorcerer.

Marion said, "I want to answer your question, but first I need you to excuse me for a minute. I'll be back."

Crocker looked at his watch. It was almost 2300. Time was clicking past as they talked.

He walked over to Lane and pointed to his timepiece.

"I know," Lane said.

"Then what the fuck are we waiting for?"

"You'll see."

Ten minutes later, car doors slammed outside and CIA station chief Max Jenson entered with a Hispanic deputy. Jenson was a tall fair-haired man in his late forties who looked as big and strong as a defensive tackle. He leaned on the edge of a table and asked for a quick update, which Lane provided.

Then Marion returned with a short woman who wore a black-and-silver wrestler's mask. He said, "This is Maria. She and other members of her family have been working for El Chacal for years. Now she's cooperating with us."

Ivan Jouma, the Jackal, lay in a lounge chair watching a pre-release DVD of *The Lone Ranger* starring Armie Hammer and Johnny Depp. What he saw was a working edit without music or sound effects. When Depp first appeared on the screen dressed as a bare-chested Tonto with white-and-black face paint and a black crow on his head, Ivan frowned.

"What the fuck?" he asked in Spanish. "Is he trying to look like a *brujo* or a *nagual?* Or is he making a joke?"

"I can't tell," the gray-haired doctor answered as he measured Jouma's blood pressure. He knew that a *brujo* was an Indian witch doctor and a *nagual* someone who reputedly had the ability to transform into an animal. But as a man deeply rooted in science, he didn't believe in either.

"How are the *gringas?*" Ivan asked.

"The mother became very agitated and had to be sedated, but the younger one is calm."

"Good-looking ladies. I wonder what they're worth."

"How is your appetite, *Jefe?*" asked the doctor, changing the subject and pressing the skin under Ivan's right ribs.

"Bad." Ivan winced.

"Pain?"

"All the time."

"Energy level?"

"Sucks."

The doctor stopped, lowered Ivan's shirt, and checked the results of the latest blood tests, which revealed that the hepatitis C type 1 that his client had been suffering from for years had reached the acute stage.

"What do you think, Doc?" Jouma asked.

The doctor rubbed his chin. In his estimation, the infection caused by the virus now affected eighty-five percent of Jouma's liver. The oral ribavirin he'd given him and the interferon alphas he had injected twice a week for the last three years were no longer working. The side effects of the interferon included agitation, depression, and flulike symptoms.

Jouma froze the film on a frame of Johnny Depp walking

along the top of a moving train. "If you have something to tell me, give it to me like a man," he ordered. "Don't be afraid."

The doctor picked a folder off the cabinet to his right that had Olivia Clark's name on it. After quickly confirming that the results of the recent blood tests matched the information on her stolen medical chart, he said, "*Jefe*, I recommend that we go ahead with the procedure."

Jouma nodded and popped an Altoids peppermint into his dry mouth. "Fine. If that's your opinion, we do it."

The doctor cleared his throat. He wanted to clearly explain the risks, which included the body's rejection of the new organ, infection, depression caused by the very long period of convalescence, and the danger of chemical dependency because of the need for strong painkillers.

There was peril for him, too, because if anything went wrong, he would be blamed and probably killed in a painful manner.

But before he could articulate any of this, Jouma's private cell phone rang.

He picked it up and barked, "What?" in Spanish.

As the doctor reviewed the results of the Doppler ultrasound, echocardiograms, and blood tests one more time, Jouma listened, frowned, then asked into the phone, "Who told you this? The *gringo?*" Jouma nodded. "You think we can trust him?"

As the doctor listened to the *jefe* talk, he considered possible clinics in Mexico and nearby countries where the procedure could be performed.

He saw Jouma glance at his diamond-encrusted Hublot Big

Bang chronograph watch, which retailed for over a million dollars.

"Move the merchandise to Tapachula and call the Federales," Jouma barked into the phone. "Then call that video guy, Nelson. I want to record the *señora*'s final words, then send them to her stupid husband."

CHAPTER TEN

Expect problems and eat them for breakfast.
—Alfred A. Montapert

IT WAS a few minutes past 0500 by the time they launched—Crocker in the first SUV with Suárez, and Akil and Mancini following in the dark-blue Suburban with Davis and Nieves. They wore an assortment of straw hats and baseball caps pulled down low, sneakers, boots, and casual clothes to look like gardeners or day workers.

Underneath they had on lightweight eight-millimeter-thick Level III-A+ Dragon Skin Pinnacle Armor capable of stopping 7.62x25mm steel-cased lead-core bullets traveling at 1,450 feet per second. In warm weather the specially designed DuPont Supplex shoulder straps and carrier were designed to wick moisture and excess heat from the body to the surface of the fabric for release, but Crocker felt sweat dripping down his chest to his stomach and into the front of his jeans.

The sun hadn't even begun to rise and the air was already dense and hot. They were driving west down a two-lane road past ranches, factories, subdivisions, and rough hills. Short, squat Maria, seated next to Suárez at the wheel, told him in Spanish to turn off at a dirt road. They bounced for a few minutes past a pen filled with chickens and pigs and stopped at a fence.

Akil hopped out and clipped the lock on the gate. Then they rolled into a scruffy little yard, parked behind some trees, and walked twenty feet to a shed. Maria pointed to a locked wooden box next to where some old clothes were hanging. Suárez kicked it open and retrieved two sets of keys.

"*Por aqui,*" Maria said as she led the men to two old pickup trucks loaded with lawn mowers, weed whackers, leaf blowers, rakes, clippers, and other assorted gardening equipment. She still wore the black-and-silver wrestler's mask. Judging from her hands, she appeared to be a woman in her twenties. She stood about five feet two and was soft and round, with black hair.

"When are these guys going to show up and find their trucks missing?" Crocker asked Suárez.

Suárez spoke to Maria and translated back. "She says they don't work anymore. We gave them green cards, so they closed the business and are moving to the States."

"Where in the States?" Akil asked.

"Orange County."

According to the arrangement Lane had made with Maria, each man had been paid thirty thousand dollars, and they'd been given an additional twenty thousand for the two trucks.

The vehicles were hardly worth it—a beat-up black regular-cab Ford F-150 with a missing front fender and

176,000 miles on the odometer, and an extended-cab silver Chevy S-10. But they worked, as Suárez and Mancini discovered when they drove them out of the yard and back onto the paved road.

The sun started to rise to their right, turning the dusty, polluted air an unhealthy-looking shade of brownish yellow.

From the passenger seat of the lead Ford, Crocker once again consulted the hand-drawn sketch of the estate Maria had given them. "There's only one entrance? She's sure of that?" he asked Suárez.

Maria sat between them praying quietly with a pink rosary clutched in her hands.

"That's what she said. Yes."

"Which one of the Clarks is upstairs?"

Suárez checked with Maria. She pointed to a room on the sketch.

"They keep Mrs. Clark in one of the front bedrooms upstairs. Her daughter is staying in the guest house at the back of the estate."

"And they're both watched by armed guards?"

Maria nodded.

"How many guards inside the house?"

"Usually four or five besides the two watching the women."

"Where?" Crocker asked.

"Two are at the front gate, two in the backyard, one maybe on the first floor."

"Video surveillance?"

Suárez asked Maria, then translated to Crocker, "Eleven cameras total. Two at the front gate, two at the front and back of the main house, four along the outside wall perimeter, two at the front and side doors to the guest house, another at the balcony door to the main house."

They had been over the layout a half dozen times, but still Crocker felt unease about the mission. He thought maybe it had to do with the tragic outcome of the op in Syria, or the fact that this mission had been thrown together so quickly, or that Maria was their source.

According to what Bob Marion had told them back at the safe house, she and members of her family had been employed by El Chacal for years. Recently a half sister and cousin who worked in one of his meth plants had been accused of stealing and buried alive.

Maria instructed Suárez to take a right at the next traffic light. An old man and a boy at the corner pulled a wagon full of yellow flowers. The team waited for a mangy dog to cross ahead of them.

Part of Crocker's unease had to do with operating in Mexico, where it seemed *gringos* were distrusted and *gringo* government agents like them were considered the enemy.

He forced himself to think positively.

Maria pointed to a McDonald's with blue-and-gold plastic monkey bars on the next block. Suárez pulled over.

"Why are we stopping?" Crocker asked.

"She's getting out," Suárez answered.

"Muchas gracias," Crocker said as he slipped out so she could exit.

"Vaya con Dios, Señor," she muttered through the hole in the wrestler's mask.

He watched through the rearview mirror as she turned her

back to them, removed the mask, and tossed it into a box of trash.

They were on their own now, armed with SIG Sauer side arms, HK45CTs, MP7s, HK416s, M-79s, explosives, and handheld USMC ISR radios—all of which were concealed in different parts of the trucks. The neighborhood they entered was quiet, with high walls topped by barbed wire and broken glass. Morning sunlight simmered off the asphalt road.

Crocker saw a tall, freshly painted burnt-sienna wall and palm trees ahead.

"That's it," Suárez remarked.

"Just like Carlos said."

"What?"

"The palm trees, Suárez. Pay attention."

They turned in front of the tall green gate and stopped.

"Should I honk?" Suárez asked.

"Honk once," Crocker said, pulling the faded New York Yankees cap lower over his eyes. He held the SIG Sauer P226 alongside the seat and conducted a press check to ensure there was a chambered round.

A guard poked his dark face over the wall to the right; then the gate swung open. Crocker spotted big trees heavy with lemons and other fruit, and walls covered with flowering vines.

The guard, who had an AK-47 slung over his shoulder, walked to the driver's window, said something to Suárez, then waved them in.

"What did he say?"

"A snake bit one of the dogs last night in the back near some mango trees. He warned us to watch out."

"Dogs?"

"Maria didn't say anything about dogs," Suárez said.

"Dogs we can handle," Crocker whispered back.

They were in about thirty yards before they saw the main house on their left. It appeared smaller than what Maria had described, with columns and a portico at the entrance and a large balcony on the second floor. Golden sunlight reflected off the windows.

They wound to the right and braked in the back by the garage, just as Maria had instructed them to do. A few seconds later, the Chevy S-10 stopped behind them.

The only person Crocker had spotted so far was the guard at the gate, which was good. The stronger the element of surprise, the better.

The six men unloaded the lawn mowers and other equipment, then grabbed their weapons. Each man had a prearranged assignment. They moved quickly—Akil and Nieves to the front gate, Davis and Mancini to the guest house, Crocker and Suárez to the main residence.

Crocker entered first through the side door, his HK416 with ten-inch barrel and suppressor ready. Standing on the tile floor in the small vestibule, he paused a moment to take everything in—sounds, smells, dimensions, shadows—all faster than the speed of light. Through the opening ahead of him, he saw the edge of a large dining room table. Past that was a hallway that led to the stairway to the second floor. On the other side of the stairway he saw a living room with modern bamboo furniture covered in cool colors.

Water flowed in the kitchen to his right. He held up two fingers to Suárez behind him and pointed to his right.

Suárez poked his head into the room and quickly came back.

"Somebody left the water running," Suárez whispered, "but there's no one in there. Fresh coffee in the coffeemaker."

Crocker signaled for him to circle through the kitchen and meet him at the stairs.

He entered the dining room weapon ready, safety off. A white cat sat curled in one of the chairs. A plate of freshly cut papaya, mango, and pineapple lay on the table. But there was no one present.

He paused for a beat and listened but heard nothing inside or out.

The living room was devoid of people, too. Just a large aquarium along one wall, where he watched a little red sea horse swim past. An issue of the Spanish-language gossip magazine *¡Hola!* with Shakira on the cover lay on the sofa. A framed poster for the movie *Donnie Brasco* hung on one of the walls.

Suárez met him at the foot of the stairs and shook his head. They climbed up the stairs two steps at a time. At the landing, Crocker turned right and Suárez turned left, according to the plan.

Another right and Crocker entered a bathroom. He stepped over two wet pink towels on the floor, crossed past the glass shower stall to his right, then carefully pushed open the door to the bedroom.

He saw an empty leather armchair with a picture of a strange skeleton-like woman above it on the wall. Stepping inside, he took in the windows facing the back of the house, and a small desk with a glass holding two paintbrushes. Turning, he saw an unmade bed to his left. A woman's suit hung in the closet over a pair of black high heels.

A tray with an uneaten chicken sandwich sat on a table opposite the bed. In the corner he saw a pair of women's slippers, a pile of women's clothes that included underwear and a pair of gray workout pants, and a half-finished paint-by-numbers art board of an Italian street with a pastry shop.

Crocker pressed the button on the side of the USMC ISR radio and said, "Omega One not here. Repeat, Omega One not in bedroom."

"No sign of Omega Two in the guest house, either," Mancini reported. "The guest house is empty. No dogs present on the property, either."

"All right. Grab any intel you find and meet at the trucks in five."

"Copy."

They were warned, Crocker said to himself. That meant the Jackal knew they were there.

A second later Akil's voice came over the radio. "Alpha One. Alpha One, it's Delta Four. The front gate is unmanned."

"What happened to the guard we saw when we entered?"

"Gone, man. Vanished."

Even more suspicious.

"Wait there, Delta Four. We're pulling out."

"Copy."

He and Suárez quickly scanned the second floor for personal items but didn't find much—some receipts in the desk drawer in one of the other bedrooms, a book in Spanish about Muhammad Ali, a closet full of men's clothes. Even the phones were gone.

"Strange," Suárez whispered.

"Very."

Nothing much, either, on the ground floor. Suárez was standing on a stool looking in kitchen cabinets when Crocker said, "Let's go."

Out the side door, he saw Davis and Mancini waiting by the trucks. Without warning, shots came from the direction of the side wall and a burst of blood rose from Davis's left collarbone. Crocker watched him spin, grab hold of the hood of the Ford pickup, and slide to the ground. Seconds later explosions rocked the front and back walls.

His ears filled with the high-pitched sounds of dogs wailing, Crocker backed inside the doorway and knelt into a crouch. Shielding his eyes from the smoke and flying debris with his left hand and turning left, he saw armed men dressed in dark camouflage with black armored vests and black masks stream through a smoking gap in the back wall. He figured they were probably charging through the front gate, too.

"Move to the main house!" he shouted into the radio. "Manny, you need help with Davis?"

"I've got him."

Nieves: "We're fucked!"

Akil: "Not happening."

Crocker: "Keep quiet and grab as much ammo as you can from the trucks. Then rendezvous in the main house!"

Lisa Clark dreamt that she was sitting in front of a *pasticceria* on an old cobblestone Italian street, admiring the yellow tulips in the little park across the street. Her head was numb and soft like a pillow and her body filled with a cottony, fuzzy warmth.

Noticing that some of the tulips hadn't been colored in yet, she filled them in with her mind, and as she did, a wave of euphoria passed through her body. The scene was perfect now. And she had created it herself according to the plan of the numbered schemata.

All the pain and anguish of the past had retreated far away.

She floated through the air like a feather. Then the air stopped moving and settled around her. Fingers touched her bare arm.

She heard someone say, "This way, *Señora*," as though he was singing a song.

Her feet touched the ground. Gravel tickled her feet through the leather sandals. The air was fragrant with the smells of grass and flowers.

Although she couldn't see, everything felt as though it fit together in a perfect God-like order.

She heard a voice whisper to her right, "Mom."

She recognized the voice of her daughter, Olivia, which thrilled her. "Olivia."

"Mom, I'm blindfolded. Are you there?"

"Yes, darling."

"Are you okay?"

"Yes. Yes, absolutely."

"Mom...Mom, I love you."

"I love you, too," Lisa responded. "Is something wrong?"

"Are you serious, Mom? Did they give you something?"

"Maybe...it's not important."

"Do you understand what's going on? Do you know where they're taking us?"

The urgency in her daughter's voice was something that she didn't understand and that almost offended her. She had opened her mouth to say something, when a man grunted "Quiet!" and squeezed her arm tightly until it hurt.

Crocker knelt over Davis on the tile kitchen floor and applied pressure to the wound with his left while reaching for a blowout patch in his emergency medical kit with his right. Rounds flew over his head and slammed into the wall and refrigerator behind him. There was glass strewn everywhere, spent shells and smoke. Suárez knelt behind a window to his right picking off the enemy, who had taken cover behind trees, chairs, bushes, and several modern sculptures in the yard.

"Who are they?" Suárez shouted as dogs continued to wail and yelp from somewhere in the backyard.

"Zetas, cops, fucking aliens. Just take 'em down!"

"With pleasure!"

Urgent voices screamed over the radio. "Boss, taking fire out front!"

"Two tangos down near the gate!"

"We need refo! The mofos keep coming!"

Before he could answer, he had to stem the flow of blood so Davis didn't bleed out.

He spoke to Davis in a low voice throughout the whole procedure. "Just a nick. Routine. I'll have you patched up in a second, then we'll get you out of here."

The round had entered right below Davis's left clavicle and

exited his back near the spine. With the bleeding in the front staunched, Crocker lifted him enough to feel through the blood on his back.

There seemed to be no structural damage, which was a huge relief.

"Missed your spine," Crocker said as he applied a second blowout patch to the gaping wound in back. "You're a lucky man."

"Thank God..." Davis's eyes had rolled back in their sockets. His skin had turned pale and was covered with sweat.

It wasn't a full kit, so Crocker used what he could find—combat gauze, QuikClot, tape. Holding Davis's head up, he said, "Stay with me."

Davis swallowed and managed a tight smile. "I'm trying, boss."

Crocker stood by the side of the window, leveled his HK416, and squeezed off a three-round burst that hit some guy in a black helmet crouched behind one of the concrete planters. He heard Akil's voice over the radio by his foot: "Nieves is down. Fuck. He needs help!"

Crocker picked it up and asked, "Where?"

"The throat!"

"Keep his airway clear and open as best you can. I'll be there in a second. What's your location?"

"Second-floor balcony."

He ran in a crouch to the stairway and had dived behind the hallway wall when on his right periphery he saw a rocket rip through one of the tall windows. He covered his head as it crashed into the wall and exploded. Plaster fell; hot metal hissed through the air. But Crocker's main concern was the cell phone in his front pocket, which was their connection to the FBI safe house.

He checked it. It seemed fine. With the HK416 clutched in his right and the med kit on his back, he scurried on his hands and knees through the swirling smoke until he found Mancini pressed near a front window, aiming a Vietnam-era M-79 grenade launcher that looked like an old-fashioned blunderbuss.

"Manny…"

Mancini was completely focused on the target through the leaf-type sight. He squeezed off a 40x46mm round at an M706 armored car parked in the driveway.

The round slammed into .25-inch metal armor and exploded. Seconds later, the twin .30 cals in the turret spun their way and opened fire, tearing into the concrete around the front window.

"Fuck!" Manny shouted, ducking. Pieces of plaster and dust flew everywhere.

Crocker fished a chunk of plaster out of his right eye. "You see what you started?"

"How's Davis?"

"Not good."

Manny broke the pirate gun open and slammed in another 40mm round as Crocker jumped to the other side of the window and took aim at a black Polícia Federal truck with six or seven men in back that sped into the yard.

"We got to get him to a hospital."

Hot 5.56x45mm shells cascaded onto the floor around him. Sweat mixed with the grit on his bare chest. The armored car continued to fire, ripping away the wooden border around the window and sending pieces of glass cascading over Crocker's head and shoulders.

"Do something, Manny. That 706 is pissing me off," Crocker shouted.

"Why didn't you tell me that before?" Manny fired a beehive round that exploded near the back of the truck and released dozens of 24g metal petals that ripped into some of the men in black.

"That the best you can do?" Crocker asked.

"Kiss my ass!"

Mancini reloaded with an explosive round that hit the gas tank and caused the driver to lose control and crash into the armored car.

"Better!" Crocker shouted as he took aim at several armed men escaping in the pickup. Flames engulfed both vehicles.

"I love this fucking pirate gun," Mancini shouted, setting down the M-79 and picking up an MP7. "Simple as shit but gets the job done."

A secondary explosion caused the hood of the truck to flip in the air and land on top of an M706 turret. Two men ran from the side door, clutching AKs. Mancini calmly picked them off.

Crocker, meanwhile, had the cell phone in his blood-covered hand and was punching Lane's number.

"Lane! Lane, you hear me? It's Crocker."

"Crocker, how'd it go?"

"Bad. The house was empty. We've been ambushed by two dozen Federales with armored cars and rockets."

"No. How the hell did that happen?"

"Don't know. We're pinned down. We need relief, reinforcements, and medevac A.S.A.P.! Do you copy?"

"Medevac?"

"I've got two badly wounded men."

"Message received. I got it. I'll call the station, the governor. Hold on."

"Medevac, Lane. I don't want to lose these men!"

"No."

"Hurry!"

"I will."

CHAPTER ELEVEN

In a mad world only the mad are sane.

—Akira Kurosawa

CROCKER SLIPPED the phone into his pocket and turned to Mancini, who was reloading his MP7. The firing in front of them seemed to have let up. But the sounds from the backyard were still ferocious.

"I'm going upstairs to look after Nieves," Crocker said. "Suárez's in the back with Davis. Akil's upstairs."

Both men ducked simultaneously as an explosion sent the hood of the burning truck flying in the air.

"You want me to go back and relieve Suárez?" Mancini asked as it crashed to the pavement.

"Make sure the front is covered first."

Mancini shouted at Crocker's back, "Tell Akil to get his ass down here. I have an idea."

"I'll send him."

Upstairs on the balcony he found Akil kneeling over a prone Nieves, holding both hands on his neck.

"It's bad," Akil whispered. "He's lost a lot of blood."

"Let me see."

Akil removed his hands from the bloody mess. A round had taken a two-inch-long chunk out of the side of Nieves's neck but had missed the carotid artery. Nieves had already gone into hypovolemic shock due to the loss of blood, but his body temperature was still relatively normal, which meant that the shock wasn't severe yet.

"Hold this," Crocker said, applying a blowout patch to the wound. Then he removed his black T-shirt and said, "Now move your hands away."

He used the T-shirt to tie the bandage in place, then lifted Nieves's legs and slid a deck chair under them so that they were about a foot off the balcony floor.

"We need to get some blood in him," Crocker said.

"How?"

"Go see Manny downstairs in front. He needs you."

Just then several large explosions rocked the back of the house. Crocker grabbed his radio and shouted, "Suárez, you okay? Suárez, report!"

No answer.

He tried Mancini. "Manny?"

"Yeah, boss."

"I'm going to relieve Suárez. Any sign of medevac or reinforcements?"

"Not yet."

He found Suárez crouched by one of the back windows, fighting like a manic kid.

"Suárez?"

No answer, so Crocker kicked his foot.

Suárez frowned and pointed to his eardrums, indicating that they weren't working. Outside, past the patio and cement planters filled with geraniums, eight to ten men had taken up positions and were inching toward the house.

Crocker raked the middle of them with fire, then reloaded and continued left. He shouted, "You take the right, I'll cover the left!" Then, remembering Suárez couldn't hear, he slapped his shoulder and pointed. Suárez nodded, his face a mask of grim determination.

Crocker liked the guy more every second. Out of his right periphery he saw a flash and shouted, "Incoming!"

A second later, a shoulder-fired rocket passed through the destroyed window and exploded on impact with the cabinets on the wall behind them. Crocker felt hot shards of wood and metal burn into his back.

He heard Suárez coughing and spitting blood.

"You hit?"

Suárez shouldered his MP7 and continued firing. Crocker calculated that they would soon either run out of ammunition or be overrun.

Shouting into the radio, he said, "Manny, we need the forty mike-mike in back."

"I got something even better. We're coming."

"Make it quick!"

When he raised his head above the sill to fire, he saw three men wearing black helmets circling to the right side of the house. Then a barrage of rounds came at him, causing him to hit the floor again and bruise his mouth.

"Fuck!"

As he readjusted the sight, he saw that he was down to less

than a magazine and a half. Suárez continued to cough and choke.

"What's wrong?"

Squirming over on his belly, he grabbed Suárez under the ribs from behind and pushed up and squeezed at the same time. A piece of plaster the size of a Ping-Pong ball flew out of Suárez's mouth.

"Disgusting," Suárez said.

"Drink some water."

The shooting from the yard had intensified to the point that it was difficult to raise a weapon above the sill to return fire. But he did anyway, and as he fired heard a tremendous crash from the right side of the house.

He thought for a second that the Federales had broken through the barricaded side door, and that maybe he and his men would be joining Ritchie soon. But then a loud, incessant firing deafened him, and he saw that it was directed at the men behind the planters. He watched as they retreated and the big guns from the right mowed them down one by one. Then the guns tore into the Federales on the left side of the yard.

Suárez looked at Crocker, and Crocker looked at him, both men's expressions asking, *What the fuck is going on?* Seconds later, a black M706 armored car swung into view.

"Who's that?" Suárez asked.

It looked like the one Crocker had seen on the front drive with twin .30 cal machine guns and five-foot run-flat tires. Now it was firing at the Mexicans.

"They're on our side!" Suárez shouted with a rapturous smile on his face.

"Seems like."

Before Crocker had a chance to say anything about Mancini, Suárez stepped through the broken window with his MP7 and ran to join the mop-up activity in the yard. Crocker followed.

Five minutes later, all the Mexicans had either fled or were dead, or bleeding out. One soldier with a black mask over his face lay in a pool of blood behind one of the concrete planters. Crocker was bending down to grab the RPG-2 that lay next to him when he heard Akil's voice.

"You gonna fucking thank us, or what?"

He looked up into the slanting sunlight and saw Akil's dirt-smudged face sticking out of the side door of the M706. Without missing a beat, Crocker said, "Get your lazy ass out here and help me load Davis and Nieves inside."

"Ungrateful fuck," Akil groaned as he jumped and hit the grass.

"Nice work," Crocker said, slapping a hand to his chest.

"By the way, your back's a bloody mess."

Crocker reached around and felt sticky blood mixed with grime. It didn't seem serious, so he said, "Not a problem."

"What the fuck just happened?" Akil asked as he and Crocker climbed the steps to the balcony.

"What do you mean?"

"I mean, who were they and what the fuck was that all about?"

"That was the Mexican police," Crocker answered.

"You're kidding."

"I saw 'Federales' painted on one of the trucks."

When they reached the balcony, out of breath, Akil wiped dirt and sweat off his forehead and said, "And I thought Iraq and Afghanistan were messed up."

"Welcome to Mexico."

The bleeding from Nieves's neck seemed to have stopped, but he was still in shock, and his pulse was weak and thready. As they carefully carried him downstairs and toward the armored car, a black helicopter banked overhead.

"Medevac?" Akil asked.

Crocker squinted into the morning haze. It was a Black Hawk with POLÍCIA FEDERAL painted along the back of the fuselage. "Apparently not," he answered. "Load him inside."

The interior of the M706 was extremely hot and had room for a driver, a gunner, and eight other occupants on benches along the sides. Mancini drove while Akil manned the machine gun. Nieves lay on one bench and Davis on the other. Crocker crawled on his knees from one side to the other, monitoring each man.

"How about getting some air in this crate?" Crocker asked.

Mancini shouted, "The air conditioning doesn't seem to be working."

"Try the fan." Crocker tossed his cell phone to Suárez, seated crossed-legged on the floor. "Call Lane. Tell him where we are."

The M706 growled and lurched toward the front gate.

"No answer," Suárez shouted over the growl of the engine. "I left a message."

"Try again!"

Once they reached the street, Mancini cranked the Chrysler 361 cubic V-8 engine as fast as it would go and tried to trace his way back to the FBI safe house. The Polícia Federal Black Hawk followed about sixty feet overhead.

"What should we do about the helo?" Akil asked from the turret.

"Ignore it."

"What if it fires at us?"

"Shoot back!"

Suárez pointed to the phone and shouted, "Still no answer!"

"What the hell is Lane doing?"

He grabbed the cell phone back and tried himself. It rang and went to message. Crocker said, "Lane, we're on our way to you. We still need medical assistance, badly. Call me back!"

Nieves's pulse was growing weaker by the minute. A cool, clammy sweat covered his face and arms. His lips had started to turn blue.

"Manny," Crocker shouted, "if you see a hospital, stop!"

"What?"

"A hospital! Stop if you see a medical facility."

"I'm staying on as many well-traveled roads as I can and riding next to buses and cars, to deter the Black Hawk from shooting at us."

"Good man."

Crocker couldn't see shit—just grim, battle-weary faces and bleeding men. The big vehicle roared, hit holes in the pavement, and lurched forward like a tractor on steroids.

"Hold on!" Mancini shouted as he took a sharp curve. The metal beast tipped as if it was in danger of turning over. Crocker held Nieves so he didn't fall off the bench.

"Where the hell you get your license?" Suárez shouted.

"Mexico!" Mancini shouted back.

Crocker waved Suárez over. "Hold Nieves. I'm gonna see if that big baboon knows where he's going."

"Probably not."

Crocker squirmed forward on his belly and tried to peer through the forward slit window. "Move your big head aside so I can see," he said to Mancini.

"See what? I just turned onto the street."

"What street?"

"The street with the FBI house. It's straight ahead."

Mancini slowed the vehicle, executed a wide turn, and stopped abruptly, causing Crocker to hit his head.

"Fuck! There go another couple million brain cells."

"You don't need 'em!"

Akil laughed. Suárez hopped out the side door and rang the bell by the gate. When that didn't work, he banged on it with the butt of his weapon. When no one answered, he climbed over and opened the gate from inside.

"What the fuck happened to that Ramón guy?" Akil asked.

"Who's Ramón?"

"The old Mexican dude. The guard. Remember?"

"Maybe he took the day off."

Mancini braked to a stop on the gravel. They were all soaked with sweat and out of water.

"What do you want to do now?" Akil asked.

Crocker thought fast. "You stay here and man the thirty cals," he said. "Manny, you and Suárez help me carry Nieves and Davis out so they can get some fresh air. Then I want you to hydrate and guard the front gate. I'm gonna go find Lane."

"Got it."

"What about me?" Akil asked from the turret. "I need some fluids, too."

"Suárez, on your way to the gate, bring a water bottle for Akil. See if you can find one with a nipple on it."

"Very funny."

It was all in fun, but then it wasn't. Because as soon as Crocker stepped outside, he heard the Black Hawk roaring overhead. Looking up, he saw the helmeted gunners of the .50 cals leering down and gesturing.

He ignored them and with Suárez's help lugged Nieves inside and set him on the porch sofa.

"Anyone home?" he called out. "We need help here."

He hurried back to get Davis with Mancini's help.

Suárez shrugged when he returned. "There's no one here."

"Where the hell did they go?" Crocker asked, trying to catch his breath as he peered into the shadow-filled living room.

Suárez shrugged, then seemed to notice a dark stream of something slowly creeping out through the living room door.

"What's that?" asked Crocker.

The second he finished posing the question, he knew the answer. Stepping over the dark puddle on the tile floor, he entered the living room and was hit by the thick, musky smell of death. His eyes quickly adjusted to the darkness and made out four stacked, headless bodies in the middle of the floor.

"Holy shit."

"God have mercy," Suárez groaned at his side.

"Look." Mancini pointed to four heads lying on the coffee table like Halloween masks. Lane, red-haired Karen Steele,

Sheriff Higgins, and some blond-haired guy Crocker hadn't met. Karen had the added indignity of a severed penis stuffed in her mouth.

"Savages," Crocker groaned as he ripped down one of the mustard-colored curtains and laid it over the heads. Then he used its partner to cover the bodies.

"That's what they plan to do to us," Suárez muttered as he made the sign of the cross.

"Fuck that," Crocker growled. The savagery of the deaths unleashed a rage inside him that was almost uncontainable. Finding the handheld, he pushed a button and said, "Akil, you read me?"

"Yo. Where's my fucking water?"

"That Black Hawk still hovering over you?"

"Say fifty feet with assholes in the doors shooting me the bird."

"You got a good bead on them?"

"You know it."

"Take it down!"

"Now?"

"Yeah, now!" Crocker shouted.

"Copy."

He stood seething with anger and listened to the twin .30 cals roar outside, which had a strange calming effect. And he realized that he had reached a state of absolute freedom that he'd almost never felt before. He didn't care about orders, or protocols, or whether he died in Mexico or not. He was going to pay the fuckers back who had kidnapped Lisa and Olivia Clark, wounded Nieves and Davis, and desecrated Lane, Steele, and the others, no matter what it took.

The cacophony of firing continued. Mancini screamed in his ear. "Boss. Boss, what the hell are you doing?"

Crocker pushed him in the direction of the front gate. "You and Suárez go. Don't let anyone in the gate! Do whatever it takes."

Mancini opened his mouth to say something but was drowned out by an explosion. As the sound dissipated, Crocker heard Akil shout over the radio, "Got 'em! Mission accomplished!"

His ears followed the whining sound of the injured Black Hawk as it spun out of control, clipped the branch of a tree, and crashed somewhere in the yard. He didn't take the time to look.

"Make sure you finish off any survivors," he said into the radio. "Then stay on alert. Anyone who approaches this house either by air or on land, you shoot them unless I tell you not to."

"Yeah, boss. Balls to the wall!"

He reached Nieves as his body started to convulse. There was nothing he could do except clear his tongue with one hand so he didn't choke on it, and wrap the rug on the floor around him to keep him warm.

No more casualties, he said to himself, praying to God and remembering the recent string of rotten luck. *I can't allow another one.*

He punched one of the emergency numbers Lane had programmed into the cell phone.

A smooth woman's voice came on the line. "Who's this?"

"Crocker. I'm with Black Cell at the FBI safe house in Zapopan. It's been hit. Four people are dead."

"What do you mean, it's been hit?" the CIA station duty officer asked.

"You heard me. Find Jenson and tell him Crocker called and the mission went to shit. We just got back to the safe house and found Lane, Steele, and two others dead in the living room. Decapitated."

"Lane? David Lane?"

"Yes!"

The woman on the other end gasped, "Oh, my God!"

"It's awful."

"David Lane?"

"Yes."

"That was you who battled the police in Puerto del Hiero?" she asked.

"Yes," Crocker answered. "We were ambushed by Federales. We're back at the safe house now. I've got two severely injured men with me who need emergency medical assistance. I'm not going to let them die. How long is it going to take you to get a team out here?"

"I'll have to check."

"Where are you?"

"Mexico City. Hold on."

She came back half a minute later and said, "Twenty minutes, maybe less."

"They'll be dead by then," Crocker responded. "Is there a hospital nearby?"

"You're in Zapopan now?"

"Correct."

"Hospital San Javier is off Calle Parra about three minutes away."

"I need directions."

She transmitted them over the phone, and Crocker scribbled them down—a right at the first intersection and two lefts past a big park. "We're going there now," he said.

"How?"

"We've got an M706 that we took from the Federal Police."

"You're kidding, right?"

"Have your people meet us at the hospital. Call the consul, the ambassador, the mayor, anyone you think can help. We're going in armed and the Mexicans are on our tail."

"That's ill advised. Let me get Mr. Jenson on the line."

"Goodbye."

Crocker radioed Suárez and Mancini and asked them if they saw any police activity on the street.

"Not yet," Mancini reported.

"Any sign of Ramón?"

"Negative."

"Okay," Crocker said. "I want you to hurry back here and help reload Nieves and Davis onto the 706."

"Aye-aye."

Through the screen porch door, he watched the Black Hawk continue to burn out at the far end of the swimming pool as the men ran toward him.

They reloaded the two injured men; then Mancini climbed into the driver's seat and asked, "Where're we going?"

Crocker read the directions. Five minutes later, he pointed to the INGRESO DE EMERGENCIAS sign and Mancini steered the metal beast up to the entrance and stopped in front of a circular green-glassed atrium.

Seeing the armored car, the guard at the entrance dropped

the M-1 he was holding and ran into the two-story hospital. The four-man construction crew that was repaving an outdoor staircase watched openmouthed as the grime-covered Americans stepped out of the vehicle, armed and ready. Crocker was still bare-chested. He and Suárez were bleeding from superficial wounds to their faces and backs.

Suárez took charge, grabbing orderlies and shouting instructions in Spanish.

Medical personnel wearing light-green tunics scrambled. Gurneys and nurses appeared. The wounded men were wheeled inside.

A weary Crocker turned to Mancini and said, "Relieve Akil in the M706. You and Suárez guard the door. Don't let anyone in or out."

"Looks like we're taking the whole hospital hostage."

"If that's what it takes to save our men, yes."

CHAPTER TWELVE

Common sense is not so common.

—Voltaire

AN HOUR later, Crocker stood as he watched a young Mexican doctor pass through swinging double doors and remove the white surgical mask from his face. He squinted, expecting the worst.

"The American consul and governor of the state of Jalisco are in the waiting room and want to talk to you," the tall doctor said, looking at the scratches that had bled through the short-sleeved medical shirt a nurse had given Crocker. "Maybe we should clean you up first."

"Not necessary," Crocker answered, peering into the man's small brown eyes.

He stood at least an inch taller than Crocker, who was six two. The sterling-silver plate on the front pocket of his white coat read RUBÉN WERNER. Crocker's first wife, who was a German teacher, had told him that *Werner* meant "uncertain" in German.

"How are my men?" he asked.

"The blond gentleman…"

"Davis."

"I don't know if I should be talking to you about this."

"Why not?"

"Because this is an extraordinary situation, and one that I find deplorable."

"I don't give a shit what you think. Tell me about my men."

The doctor tightened his jaw and nodded. "Mr. Davis," he pronounced slowly. "His collarbone was badly fractured. We've cleaned the wound and set the bone for the time being, but he's probably going to need a bone graft of some kind."

"When?"

"I've called a specialist from Mexico City who will arrive tomorrow."

Crocker had spent the last sixty minutes thinking ahead and dealing with hard realities. He knew that the hospital was surrounded by Mexican police and army units that were threatening to raid the building.

"Davis can't be moved?" he asked.

"Not for the next several days, until the injury is set properly and there's no risk of infection."

"What about Nieves?" Crocker asked.

"Nieves is more problematic. As you know, he lost a great deal of blood. We've given him transfusions, so his vital signs and stats are improving. But he's still in a coma."

Crocker nodded. At least he wasn't dead.

He said, "Thanks, Doc. I appreciate what you've done."

He followed Dr. Werner down a long hall, his dirty, bloody

hiking boots echoing off the pale-blue walls. Nurses and orderlies poked their heads out of rooms and hallways to steal a glance at him. He was totally focused on getting his men out of there and continuing to pursue the Jackal. And he was very aware that the last hours of Lisa and Olivia Clark's lives were passing by, if they weren't dead already.

Crocker was so tired that he started to hallucinate. The nurse in the room to his right turned into his mother. Several orderlies standing ahead turned into schoolgirls in uniforms.

Staring at them, he remembered a mission he had gone on with Clark and Ritchie during the First Gulf War. It involved taking out six armed MA2-543 SCUD Transporter/Erector/Launcher missile installations hidden in the garden of a girls' high school.

They had dyed their beards and mustaches black, parachuted onto a soccer field about a quarter mile away from the school in the middle of the night, taken out the six Iraqi guards, and disabled both the vehicles and the Shabab-2 engines of the thirty-four-foot-long Al-Hussein rockets.

Mission accomplished, they had retreated to an abandoned chemical plant north of the city and hidden in a drainage pipe, where Clark was bitten by a desert horned viper—one of several very lethal snakes native to Iraq.

Crocker had elevated Clark's wrist, cleansed the wound, tying a not-too-tight tourniquet three inches above the wrist, and applied a Sawyer venom extractor he kept in his EM kit, which looked like a large yellow syringe.

He saw the extractor now. Blood oozed out of it.

"Boss."

"What?"

Crocker blinked and realized that he and the doctor were standing in a large waiting room. Thirty or so men—visitors to the hospital and personnel—stared at him. They looked up from their positions on the floor, standing, and sitting in green chairs.

Mancini stood facing him with an MP7 strapped across his chest. "You okay, boss?"

Crocker nodded.

"We released all the women and children."

"Good."

"The Mexican commander outside has been demanding our surrender and I've been telling him to go to hell. I don't trust any of them."

"Neither do I."

"Suárez has been outstanding."

A helicopter passed over the building, rattling the windows. Through the double doors he saw tanks, news vans, and soldiers in riot gear. They looked real.

"The consul and governor are waiting in the administrator's office, down the hall," Mancini said, pointing to a narrow fluorescent-lit hallway to his right.

"Thanks. See if you can find me a glass of water or a cup of coffee."

Crocker turned the knob of the pale beige door and entered, holding his HK416 and SIG Sauer. The five men inside regarded him with varying degrees of fear, contempt, and suspicion, then introduced themselves one by one.

The U.S. consul was young and full faced, with short hair and a dark beard. He seemed completely overwhelmed. The governor of Jalisco was a good-looking man with gray hair, dressed in an expensive suit and cowboy boots. He acted like someone who was pleased with himself, which struck Crocker as completely inappropriate.

The other three men included the hospital administrator and two of the governor's aides. A male nurse brought bottles of water, a cup of black coffee for Crocker, and a bowl of fruit.

Crocker downed the coffee and drank half a bottle of water. His ability to focus quickly improved. In blunt language he described what had transpired that morning, starting with the raid on the house in Puerto del Hiero and the battle with police.

The governor interrupted. "You and your men are in my country illegally, and you have committed criminal acts. I advise you to surrender immediately."

"That's not going to happen," Crocker countered.

"If you surrender now, I'll try to arrange your safe passage back to the United States, but I can't guarantee that."

"We're not interested in leaving until we've completed our mission, which is to rescue Lisa and Olivia Clark."

"Our security forces are capable of doing that," the governor said.

Crocker shook his head and glanced at the clock on the wall, which reminded him that valuable time was ticking past.

The consul tried to act as conciliator, explaining the positions of both governments and the negative effect the Clarks' deaths would have on U.S.-Mexican relations.

The governor stepped forward aggressively and pointed a finger at Crocker. "As Mexicans, we won't tolerate violations and insults to our sovereignty."

Crocker wanted to clock him in the mouth but held himself

back. Turning to the consul, he said, "Get some people in here who make sense."

An hour later the CIA station chief, Max Jenson, arrived with the Mexican deputy minister of defense.

The three men retired to the administrator's office, and within fifteen minutes, a deal was worked out. First, they waited for a helicopter to ferry Nieves and Davis to a hospital in Mexico City. Then Crocker and his men relinquished control over the hospital and the M706 and were released into the custody of Jenson and the U.S. consul. The Mexican deputy minister promised that once the two wounded men were healthy enough, they would be transferred to a recovery center in the States.

As he sat in the back of an SUV that sped through the streets of Guadalajara, Crocker's body begged to sleep, but his brain wouldn't let him, pushing the name Maria to the surface over and over.

Once he focused enough to understand who Maria was and why she was important, he said out loud, "We've got to find her."

But no one responded. Mancini, Akil, and Suárez sat behind him, snoring, and the driver kept staring ahead.

Jenson in the passenger seat finished his cell phone call, pulled the buds out of his ears, turned back to Crocker, and said, "I have good news and bad. The good news is that Nieves was given a blood transfusion and is responding to pain and verbal stimuli."

"He and Davis have arrived in Mexico City?"

"Yes."

"What's the bad news?" Crocker asked.

"We've got nothing on the Clarks' new location."

"What about the Jackal?" Mancini asked.

"Nothing on him, either."

"We need to find Maria," suggested Crocker.

The sandy-haired CIA officer at the wheel looked over this shoulder and finally spoke. "Maria isn't her real name."

"What is it?"

"Claudia Matamoros."

"Find her," Jenson barked, looking at his watch. "We've got nine hours."

Lisa dreamt that she was in the woods being chased by a pack of jackals like the ones she'd seen in the backyard. Her lungs burned and the muscles in her calves ached as she ran over the mossy, leaf-covered ground, trying to keep from slipping. Struggling, she veered right, into the cover of high green grass that bordered a body of water.

The jackals snarled and howled behind her. She couldn't imagine why they were so angry, or what she had done to put herself in this horrible situation.

But it must have been something personal, because she sensed their hatred as they clawed the ground and closed the gap between her and them.

Six feet beyond the tall grass lay a river that fed into a silver-colored lake. She ran as fast as she could, jumped, and landed on the soggy edge of the far side with a splash. The jackals whined and howled on the other side. But when she tried to pull herself out of the muck, she discovered that her legs were stuck.

Seeing her distress, one of the jackals jumped into the water and started to swim toward her. She saw its hungry yellow eyes draw closer and struggled to pull free. The animal was practically on her. She saw its long teeth and smelled its hot, disgusting breath.

As it bit into her shoulder, she screamed, "No!" and awoke in a room filled with pale-blue light.

El Chacal leaned over her and shook her shoulder gently.

"Mrs. Clark," he whispered with a sensual Mexican accent. "Mrs. Clark, wake up."

The bed had four wooden posts. The windows were covered with long blue curtains. A young man in a white shirt and dark pants stood near the door.

"Mrs. Clark..." the Jackal whispered. "Can you hear me, Mrs. Clark?"

The whites of El Chacal's eyes were yellow. His lips bloodless and cracked.

"Mrs. Clark," he said. "I have good news for you. Your stay with us is almost over."

"Really?" she asked, a big wad of emotion gathering in her chest.

"Yes. But before you go, I want you to record a statement. You think you can do that for me?"

Tears of relief gathered in her eyes. "A statement?"

"Yes, a statement. That's all I ask. I'll send someone to help you. But first, you need to take a shower and get dressed."

"Of course," she said, sitting up and discovering that her white cotton nightgown was drenched in sweat. "Thank you."

*   *   *

Crocker was pulling on the fresh light-green tunic and pants he had grabbed at the hospital, when Jenson, in the passenger seat, turned to him and said, "Claudia's father, mother, brother, and aunt have already left for Dallas. But Claudia is still trying to recover her five-year-old son, who has been living with his father at an amusement park on the other side of town. My people think she's there now."

"Hit the gas!" Crocker exclaimed.

It took them forty minutes to find the amusement park, which sat behind a Ford dealership off the south highway. It was a sad, grimy place with a tall, rusted Ferris wheel, a pit for bumper cars, a roller coaster that was out of order, and an assortment of game booths and lesser rides.

The sandy-haired CIA officer rolled the black Range Rover with blacked-out windows into the dust-filled lot and parked.

Despite its condition, the place was filled with lower-class Mexican mothers and children, many of whom were carrying balloons. Directly ahead of them was a bumper car ride with a long line of excited children.

Jenson addressed Crocker and his men in back. "The father's name is Moco Taveras. You think you guys can handle this?"

"Is Elvis dead?"

"You going dressed like that?" he asked Crocker.

"Why not?"

The four SEALs strode to the ticket window, where Suárez paid the forty-peso admission for all four men, then asked the big woman behind the counter where they could find Moco Taveras.

She shrugged as though she'd never heard of him.

After he handed the ticket woman another three hundred pesos (approximately twenty-four dollars), she said, "Moco's running the Ferris wheel today."

Crocker, Mancini, and Akil sipped cold sodas as they watched Suárez approach the attraction and a mustached man with a blue bandana tied around his forehead.

Suárez told Moco he worked for the FBI and had money for Claudia. Moco suggested that Suárez leave the money with him and he'd make sure to give it to his wife. When that didn't work, he pointed in the direction of the bumper car pavilion.

As Suárez walked away, Crocker saw Moco reach for his cell phone. A minute later, he saw Claudia (Maria) emerge from the pavilion in a blue top and tan pants, clutching a dark-haired little boy by the hand.

The moment she recognized him, she pushed the boy toward the Ferris wheel, turned, and ran in the opposite direction.

Suárez stopped the boy, and Akil and Crocker pursued her.

It was a short chase. Crocker snatched her off her feet and carried her to the Range Rover. She kicked and screamed, but neither Moco nor anyone else intervened.

Crocker set her on the middle seat and sat next to her as she clutched her son. All of them were dusty, sweating, and out of breath. Minus the wrestler's mask, Claudia had a round, pleasant face.

Suárez asked her a question in Spanish, and Claudia wept and responded at the same time. She swore that she hadn't alerted the narcoterrorists at the house and had no motive for betraying the Americans, who were moving her family to the States.

Crocker sensed that she was telling the truth.

"Does she know where the American women are now?" he asked.

Suárez translated. Claudia shook her head and said something.

"She doesn't," Suárez said. "She says El Chacal owns houses, apartments, and properties all over the country."

"Does she have any way of getting in touch with people who do know?"

Claudia shook her head vigorously and said something in Spanish.

"No," Suárez said.

"Does she have any idea who betrayed us?"

She thought about it, then nodded.

"Who?"

"Señor Marion," she said.

"Bob Marion, the security consultant?"

"Jes."

It seemed like a stab in the dark, but it was all they had and the clock was ticking.

Jenson said, "Let's head back into the city. I'll see if my people can locate Marion. He works for Global Banking and Investments downtown."

Crocker struggled to stay awake as the sandy-haired CIA officer spun the vehicle onto an *autopista* and sped into town. All he saw were cars flashing by and patches of blue sky.

He dreamt he was standing on a rock casting a line into a

river. Three minutes later, he opened his eyes and saw that they were passing a silver bus.

"This Marion guy was at the safe house when the raid was discussed?" Akil asked from the backseat.

"He was the dark-haired guy with the two-day growth and the smug look on his face," Mancini answered.

Crocker tried to focus. He remembered that there had been something about Marion he hadn't liked.

Five minutes later Jenson removed the buds from his ears and reported, "He's attending a cocktail party in the Emiliano Zapata Room of the Hotel Demetria, which is near the university, downtown."

"Marion?" Crocker asked.

"Yeah, Marion."

"Where's that exactly?" the driver asked.

"Twenty-two nineteen Avenida de la Paz. I'll punch it in the GPS."

Crocker slipped in and out of consciousness, but on some subconscious level his mind was busy trying to catch up with the events of the day. He absorbed information and processed new situations faster than most people. The image of the four heads on the coffee table kept reappearing.

He was jarred awake as the Range Rover hit a speed bump and lurched left.

"Sorry," the driver muttered.

Outside he saw a beautiful, idyllic afternoon with sidewalks jammed full of determined-looking businesspeople and shoppers. Claudia sat leaning against the opposite door with her son in her lap.

The CIA officer pulled to the curb in front of a sleek hotel tower with a fountain out front. Atlas stood in the middle holding a metal globe on his back.

"Who's going up?" Jenson asked.

"I'll go with Suárez," Crocker said, glancing at his watch. The deadline was eight hours away.

"Not dressed like that."

They compared sizes and exchanged clothes. Crocker got Jenson's black pants and pullover. Suárez wore the driver's polo and chinos.

"That's better," Jenson concluded. "Grab him and take him down to the parking lot. We'll meet you there."

They entered the modern black-marble lobby wearing their same blood-covered black boots.

"High class," Suárez whispered.

"Looks more like a modern art museum than a hotel."

The clerk at the front desk turned his nose up at them like they smelled bad. "Twelfth floor," he said. "But invitation only."

They rode up alone, watching footage of masked Mexican soldiers roaming the grounds of the FBI compound on the elevator TV. It had the effect of a flashback from a bad dream.

Two burly guys in black suits stopped them at the double doors to the Emiliano Zapata Room.

"We're from the U.S. embassy," Suárez said in Spanish. "We have an important message to deliver to someone inside."

One of the guards looked them over and asked, "What's the VIP's name?"

"Señor Bob Marion."

"Wait here."

Crocker pushed past as one guard consulted a guest list on a table by the door and another turned to greet a short man in a gray suit.

"*¡Que cosa!*" the guard shouted.

Crocker quickly scanned the high-ceilinged room. There were no people in the center. Instead, large ceramic objects were displayed on tables. One of them looked like a huge gourd. People crowded under columned corridors on all four sides of the room. In the far left corner of the center space a jazz quartet played "A Night in Tunisia" by Dizzy Gillespie, which was one of Crocker's favorite jazz tunes. To his right, he caught a glimpse of a woman with red lipstick throwing her head back and laughing. She stood next to a potted tree.

In the dim, atmospheric light he saw Bob Marion standing with his back to her, leaning one hand on the side of the planter. He wore a dark-gray suit and a blue shirt open at the collar. His other hand held a cocktail.

Crocker glanced over his shoulder to see if the guards were following him—they weren't so far—then crossed the room.

Marion stood conversing with a tall, thin woman in a tight dress.

Crocker approached and said, "Excuse me, Bob. We met at Lane's house a couple nights ago."

Marion looked perplexed. "Oh, yeah."

"Yeah."

Marion seemed to sense that something was wrong. But before he could slip away, Crocker grabbed him by the forearm. He had the SIG Sauer hidden under the back of his black pullover.

"Bob, I need to talk to you in private," Crocker said.

Marion maintained his cool. "Now?" he asked, trying to shake free. "This is a little awkward. This lady and I are discussing something important."

Crocker wouldn't let go. "It can't wait."

"Really, we have to do this now?"

Crocker tightened his grip on Marion's arm.

"Give me a minute and I'll meet you in the lobby," Marion offered.

Crocker escorted him to a door in the corner, pushed it open, and punched the call button for the service elevator.

Marion started to struggle. "I don't know what you think you're—"

When the elevator door opened, Crocker shoved him inside, so that he stumbled backward and hit his head on the back wall of the car.

"What the hell is wrong with you?" Marion groaned, holding himself up by the brass rail.

Crocker pushed the button for the basement, then pulled Marion up by the front of his suit. "I'm a little fucking upset. First, me and my men were ambushed when we got to the house in Puerto del Hiero. And when we returned to the FBI safe house, we found Lane, Steele, and two others dead with their heads cut off."

"What?"

Crocker clocked him hard in the solar plexus.

Marion doubled over and groaned, "Maria."

"You mean Claudia. She's with us now, and she says it was you."

"No."

The elevator door opened into the badly lit basement. Crocker tried to quickly get his bearings, when Marion pushed him and bolted. But Crocker managed to stick his right foot out and trip him from behind, causing Marion to fall face-first to the concrete floor. Crocker picked him up by the back of his suit and saw blood dripping from his nose onto the front of his blue shirt.

"You'll pay for this," Marion growled.

"No, you will," Crocker said, holding the SIG Sauer 226 to Marion's head. With his left, he removed the walkie-talkie from his back pocket and spoke into it. "I'm in the basement, by the service dock, and I've got Marion with me."

Seconds later the black Range Rover screeched to a stop in front of them and the back door opened. Crocker shoved Marion inside.

"What have we got here?" Max Jenson asked, leaning over the passenger seat.

Crocker: "Wait. Where's Suárez?"

Mancini: "He's meeting us out front."

"Okay," Crocker instructed. "Then find a deserted place to park."

The CIA driver found an empty parking lot behind an office building under construction two blocks away. The workers had either quit early or had taken the day off.

The SUV sat in the shade with Mancini, Akil, and Suárez crowded in back and Crocker, Marion, Claudia, and her son on the middle bench. Marion held a handkerchief to his bleeding nose.

Jenson grabbed him by the front of his jacket and pulled him up against the back of the passenger seat. "Where's the fucking Jackal?" he shouted. "Where's he holding the Clark women?"

"I don't know."

"Bullshit!" Jenson reached out and grabbed Marion by his wounded nose as Claudia covered her son's eyes. "You can make this easy or real, real hard on yourself. Your choice."

"Okay. Okay. Let go!"

Jenson loosened his grip.

"I don't have contact with the Jackal or his men," Marion explained. "Never have. But I think I see what happened."

"What?"

"Ivan Jouma is a client."

"You mean of Global Banking and Investments?" Jenson asked.

"Yes. We help him locate investment opportunities."

"The fuck you do!" Jenson screamed, his neck and face turning red with anger. "You help him launder drug money, through Guatemalan cutouts into U.S. banks."

"I know nothing about that."

Jenson slammed Marion in the chest so that he rebounded hard against the back of the seat. "Don't give me bullshit, or your financial doublespeak! You work for the enemy and were pretending to help the FBI. When you heard that these brave men were going to raid the house where Lisa and Olivia Clark were being held, you called the Jackal and warned him. Didn't you?"

"No!"

"You lie to me, and I'll break every bone in your body, then throw you in a secret Polish prison for the rest of your life where you'll rot to death. I'll grab your wife and I'll sell her to the Russian mob."

"I don't have a wife."

Jenson reared back his fist as though he was about to clock him.

Marion held up his hands and pleaded, "All right. All right. Maybe I made a mistake. But I didn't call Jouma or any of his people. Legally, I'm not allowed to have any direct contact with them."

"Then what did you do?" Jenson screamed.

"I told an associate."

"You mentioned the impending raid to someone else who works at GBI?"

"Yes."

"What's his name?"

"Do I need to tell you that?"

"Hell, yes."

"All right . . . Tony Alvarez."

"You sure about that?" Jenson asked.

"Yes."

"You'll wager your life on it?"

"I will."

Crocker asked, "You got your cell phone with you?"

Marion nodded. "I do."

"Call him. Find out where he is."

"Tell him you have some more information but think your cell phone is tapped and need to see him in person," Jenson added.

As Marion made the call, Crocker checked his watch. Less than eight hours remained until the midnight deadline, and the minutes were ticking away.

SEAL TEAM SIX THE JACKAL

*   *   *

A medium-height guy in a fancy suit, no tie, stood in front of a shiny thirty-six-story office building on Avenida Hidalgo, which was about a quarter mile away from the FBI safe house where Lane and the others had been brutally executed. He looked pleased with himself, listening to his iPod and looking down at his Sony Ericsson Black Diamond, then up at two tight-suited *señoritas* strolling past on stacked heels.

When he smiled, they smiled back.

"That's him," Marion said, pointing.

Crocker thought he seemed like a typical banker—bland looking, self-important, expensively dressed.

The CIA driver braked the Range Rover in the bus lane, and Suárez and Crocker got out, grabbed the guy by the front of his suit, and threw him into the front passenger seat.

By the time Crocker slid back in, Jenson already had his hand around Alvarez's throat and was choking him so hard he couldn't speak.

So Crocker said, "Max, ease up. Let him talk."

Alvarez coughed, looked deeply offended, and feigned innocence at first. But when Jenson explained who he was, and how he was so pissed off he was going to order the men in the SUV to beat Alvarez to a bloody pulp and then throw his useless body into a secret Polish prison for the rest of his life, Alvarez started to talk.

He admitted that he had called one of the Jackal's associates and told him about the upcoming raid.

"Where is he now?" Jenson asked, showing remarkable restraint this time, Crocker thought, because he wanted to punch Alvarez in the face himself.

"I don't know," Alvarez said. "I really don't. And I don't think it's fair to hold me accountable for what happened, because I had nothing to do with that. I was simply passing information on to a client."

Without warning, Jenson reared his right fist back and smacked Alvarez in the mouth so hard that his head slammed against the passenger-side window.

"I really don't like you," Jenson said, grabbing him by the neck and getting ready to smack him again as Claudia shielded her son's eyes. "You've got five minutes to find out where the Jackal is and where he's holding the Clark women before I tell these men to take you to the top of the building and push you off."

"I thought I told you—"

"Five minutes!" Jenson shouted.

Alvarez started scrolling through programmed numbers on his Sony Ericsson and making calls. He nodded and stammered as Jenson measured time on his watch.

"Four minutes, forty-five seconds!" Jenson shouted.

"Okay. Okay," Alvarez said, holding up his hand and listening, bloody slobber oozing out the corner of his mouth.

"Five!"

"Okay. Okay. I got it!" Alvarez exclaimed as he pointed to the phone.

In a quaking voice, he informed them that the Clark women were being held on a ranch near Tapachula. But his source couldn't confirm that the Jackal was with them.

"Where's the fucking Jackal?" Jenson shouted so loud that Crocker's eardrums hurt.

"No one knows for sure. He's probably with the women."

"Forget the Jackal," Crocker interjected. "Where's Tapachula?"

"In the southern state of Chiapas, near the Guatemalan border," Jenson answered.

"Get us there! Now!"

CHAPTER THIRTEEN

If Jesus was a Jew, how come he has a Mexican first name?

—Billy Connolly

LISA CLARK checked her hair and makeup in the oval mirror, telling herself that the ordeal would soon be over and she'd be reunited with her husband, son, and daughter. Excitement coursed through her body and lit her skin and eyes from within.

That glow had been missing for days. Seeing it now, her confidence grew. But she also had doubts, fears, and questions that she struggled to hold back.

"What do you think, *Señora?*" the young woman with the brush in one hand and a can of hair spray in the other asked.

"Are you going to do my daughter's hair, too?"

"Oh, yes." The woman nodded. "The *señorita*, she bery beautiful. She bery nice girl."

"Thank you."

"Jou should be bery proud."

"I am."

Lisa stood, buttoned the white blouse, and then stepped into the blue skirt and zipped it up on the side. As before, the clothes fit perfectly. Waiting for her on the bed were a jacket and a string of pearls. Black high heels rested on the floor.

She'd been through this routine hundreds of times before, preparing herself to face the public. The fact that she was going to look good pleased her.

Lisa wiped a smudge of lipstick from her front teeth, smiled into the mirror, then turned to the armed man standing near the door. "I'm ready if the *jefe* is," she announced.

"Him not yet, *Señora*. But he will come soon."

It took nearly an hour to squeeze through rush-hour Guadalajara traffic and reach the airport. Crocker and the three remaining members of Black Cell waited in a small room for the CIA Gulfstream IV to arrive, while Jenson paced and ranted into his cell phone, "Where's the fucking aircraft?...Make goddamn sure there's someone to meet us at the airport....Alert our people there....I want the exact location of the ranch....We're going to need weapons and equipment."

Crocker was more interested in what the female CIA officer who was with them was trying to do: confirm the information that had been given to them by Alvarez.

Forty minutes later, when the aircraft taxied to the tarmac in front of them, she still hadn't been successful.

"It's the best we've got," Jenson said, glancing at his watch.

As soon as Crocker hit the seat, he fell asleep and dreamt he was watching Holly kneel on a white tile floor and wash a baby boy in a bathtub. The baby's skin glowed, lighting the room pink. When he burped, gray smoke poured out of his mouth and he started to cry.

Holly looked back at Crocker.

He picked the baby up and held him to his chest, but the smoke kept coming.

"Holly?" he asked. "Holly, what's going on?"

She didn't answer and he couldn't find her through the gathering smoke.

"Holly…"

Two hours later, when the wheels hit the tarmac, he awoke, feeling anxious about Holly and not immediately understanding why.

The reason became apparent the moment he glanced at the new Suunto watch Holly had given him recently after the last one had been destroyed in Foz do Iguaçu, Brazil. This was the Core Lava Red model with all the bells and whistles, including altimeter, barometer, and a compass with weather information. It looked cool as hell, too.

It showed 2108 hours on the 15th.

Yesterday had been Holly's forty-second birthday and he'd forgotten to call. This wasn't the first time he'd failed to reach her on a wedding anniversary or birthday. A voice in his head reminded him of all the long absences, hardships, and funerals she'd had to endure because of him. It told him he didn't deserve her.

Maybe the voice was right.

Outside the oval window, low buildings, lights, and semitropical foliage passed. The landscape looked flat and wild.

He heard Max Jenson growl something from behind him

and remembered that the CIA station chief had accompanied them. Crocker picked out some of the words Jenson was growling into his cell phone, including "Mexican government" and "permissions."

The plane came to a stop in front of a low military-style building guarded by armed men in camouflage uniforms with black balaclavas over their faces. The door opened and they passed through the florid air and entered an air-conditioned room. Jenson behind him shouted into a cell phone, "Over my dead body we're letting them do this. You understand me? No goddamn way!"

If Jenson was saying he wasn't going to allow the Mexican government to get involved, Crocker couldn't agree more, not after what had happened in Guadalajara.

A tense young bearded CIA officer named Becker greeted them and pointed to a tray of sandwiches, bottles of water, and cans of soda that sat on a cabinet along the wall. "You probably want to refuel now, because we're going to have to move fast."

"What the fuck are we waiting for?" Jenson growled.

"The recon team should be arriving soon with photos of the ranch and other surveillance."

"Should be?"

"Will be, sir."

"Tell 'em to fucking hurry!" Jenson shouted with his hand over the phone. "We've got the lives of two American women on the line. We screw this up and we'll all be fired."

The tension, unsettled sleep, and guilt about missing Holly's birthday had drained Crocker's appetite. So he popped a can of Pepsi and looked out the windows of the temporary structure to the masked men standing guard outside.

Becker sidled up to him and said, "I might be able to find you a yogurt or some energy bars, if you don't want a sandwich."

"I'm fine. Who are they?" he asked, pointing to the men outside.

"Mexican soldiers from the GAFE. Army special forces."

"Can we trust them?"

Becker shrugged. "Can you trust anyone connected to this government? I've got body armor and all kinds of ordnance in the next room, when you're ready."

"Mancini's the guy you want to talk to about that," Crocker said, pointing to Mancini, who was wolfing down a roast beef sandwich. Crocker's three men sat in folding chairs in a corner of the room eating quietly.

Crocker knew what they were doing—preparing themselves mentally for the mission ahead. He needed to find the time to do that, too.

First he walked over to Mancini and told him about Becker and the ordnance. As the two men exited, Becker looked back at Crocker and said, "Your CO requested that you call him."

"Now?"

"As soon as you can. I set up a secure phone in the office across the hall."

He didn't like it—the confusion, the uncertainty, the fact that they were still relying on Mexican officials.

The office was barely large enough to accommodate a metal desk and chair. Sutter picked up in his office on the second ring, even though it was an hour ahead, 2214 in Virginia Beach.

"Sir, it's Crocker," he said. "Mancini, Akil, Suárez, and I are currently in southern Mexico getting ready to launch a rescue mission."

"Another one?" Sutter asked.

"It will be our second, sir. We're with the station chief now."

"Whatever you do, you'd better execute it soon."

"We're waiting for an intel update," said Crocker.

"I hope it's more accurate this time."

"So do I. Someone on the inside warned them back in Guadalajara."

"All I can say is, I can't think of anyone better prepared and more capable of rescuing the hostages."

"Thank you, sir."

"Before I sign off, I got a piece of good news. Davis returned this afternoon and he's on his way to recovery."

"I'm very glad to hear that. Please give him my best."

"I will. I know he misses you guys."

"We miss him, too."

"I just wanted to make sure that you're still alive and not rotting away in some Mexican prison."

"We came close."

"Keep doing what you're there to do. We'll get you home."

"I appreciate that, sir."

"Oh, and one more thing. I got a call from the Fairfax County sheriff's department. They want to talk to you about some break-in. You know anything about that?"

"I'm not sure, sir," Crocker lied. "But I'll call them when I return."

*　　　*　　　*

Two guards escorted Lisa down a hallway, into a long room with several doors leading into hallways and other rooms. It featured a tile floor, a large metal candelabra on the ceiling, and high-backed wood-and-leather chairs along the walls. At the end hung a black flag with a red, white, and green map of Mexico in the middle, and a big "Z."

"Where's my daughter?" Lisa asked.

The guards led her over to a high-backed chair in front of the flag and indicated that she should sit.

Before she did, she asked, "Is the *jefe* coming?"

Instead of answering, they stepped away and stood to either side of her with their arms crossed.

Facing her about ten feet away was a man with a beard and long hair. He leaned over a video camera on a tripod and adjusted the lens. Black cords snaked from the camera to some kind of electronic receiver at the opposite wall.

About a foot in front of the camera and to either side stood two large professional studio umbrella lamps.

"Hello," Lisa called. "Do you know if the *jefe* is coming?"

The photographer looked up and smiled at her with a mouthful of large uneven teeth. His face reminded her of the skinny actor from the movie *Y Tu Mamá También*, whose name she couldn't remember.

"El Chacal? No, Mrs. Clark," the man answered. "I'm just the camera operator. My name is Nelson. I'm checking to make sure all the cables are properly connected. I should be ready for you in a minute."

His casual manner, the camera, and the strange flag all

started to unnerve her. It wasn't what she had expected. Her pulse quickened and her mouth turned dry.

"The *jefe* wants me to make a statement," she said, trying to get a handle on what was going on.

"Yes, he does, *Señora*. Yes."

"But you don't expect him to be here."

"No, I don't. No," Nelson answered, shaking his head.

"What about my daughter?"

"I know nothing about her."

"Do you know if she's here, in this house?"

Nelson shrugged.

"So I should assume she won't be here when I make my statement."

"I guess not, *Señora*. I don't know."

"Did El Chacal tell you what he wants me to say?" Lisa asked.

"No. To tell you the truth, I've never met him. But I would think he wants you to be honest. You know, speak from the heart," Nelson said, slapping his chest. "Maybe talk about what this experience has meant to you, how you've been treated, what you've learned."

"Okay," Lisa said, trying to clear her throat. "I was expecting something else."

"Like maybe a script, *Señora?*" Nelson asked, smiling. "Or a speech? No, we don't have a script. This is more like reality TV, you know, improvisation. Why don't you sit and I'll adjust the light."

She did, and almost immediately Nelson switched on the two large lamps. "If these are in your eyes, please tell me."

"They are," Lisa replied, shielding her face with her hands

as the confidence drained out of her. It was replaced by a queasy panic.

She asked herself, *What if this is some kind of test, and if I don't say the right things, Olivia and I won't be released?*

A Mexican American CIA agent and another Mexican man wearing a black mask stood on one side of the table with Becker and CIA station chief Max Jenson behind them. The members of Black Cell faced them. The two Kawasaki KLR 650 dirt bikes that the men had ridden in on were visible through the window past Becker's shoulder.

Jenson stepped forward, leaned his long body on the table, and rubbed his eyes. In the middle of the table sat an olive-green backpack. He pointed at it, then spoke.

"We're running out of time, but I want to explain a couple things quickly. This man to my right is Gomez. He works for us. I don't know the identity of the individual on my left, so Gomez will fill us in."

Gomez jutted out his round chin and scratched under it. He stood about five ten and was built like a wrestler. His face was covered with several days' growth of beard and he had a haunted look in his eyes. "This man doesn't have a name or a face," he announced in a gruff, nasal voice, "because he's both an important asset and a member of the Mexican government security service."

"Who is he hiding from, us or them?" Jenson asked.

"Them," the masked man answered in accented English.

"Good answer."

Crocker wasn't sure he trusted any of them, and Jenson

seemed to sense that. He looked at Crocker with an expression that asked: *Do you want to go on with this, or not?*

Crocker nodded.

"Okay," Jenson said. "Show us quickly what you found."

The masked man opened the backpack and turned it over. Two dozen photos, maps, and diagrams spilled onto the table. He selected one that showed a strange, German-looking red clapboard house photographed through the bars of a gate.

"This is Las Lagrimas," Gomez stated as the masked man handed the photo to Crocker. "*Lagrimas* means 'tears' in Spanish."

"Is that significant?" Jenson grunted.

"Not really. No."

"Then let's stick to what these men need to know in order to carry out their mission."

"Okay."

"Las Lagrimas is one of six ranches, nine estates, and five apartments owned by Z-Thirteen throughout the country," Gomez stated.

"What's Z-Thirteen?" Crocker asked.

"That's the Zeta designation for El Chacal."

Jenson groaned, "Let's not waste time."

"Las Lagrimas is a cattle and sheep ranch formerly owned by an American rancher named Stanley Klausner, who died mysteriously in ninety-four as a result of what some say was his involvement in the Contra War in Nicaragua. Klausner was born in Germany, which explains the design of the house."

"Cut to the fucking chase," Jenson warned.

"The setup is pretty straightforward," Gomez continued.

"A main house, concrete airstrip and hangar, pool and cabanas, stables, and several equipment sheds on approximately five hundred acres. In Klausner's day, it was an active ranch. All that remain are a few head of cattle, a couple horses, and some avocado and lemon trees. The Jackal uses it as a vacation house."

"What the fuck does that mean?" Jenson asked.

"He's rarely there and when he is, he rides horses, hangs at the pool with young babes, and generally chills."

"Move on."

Gomez separated a satellite surveillance photo from the documents on the table and pointed to the main house.

"The two-story ranch house was built in a German style with a portico that runs all around it. It's about four thousand square feet, with formal dining room, living room, library, and kitchen downstairs, and four bedrooms, or three bedrooms and a study, and two bathrooms on the second floor."

Jenson glanced at his watch and grunted, "Hurry up."

"The whole ranch is enclosed by an eight-foot-high security fence topped with barbed wire and cameras. The front gate is guarded by armed men twenty-four/seven. And we found another interesting thing."

Gomez located another satellite photo of the ranch. "This one was taken about 1600 today. In an earlier photo, taken at 0940, there was a Learjet on the runway. In the later picture the aircraft is gone."

"Meaning?"

"Unsure."

"Are the Clark women still there?" Crocker asked.

Gomez turned to the masked man, who nodded.

"We believe so. Yes."

"What about the Jackal?"

The masked man nodded again.

"You've personally seen him and the women?" Crocker asked.

"No, but he knows someone who has," Gomez answered.

"And they're alive?"

"We believe so. Yes."

It wasn't a whole lot to go on, but under the circumstances, it would have to do.

"What's this?" Crocker asked, pointing to a river that snaked behind the ranch.

"That's the Coatan River," Gomez answered. "About a half million Central Americans pass over it a year on their way to the States."

"Why the fuck is that relevant?" Jenson snarled.

"Because it's not well monitored," Gomez explained. "Bandits and hustlers use big rafts with inflated truck-tire inner tubes to transport drugs and contraband across it day and night. And nobody stops them, because they're working with the Zetas, MS-13, or one of several Guatemalan gangs."

Jenson slapped his big hands together and, looking at Crocker, asked, "What do you think?"

Crocker glanced at his watch. They were eighty-three minutes away from the deadline. "How many guards and how are they armed?" he asked.

Gomez looked at the masked man, who held up ten fingers.

"Expect ten to a dozen with automatic weapons. The last time we looked, which was about an hour ago, they were stationed around the house. Four or five at the front gate, a few in back. I would expect more inside the house itself."

"Thanks."

"Anything else?"

Crocker looked at Mancini, who shook his head.

"All right, let's get these guys geared up," said Jenson as he set a hand on Crocker's shoulder. "Come with me."

Outside, the night air was still and thick. Hundreds of male cicadas and spittlebugs clicked around them in unison, announcing to the females that they were ready to mate. Jenson strode to the corner of the aluminum building and lit a cigarette as Crocker watched a falling star streak across the sky and fade.

"We got a problem," Jenson said, drawing on the Camel Light, his forehead furrowed. "A big fucking headache."

"What?"

"Washington hasn't given us authorization. They're waiting for permission from the Peña Nieto government, and I can tell you that the Mexicans want to execute the raid themselves. The problem is they don't know what we know in terms of intel, and I don't plan to tell 'em."

"Don't," Crocker answered, more aware than ever of the minutes ticking by. "We can't trust them. We both know that."

"But I also know this White House, and they don't want to risk their relationship with the new Mexican president, so they're not giving us the green light."

Crocker grimaced.

"It's a goddamn mess, and it's been dumped in our laps."

"You think the Jackal will carry out his threat and execute the Clark women?" Crocker asked.

"Based on everything I've heard about him, I believe he will."

Crocker slapped Jenson on the shoulder. "Then let's go!"

"We could both lose our jobs for this, if we're not shot by the Mexicans first."

"Right is right."

"I won't argue with that." Jenson stepped closer and lowered his voice. "I don't trust these sons-a-bitches guarding us, either. They probably got orders to follow you to the ranch."

"We'll use deception. Let's go."

Lisa sat in the chair with her hands folded in her lap, sweating. For some reason, the air conditioner had been turned off, which caused her to become increasingly uncomfortable.

Ten minutes grew to twenty, then thirty. She prayed silently, *God, if you get my daughter and me out of here alive, I'll dedicate myself to being a better person. I realize I've made mistakes in the past, and I understand now that politics and seeking power are not the right path for me. All I want to do in the future is love and nurture my family and help people in need.*

She looked up at Nelson and a third armed guard who stood near the camera, whispering. This one seemed rougher than the others and had black tears tattooed down the side of his wide face. He whispered something to Nelson, slapped him in the chest with the back of his right hand, and chuckled cruelly like someone who had just twisted the head off a cat. Then he turned to Lisa with a look that sent a chill through her body.

"*¿Lista, Señora?*" the guard asked leeringly.

She looked away, pretending not to understand and wishing she could turn invisible. *If only one of us survives this, let it be my daughter*, she prayed silently. *She's a good, decent girl with a big heart. Please spare her.*

A cell phone rang to a hip-hop rhythm. The guard beside Nelson answered, "*Sí, Jefe…*"

She had hoped to hear footsteps and watch El Chacal and Olivia enter through one of the doors. But she realized now that wasn't going to happen.

As the guard whispered into the phone, he looked at her and nodded. The unease she felt was almost unbearable. "Lord God, I place all my trust in you," she said, closing her eyes. "I love you more than I ever could have imagined."

The guard slipped the phone back in his pocket, then nodded at Nelson, who flipped on the umbrella lights again. They startled her.

Suddenly he seemed to be in a hurry. He said, "We only have fifteen minutes, *Señora*, so you have to talk fast."

"Okay, but what about my daughter?" she asked nervously, sweat dripping down her face and ruining her makeup.

"I don't know about her, *Señora*. I don't know anything. My job is to record your statement."

"Does he?" Lisa asked, pointing to the guard.

"Chamale? No."

"What happens after I record my statement?"

"You will go with Chamale. Stop asking questions."

CHAPTER FOURTEEN

Knowing is not enough, we must apply. Willing is not enough, we must do.

—Bruce Lee

CROCKER AND the three other SEALs made a big show of saying goodbye and wishing good luck to Becker, Max Jenson, and the masked Mexican, who climbed into the dark-blue Suburban, armed and wearing black helmets, then drove off.

They waited five minutes until the Mexican soldiers guarding the building jumped into their jeeps and followed them, then exited out the back door, through thick foliage, to an old Ford Explorer parked by an equipment shed. Gomez flicked on the yellow parking lights, and they climbed inside.

Gomez, who resembled a young Edward James Olmos, said, "The weapons and ammo are in back. Grab what you need."

Mancini passed an MP7 submachine gun with suppressor and M3X weapons light, a SOG knife, a cylindrical M14 incendiary grenade (which could produce enough heat to melt through an engine block), an MK141 Mod 0 stun grenade, two M68 frag grenades, an HK-45CT handgun, and three extra mags for each of them up to Crocker in the passenger seat.

He stuck the mags into the pouches of the low-profile vest he'd strapped over his black tee and slipped the handgun into the sleeve under his left arm, since he was a right-handed shooter. They had no armor, which meant they didn't have protective ceramic plates to insert in the vests.

Crocker didn't mind, because he wanted them to move as fast and as stealthily as possible. Each operator also wore an INVISIO M4 headset with vibration-sensing bone conduction so they could communicate with one another, and NVGs, but no helmets.

"We're about five minutes away," Gomez announced as he steered onto a two-lane asphalt road that took them past a movie theater playing *Iron Man 3*. Among the crowd gathered outside was someone dressed in an Iron Man suit, posing with his arms held triumphantly over his head.

"Fool," Manicini grumbled.

"Lighten up," Akil said. "He's just having fun."

"Maybe we should recruit him," Suárez remarked.

"Good idea."

"How do you want to do this?" Gomez asked Crocker as he glanced in the rearview mirror to make sure they weren't being followed.

"Get us as close as you can without being detected," Crocker replied, screwing a six-inch suppressor into the barrel of his MP7. "You brought bolt cutters, right?"

"Two Porter thirty-six-inchers. Top of the line."

"Good. We'll cut through the fence along the river and enter from the back. Once we're in, Manny, you and Akil deploy into the yard around the near side, to your left. Disable the side door, then secure the front door and front gate. Then clear through the front entrance into the bottom floor."

"What do you mean by disable?" Mancini asked.

"Bar it, block it, deploy an M14 to melt the lock, whatever," Crocker answered. "We need to prevent people from escaping the house."

"Got it."

"Call Suárez or me if you need help securing the front. And try not to shoot us, because we'll be entering through the back portico and heading for the stairway."

"How many enemy should we expect?" asked Akil.

"You said ten, right?" Crocker said, turning to Gomez.

"Anywhere from six to fifteen."

Akil: "Piece of cake."

"We don't want anyone escaping," Crocker continued. "Look for the hostages and clear them out of there."

"Two blond babes. Not a problem," cracked Akil.

"We don't want them getting hurt."

Mancini: "No."

"Suárez, once the first deck is secure, you and I are going to climb up to the balcony and attack the second. While we do that, Mancini and Akil will cover the bottom of the main stairway."

Akil: "Clever, boss."

"Don't fuck around."

"Floor plan?" asked Mancini.

"You saw what they showed us. You want me to go over it again?"

"Not necessary."

"What about me?" Gomez asked. "What do you want me to do?"

"You'll bring the Explorer around and block the front gate. Don't let anyone escape. Can you do that?"

"Yes."

"What about creating a diversion?" Mancini asked.

"No time," Crocker answered, glancing at his watch. "It looks like we're going to be hitting them within five or ten minutes of the deadline, maybe less. So they'll be on alert. Which brings me to another point: This all has to be quick and precise. As soon as we're compromised, we've got to get to the hostages within thirty seconds. Otherwise, they'll be executed."

They had passed through the commercial part of town and were climbing through thick foliage, past homes and ranches. A half-moon shone ahead. Crocker's heart raced like crazy. The problems with this mission were almost too numerous to consider. For one thing, they had no exit strategy, and there was no time to try to cobble one together now.

Gomez pulled to the shoulder just before the road curved right.

"This it?" Crocker asked.

"On the other end of this curve is a dirt road that runs about fifteen hundred yards to the Coatan River. I'll let you out at the end of that. From there, you've got about sixty yards of brush until you reach the fence."

"How long do you think we have until the Federales arrive?" Crocker asked.

"Good question," Akil said from the backseat.

"Say, fifteen minutes," Gomez answered. "Twenty at the most."

"Maintaining the element of surprise is critical," Crocker reminded them. "We don't know for sure, but we expect the hostages are on the second deck."

"Keep alert for booby traps."

"Let's launch this fucker."

"This one's for Ritchie!"

"For Ritchie. Go!"

Senator Jesse Clark sat in his Capitol Hill office, sipping from a glass of iced tea and waiting for the live stream to appear on his computer. Accompanying him were three aides, an FBI hostage crisis expert, and two deputies from the White House National Security Council.

A female aide looked at her watch and said, "Should be any minute now."

An instant later the feed went live with the camera tightly focused on Lisa's tense face.

"Lord have mercy," Clark muttered.

"She looks good," the aide whispered. "Very poised."

"Always does."

On the live stream, Lisa looked up, bit her top lip, and started to speak.

"My captor has asked me to record a brief statement about my experience here. He has given me no guidelines, so I'm speaking freely, choosing my own words. First, I want to say that while this ordeal has been difficult and even frightening at times, I have been treated well. I haven't been threatened. And although I have had very little contact with my daughter,

I have no reason to believe that her treatment has been any different from mine."

As she spoke, the camera slowly pulled back, revealing the chair she was sitting in, her suit, and the black flag behind her.

"What's that?" asked a male aide in a whisper.

"A strange variation of the Zapatista flag," the NSC deputy answered.

"Shhh!" said Clark's female aide.

Lisa continued: "Early in my captivity, the man who had been holding us explained his reasons for kidnapping us, which have to do with what he believes is a pattern of prejudice and unfair treatment of Mexicans by the United States government that he says continues today in the war against drugs. I admit that my understanding of the situation is limited. After I'm released, I plan to dedicate myself to the study of Mexican-U.S. relations and to righting any injustices perpetrated by the United States. Finally, I love my family and my country, and I'm proud to be part of both of them. God bless us all."

Lisa managed to hold her composure until the last four words, when her voice cracked and her lips started to tremble.

Suddenly, the screen turned black.

"What dignity," one of Clark's Senate aides said. "I think she did an amazing job."

"I agree," opined the FBI hostage expert.

"Remarkable."

The six people in the room turned to Clark, who had a stunned, pained look on his face. It was as though seeing his wife and hearing the anguish in her voice had made the crisis more personal and immediate than it ever had been before.

"She said 'after I'm released,'" the senator announced as he wiped a tear from his eye. "You hear that?"

"Yes, sir."

"'After I'm released,'" he repeated. "Does that mean she knows something we don't?"

"Knows what?" asked the FBI expert.

"Knows that he's letting her free."

"Unclear, Senator," the FBI officer answered. "She's probably unaware of the deadline and her kidnapper's demands. That's usually the way these situations work. As a kidnapper, you don't tell the hostages anything they don't need to know."

"Oh…"

"But I thought she sounded and looked good," the deputy from the White House NSC offered.

"Me, too," said the FBI hostage expert.

"What happens now?" Senator Clark asked.

The FBI expert glanced at the ticking Tiffany clock on the corner of his desk, which showed twelve minutes before the deadline. "Well, right about now the commandos from the Mexican GAFE have moved into position and are surrounding the site," he said in a confident voice. "We should hear something in a matter of minutes. These men are highly trained in hostage rescue. There's no reason to believe they won't achieve positive results."

"I hope so," Senator Clark said, turning and glancing at the framed photos of his wife and daughter on the wooden credenza behind his desk. "The president is confident?"

"Yes, he is, sir," the NSC deputy answered.

Senator Clark stood, bowed his head, and extended his arm. "Eleven minutes. Please join hands with me in prayer."

*   *   *

Crocker, Akil, and Suárez knelt behind thick foliage at the corner of the fence, sweat beading on their faces, even though it was almost midnight, as the Coatan River gurgled in the background. Mancini returned to report that he had disabled the security cameras along the top of the chain-link fence.

"All of them?" Crocker whispered.

"The three that run along this side."

"Good."

But they had other problems, which Crocker pointed to past the aluminum fence ahead. Up a graded embankment and approximately fifty yards away stood three armed men near the back of the house. One of them held two pit bulls on a leash.

The SEALs had no sniper rifle in their possession. So taking the men and dogs out without alerting the guards inside the house was nearly impossible. Suppressed weapons aren't completely silent, and even though some of the MP7s featured high-end scopes, none of them had been calibrated, and there was no time to do that now.

"You guys wait here, and I'll go around from the side and surprise them," Akil offered.

"No time," Crocker answered, glancing at his watch. They had eight minutes until the deadline.

"What, then?"

"Hand me the shotgun, some breaching rounds, a couple gas masks, and three CS gas grenades," Crocker whispered. The shotgun was an M870 single-fire twelve-gauge with a ten-inch barrel.

"We have no gas masks," said Mancini.

"Then nix the masks."

"What you gonna do?" Akil asked.

"Secure the hostages."

"How?"

"Rush the side door, blow the fucker open if I have to, enter the house."

"Boss—"

"The second you hear me, take out the three guards and the dogs and clear your way to the front gate. Then enter the house. I'll be on the second deck."

Mancini nodded. "We've got your back."

Crocker checked his watch again. "Six minutes." Then to Suárez: "Bring a bolt cutter and come with me."

Thirty seconds later, they reached a point along the fence parallel to the side door. It took another thirty seconds for Suárez to snip through the aluminum threads and pull them back enough for Crocker to crawl through. The pit bulls started to bark.

Crocker gave Suárez a thumbs-up, then gestured for him to wait at the fence.

Suárez nodded and mouthed the words *Good luck*.

Crocker dashed in a crouch to the portico and climbed three wooden steps to the side door, only to find it bolted shut. He slammed an M1030 breaching cartridge into the M870, aimed it at the lock, turned his head away, and fired.

Under ideal circumstances he would have been wearing eye protection. But he did the best he could, squinting through the smoke and falling debris and seeing that the wooden door had sprung open. He entered, quickly scanned the large rooms from the hallway, then headed for the stairway.

The three remaining members of Black Cell waited behind the fence with their weapons at ready. As soon as the shotgun blast went off, the three heavily armed Mexican guards came running toward them, just as they had anticipated. One was shouting into a radio; another held the two pit bulls on a chain.

When the Mexicans approached within twenty yards of the fence, the SEALs opened fire with MP7s and cut them down in a mangle of screams, blood, falling limbs, and smoke. Akil was on his belly halfway through the fence when he saw that one of the pit bulls had pulled free and was charging at him full speed. He reached for his weapon but couldn't maneuver it through the fence because the right shoulder strap of his LBT low-profile vest had gotten stuck on the end of one of the aluminum threads. "I need help here!" he exclaimed, grabbing the handle of his SOG knife with his left.

Neither of the other two SEALs was in a position to assist him—Mancini was in the process of crawling under the fence on the other side of a rosemary bush and therefore had no clear line of fire. Still, he squeezed off a couple of rounds that skittered along the ground and missed the charging dog. Suárez was already in the yard and out of sight, as he had entered at the same spot as Crocker.

So all Akil could do was focus intently on the massive mouth of the dog, which charged within six feet of him and lunged, eyes fierce and full of fury, sharp incisors bared.

At the last second Akil pulled his head back through the

hole in the fence, so that the dog slammed into it with a hor-rific growl. Akil felt teeth graze the flesh near his shoulder. The beast was trying to bite through the aluminum and get at his neck.

Akil pushed his left hand through the opening and sank the blade of the SOG knife into the dog's neck. Hot blood spilled over his hand and down his arm as the dog's eyes shifted from surprise, to anger, to recognition that he was dying in a mat-ter of seconds.

"Sorry, mutt," Akil moaned.

The dog exhaled its last breath, trembled, and went still.

Counting the seconds until the deadline in his head, Crocker hurried toward the stairway, weapons at ready. He glimpsed an olive-green pickup and armed men through the tall win-dows and white smoke, pulled the pins on two of the CS gas grenades, threw them toward the front door, then started to climb. *Boom...boom!* The house shook.

Ninety seconds.

He took the wooden steps two at a time, his heart thump-ing like a piston, the odorless smoke already finding its way into his eyes. Someone was moving above, and he heard shooting outside along the side of the house where the SEALs had entered.

Sixty.

All his senses on high alert and both the shotgun and MP7 off-safety, straight finger, he reached the landing and was con-fronted with a choice. A horseshoe balcony ran along the stair-way opening on the second deck with two doors on either side and three more doors behind him, facing the front of the house.

Hearing something in the room to his left, he crossed and kicked the door open. Someone was leaning out the window. In a split second he ID'd that person as a male and released a salvo from the MP7 that ripped a T in him—eyes, to nose, to sternum. The man crumpled and turned, trying to hold in the white-and-purple putrid-smelling organs that were spilling out of his stomach. The room contained a desk covered with medical equipment (stethoscope, sutures, syringes, scissors, glass vials), a scale, an unmade bed, and a can of Coke.

No hostages!

Crocker took a deep breath and backed out, crossed to the other back bedroom, and stopped. The door was locked. *Ten seconds!* exclaimed a voice in his head. From the front of the house, he heard men shouting in Spanish, a vehicle starting, and weapons discharging.

Crocker reared his right foot to kick the door open, but something told him not to. So he loaded another M1030 cartridge into the 870 and fired at the lock. A second after the door sprang, the entire wall in front of him exploded, lifting him off his feet and throwing him against the wooden rail. He held on to keep from falling over. Shards of wood and metal embedded themselves in his face, neck, arms, and chest. His head wobbling, he struggled not to lose consciousness.

Zero, the voice announced as he breathed deeply to clear his head. All that accomplished was to fill his lungs with smoke.

Tears muddled his vision. Through the dust, smoke, and flames, he heard a door creaking open behind him and footsteps running along the second-deck landing. The MP7 lay out of reach, so he grabbed the M870 that lay alongside him. Feeling along the pouch near his waist, he inserted another cartridge. Turning from a seated position, he spotted the blurry form of a man emerging from the bedroom to his left, holding an M4.

Crocker fired first. The M1030 breaching round hit the man smack in the middle of the chest and exploded. Crocker pulled himself up, ran, and stepped over the man as smoke rose from the ghastly hole in his chest. The man's hair stood straight up.

Suárez and Mancini crouched behind an avocado tree along the front side of the house as white smoke spilled out of the barrels of their MP7s. The bodies of two Mexicans they had just taken down lay bleeding out on the concrete driveway next to a military-green Toyota pickup. Beyond the pickup rose a big black metal gate and a fence covered in red bougainvillea.

Mancini raised two fingers and pointed to the front of the house to indicate that two other Mexican guards had retreated through the front door.

Suárez nodded.

Using hand signals, Mancini instructed Suárez to enter through the side door, which was to their right and about ten yards behind them, while he circled around and bum-rushed the front.

The idea was to trap the two retreating Mexicans in a crossfire before they reached the stairs.

Mancini tapped the top of his head and nodded. Suárez tore across the lawn to the shattered side door. He entered and was immediately hit by a wave of heat and smoke. A fire had broken out on the other side of the front hall and was spreading quickly through the wooden structure.

Through the smoke, Suárez spotted two men kneeling along a wall near the stairway, and he circled to his right through a breakfast room, kitchen, back porch, and media room, to try to surprise them from the other side. The dark-wood-paneled media room was filled with white smoke. Still, he made out boxes of Cuban cigars and glass cases filled with DVDs.

Using his left foot, he slowly pulled open the door and stepped into the hallway. The combination of tear gas, smoke, and heat blinded him for a second and squeezed his throat. Still, he kept his head enough to see something move to his left along the floor.

As he turned, shots rang out. One of them slammed into the door near his chin. Another cut through the web of skin between his right thumb and forefinger and clattered along the stock of his weapon, causing him to let it go.

The MP7 hit the floor. So Suárez reached for his handgun, and in that second he knew he was fucked. He heard a weapon discharge and clenched the muscles in his chest and stomach to try to repel the bullets. But mysteriously, they didn't come. Instead, they tore into the men along the wall, who screamed and grunted.

Looking up, he saw Mancini step through the white mist, gray smoke still wafting out of the end of his weapon.

"You okay?" Mancini whispered.

"Flesh wound," Suárez whispered back, pointing to his hand, then bending to recover his weapon from the floor. His arms shook. What he really wanted to say was: *Thank you for saving my life.*

* * *

Choking on cordite, smoke, and tear gas rising from the second deck, his eyes raw and teary, Crocker entered the front bedroom, his mind operating at warp speed, picking up impressions—two windows in front of him, a white wrought iron king-sized bed in the middle, and stretched over the bed, a blue plastic sheet, which had ballooned a foot and a half on the top and sides. A clear plastic tube traveled from the bed to a tank of gas near the wall to his right.

Otherwise, the room was empty. A terrific firing erupted outside, shattering glass and ripping through the clapboard walls.

He knelt, dropped the M870 on the floor, located the SOG knife in his vest, and slit the plastic open in one long, careful motion. A pungent gas leaked out.

A chlorine compound, Crocker said to himself, reaching into his admin pouch, feeling for a blue bandana, and tying it over his nose and mouth. Spinning to his right, he rose and kicked out the window, then tightened the knob on the tank, which had an elaborate timer attached.

Under the sheet, he spotted one woman, not two. It looked like Mrs. Clark, and she appeared unconscious. Six leather straps bound her tightly to the bed. Kneeling on its edge, he sawed through the restraints, carefully lifted her into his arms, carried her like a baby to the bathroom, and shut the door. Patches of livid red covered the skin on her face and neck, and her lips had turned purple. He set her down on the green tile floor, pulled open the bathroom window, then felt for a pulse along her neck.

It was weak, but she was still breathing, so he held her airway open.

Akil's voice filled his ears. "Boss, boss..."

Crocker thought he was hearing him through the headset, but when he looked up through tear-filled eyes, he saw Akil standing in the other doorway—the one that opened to the landing. The left side of his head and his left arm were covered with blood.

"Boss."

"You intact?"

"Hell, yeah. You locate the other one?"

Crocker shook his head vigorously and pointed to the other front bedroom. His throat, ears, and eyes burned, and he was sweating excessively because of exposure to the chlorine gas.

"The downstairs is on fire," Akil announced.

"Then go, quick! Find her."

Akil nodded, turned, and ran, and Crocker heard Mrs. Clark moan. He watched her gasp for breath and cough and a second later throw up greenish-yellow bile all over his arms.

He was pleased to see it, and the surprised look on her face, as he held her mouth open with his left hand and cleared her throat with his right.

"You're okay," he whispered. "Bear with me. Try not to make a sound."

He walked to the stall shower, turned on the water, then picked up Lisa and carried her inside. Feeling the cool water on her skin, she tried to pull away.

"No. Don't!"

"Quiet," whispered Crocker, holding her firmly. "You've

been exposed to chlorine gas, so I have to wash it off your skin and out of your hair and eyes immediately."

"Take me home, please," she groaned.

"I will."

"Don't hurt me."

"I won't."

He propped her against the wall of the shower and pulled off her skirt and blouse. She stared at him in shock as he peeled off her underwear to the pale skin underneath, covered with patches of red. She shivered against him.

He let go of her and whispered, "Wash your whole body. Nose, ears, throat, eyes, everything. I'll be right back."

She nodded, covered herself with her arms, and sank to her knees.

On the landing, he ran into Akil emerging from the other front bedroom. Smoke and flames rose from the ground floor.

"Where's the girl?" he asked urgently.

Akil shook his head.

"You check all the rooms up here?"

"Affirmative."

Crocker pointed downstairs. "Find her."

He entered the bedroom Akil had just exited, pulled a white cotton coverlet from the bed, and returned to the bathroom. There he helped Mrs. Clark out of the shower, and seeing that the patches of red were less livid, draped the coverlet around her.

"Wait here, but don't rub your skin."

Then he removed his vest and T-shirt and stood under the water himself. After quickly cleaning his hair, face, and chest, he stepped out of the shower and picked her up in his arms.

"Try to hold on to me," he said.

"Who are you?" she asked, looking up at his face, which was dripping with water, grime, and blood from the dozen or so wood and metal shards embedded in it.

"An American soldier."

"Where are we?"

"Cover your mouth and nose with the sheet and close your eyes. This might get hot."

CHAPTER FIFTEEN

Never trouble another with what you can do yourself.
—Thomas Jefferson

SUÁREZ WAS standing in the front hallway, getting ready to exit out the side door, when he saw a dark head descending through the smoke.

"Akil?" he whispered.

"No. It's me, Crocker."

Suárez hurried toward him, thinking he looked like a character in a slasher movie—soaking wet, blood dripping down his face and neck, holding a shroud-covered body in his arms.

"Dead?" Suárez whispered.

Crocker shook his head.

A grin spread across Suárez's face. "What do we do now?" he asked.

The front door was covered with flames. Crocker nodded to the side one.

Suárez ran ahead and helped Crocker clear the woman's pale legs through the doorway.

Outside, in the night air, he thought that he admired these guys more than he ever could have imagined. Not only were they the baddest of badasses, but they did their extraordinary work like it was no big deal. Another day at the office raiding a drug cartel leader's house without planning or backup. No sweat walking through fire to rescue someone from a burning house.

Suárez helped Crocker set the shrouded body on the bed of the olive-colored pickup. The person underneath it stirred, and a woman's blue eyes peered out.

Suárez patted Crocker on the shoulder and pointed.

Crocker nodded as the woman whispered weakly, "Am I okay?"

"Fine, Mrs. Clark," Crocker answered. "Lie here quietly. Breathe the fresh air. We'll get you out of here in a minute."

As he spoke, angry flames reflected in her curious eyes. Ten yards behind him, the entire left front of the house was engulfed in smoke and fire.

Remembering something, Crocker grabbed Suárez and asked, "Where's Gomez?"

"He's waiting near the gate."

"Good. Stay here."

"And do what?"

"Talk to her. Tell her a story. I'll be back."

Suárez couldn't believe what he was seeing. Crocker was actually heading to the same side door they had just exited and was about to reenter the house. "Sir?" he called softly.

Crocker paused on the lawn and spoke past his shoulder. "Don't call me sir. Call me chief, or boss if you want. Call me dickwad or motherfucker, but don't call me sir. I work for a living."

"Okay, boss."

Crocker spun on his toes and entered the house.

He found Akil in a room off the kitchen, kicking in a closet door that was covered with hand-painted vines and flowers.

"Find any sign of the other female?" Crocker asked to Akil's back.

"Only flour, maize, beans, tortillas."

"You recheck upstairs?"

"Yeah. Negative. I grabbed some medical papers, which I stuck in my vest."

"No sign of the other hostage?"

"Your ears messed up? No."

"Where's Manny?" Crocker asked.

"Out by the pool, checking the cabanas."

He'd forgotten about the grounds.

"Anything else I need to know?" asked Crocker.

"Yeah. In about five minutes the Federales are gonna be swarming all over this place," Akil growled.

"Right."

"And this guy's got an amazing porn collection and a *Pirates of the Caribbean* poster signed by Johnny Depp."

"What we need is a helo."

They checked the rooms at the rear of the house, looking for hidden chambers or a basement of some kind, before the smoke started to overwhelm them. Then they escaped out the back, where darker smoke obscured the sky. When Crocker tried to use his headset, he discovered it wasn't working, because part of it had melted from the flames and heat.

Turning to Akil and pointing to his, he asked, "Yours working?"

"My gear always works."

"Tell Manny we're on our way, and tell Suárez we'll be at the front gate in five mikes," he said to Akil, who did and reported back.

"Gomez and Suárez are both freaking out."

"Good. Let's go."

"Where?"

Crocker pointed toward the pool, which was lit from inside and looked like a cool, inviting dream. They sprinted across the lawn and past it to the cabanas, where they found striped towels, mattress pads, inflatable pool toys, and a stack of magazines.

Crocker slapped Akil on the shoulder and led the way to the stables, where they caught up with Mancini.

"Find anything?" Crocker asked.

"Horseshit and bridles," Mancini replied, kicking some of the former from the bottom of his boot.

"I was thinking in terms of a second hostage."

"I found a pink bikini in one of the cabanas and a woman's headband," Mancini replied, pulling them out of his back pocket.

"Which means a woman was there. Any woman. Anything else of significance?"

"Like a fresh grave? No."

Crocker tossed the bikini and headband to the ground as flames from the burning house licked the sky. There was still a lot of ground to cover, so he decided to bridle one of the stallions.

"Here's what we're gonna do," Crocker said, thinking out loud. "Manny, you're gonna inspect the barn and sheds along the front fence while I check out the landing strip and hangar."

"What about me?" Akil asked.

"You still have your camera?"

"Yeah."

"Run back to the gate. Have Gomez and Suárez move the vehicles away from the house. Then reenter the front gate and photograph the faces of any of the dead Mexicans you can find."

"Okay. Where?" Akil asked.

"Where what?"

"Where do you want us to move the trucks?"

"Down the road somewhere, away from the front gate so they can't be seen. Wait there when you're finished photographing the dead men. We'll find you."

The big brown horse looked anxious to move. Crocker was in a hurry, too. He grabbed it by its mane and jumped up and slid onto its back. The horse shuddered and neighed.

"How long are you gonna be?" Akil asked.

"As long as it takes."

Using the heels of his boots, he coaxed the brown horse from a trot to a gallop. Rotors of an approaching helicopter echoed in the distance. The thick night air caressed his face, reminding him of the last time he'd ridden a horse at night, as a teenager on his cousin Johnny's farm in New Hampshire— which seemed like a lifetime ago.

Reaching the square tin-roofed terminal building, he tied the stallion to a lamppost and searched. His NVGs had bit the dust somewhere in the house, so he flipped on the Maglite he carried in his low-profile vest.

A concrete airstrip stretched to his left and right and faded into darkness. Over it swirled thousands of mosquitos and other insects. He heard a siren wail in the distance. The half-moon hung crooked in the sky.

The door to the little terminal was locked, so he kicked it open and surveyed its contents: a desk, a radio, navigational equipment, and a Pirelli calendar with a naked Kate Moss leering at him from the wall. Judging from the dust on the surface of the desk, it hadn't been used in weeks. In its drawers he found some cans of soda, a loaded .38 revolver, a receipt for Jet A-1–type fuel, a chart with the variable costs of operating a Learjet 60XR per hour, a serial number (N662MS), and the purchase price ($8,950,000) and seller (Maxfly Aviation).

He stuffed the documents and the revolver into his utility pouch and moved on.

The hangar was more of the same—tools, jacks, tire blocks, spare tires, drums of Type K lubricant, a repair manual, men's overalls, cables, ropes. But no people, or anything to indicate that anyone had used it recently.

He worried for a second that maybe they had missed the other hostage in the house, and he didn't want that on his conscience. If Ritchie had been there, he would have told Crocker not to torture himself with what-ifs. Something like: *Do what you can, boss, and move on.*

The horse reared as the roof and second floor of the house collapsed, releasing a tremendous cloud of embers. Crocker ran his hand along its neck and tried to calm it down.

Sensitive creatures. There was nothing he could think of to do now but try to get out alive. Remounting, he considered the ride back to the Tapachula airstrip, where Jenson waited. As far as he knew, there was only one road back, and that would be teeming with Federales.

With no appetite for a stint in a Mexican prison or worse, he considered alternatives. The idea struck him that it might be better to have Jenson and his men fly the Gulfstream and pick them up here. That way they could get the hell out of Mexico and find medical attention for the Clark woman in another country.

He'd been so focused on keeping her alive and getting her out of the house, he didn't even ask her about her daughter. He steered the galloping horse wide of the burning house and out the gate. It was breathing hard, and its back and sides were covered with a foamy sweat, so he stopped.

Without a headset or cell phone, he had no way to communicate with anyone.

A pair of headlights flickered twice from behind some thick foliage to his right. Crocker slid off, patted the horse, and tied it to a tree. Frogs and cicadas croaked loudly around him. He made out Mancini sitting in the passenger seat of the pickup, adjusting the sight on his MP7. Akil stood beside the Explorer, parked behind the pickup.

"Where's Suárez?" Crocker asked.

"He's in the back of the pickup with Mrs. Clark," Mancini answered.

"She okay?"

"Breathing and alert."

Crocker found Gomez behind the wheel of the Explorer, looking like he was about to jump out of his skin.

222

"I want you to call Jenson and tell him to meet us here," Crocker said, leaning in the window.

"How's he going to do that?"

"He's gonna get in the goddamn plane and have the pilot land it on the landing strip behind that wall."

"That's a crazy idea."

"Maybe. But it's the only way this is gonna work." He pointed past the fence behind him. "Give him the approximate location. Tell him we'll light the runway up if he needs us to."

"Bad idea."

"Why?"

"The Mexicans are gonna get here first."

"Call him."

"I don't think—"

"Give me the fucking cell phone and I'll do it myself."

Gomez acquiesced and dialed. Crocker meantime instructed Akil to see if there was another gate to the property closer to the landing strip. Then he went to check on the woman sitting up in the back of the pickup still wrapped in the bedcover.

Suárez knelt beside her, relating a story about his grandfather's involvement in the Bay of Pigs invasion in Cuba.

"You okay?" Crocker asked, leaning over the side of the truck and feeling along her neck for her pulse, which was strong but quite a bit faster than normal.

"My throat and chest hurt, but I'm better," the woman answered. "Did you find my daughter?"

"We're still looking, ma'am." Crocker used the back of his hand to wipe sweat and blood from his forehead. "When's the last time you saw her?"

"Yesterday, or the day before. I lost track of time."

"Here at this house?"

"I'm not sure. I was drugged."

Her pupils were dilated and her skin felt hot.

"You warm enough, ma'am? You need water?"

"Suárez's been taking good care of me."

"Any difficulty breathing?"

"Not really."

"If Suárez's boring you, tell him to shut up. We'll have you out of here soon."

Akil clipped the lock on the rusted gate at the other end of the property, then waved them in. They entered, the pickup first, then the Explorer. Crocker instructed Gomez and Mancini to park the vehicles inside the hangar; then he returned the horse to the stables. From outside the little terminal building they watched the first of two fire trucks enter through the main gate.

"Lousy-as-shit response time," Mancini announced.

The house was now a pile of smoldering embers.

Following the firefighters came the Federales in two pickups, an armored personnel carrier, and a jeep.

Crocker said, "Everybody stand on the other side of the building so we can't be seen."

They were approximately two hundred yards from the main gate, but he didn't want to take any chances. "No lights, no loud noises or sudden movements. Akil and Manny, you keep an eye on the Federales and form a perimeter."

"Sure, boss."

Gomez's cell phone lit up. It was Jenson. Gomez said, "Yes, sir. Tell us what you want us to do. We're ready."

Crocker grabbed him by the elbow. "What'd he say?"

In the distance, the Mexicans were inspecting the bodies on the driveway. Red-and-blue lights flashed across the trees and sky.

"They're following the Coatan River, direction east-northeast, and are approximately five minutes away," Gomez reported.

"Tell him to stay on the line. They might not be able to see the airstrip through the smoke. Tell the pilot to keep an eye out for the fire trucks and flashing lights."

"I'll tell him."

"Where's Suárez?" Crocker asked.

Mancini nodded toward the hangar. "He's inside with Mrs. Clark, keeping her company."

"Good."

He borrowed Akil's NVGs and watched from the corner of the hangar as two more truckloads of Federales arrived. They stood in a clump inside the front gate near a firefighter in yellow who was pointing out positions throughout the property.

Then a group of black-uniformed Federales hopped into one of the black pickups and drove past the far side of the house. Crocker watched headlights wash the back fence, then inch along the back of the estate and turn left. It would be only a matter of minutes before the Federales reached them. He didn't want to risk another gun battle, or the possibility of Mrs. Clark's being seized again.

Still, he did a quick inventory and found that all that remained were three partially filled mags for the MP7s, four handguns with one mag each, one M870 shotgun with four buckshot shells, and three percussion grenades.

Hearing footsteps, he turned and saw Gomez hurrying toward him and pointing at the sky.

"Here they come!"

"Tell Suárez and Mrs. Clark. Get everyone ready and meet in front of the shack."

Seconds later, he heard a roar. Then the wing lights of the Gulfstream IV came on, illuminating the haze over the runway.

Crocker was sure that the Federales had spotted the plane already, and he saw the concerned expression on Mancini's face. To his left, Mrs. Clark slowly walked out of the hangar, wearing a pair of men's overalls and leaning on Suárez's shoulder.

"Where's the pickup?" he whispered to Mancini.

Mancini pointed over his right shoulder at headlights near the pool cabanas, approximately seventy-five yards away.

"This is gonna be close."

"Real tight."

They watched the Gulfstream land, race toward the end of the runway, brake, turn, and taxi toward them. Fortunately, the Mexicans were passing behind the cabanas and not in a position to fire at it yet. Since the plane had landed north to south and turned around, when it taxied to take off, it would be traveling north and away from the truckload of Federales.

Crocker calculated they would never be able to board everyone in time.

Turning to Gomez, he said, "Tell the pilot to keep the engines running. Tell him the enemy is on our tail, so we have to make this super-quick."

"Yes."

"Akil, you and Suárez help everyone aboard, close the door, and tell the pilot to leave. Manny, come with me."

"Where're you guys going?" Akil asked.

"Don't worry about us."

"We'll wait."

Crocker: "There's no time."

"No."

"You go. We'll fight our way out."

"Boss—"

"Don't argue. Just do it! Now!"

He and Mancini ran, crouched at the far corner of the shack, and readied their weapons. The pickup was out of view for a moment, in a gully at the near end of the stables. He saw the Gulfstream come to a full stop, saw the side door open and the stairway deploy.

Hurry!

Gomez ran toward it first, then Akil and Suárez, who was helping Mrs. Clark. She tripped and fell on her way up the stairs. Akil and Suárez supported her.

Fucking hurry!

The Federale pickup came up the berm and immediately opened fire. A big machine gun, either a .30 or .50 cal, clanged on its bed. Bullets whizzed past them in the direction of the plane, which stood completely vulnerable, like a delicate white bird.

Crocker heard the jet engine whine higher and, turning to Mancini, screamed, "Now!"

The two SEALs jumped out from behind the building and fired everything they had in a ferocious salvo of bullets that shredded the truck's front tires and shattered its windshield. Mancini groaned, grabbed his right knee, and fell to the ground. The pickup swerved left, looking for a second like it was about to turn over, then righted itself on the concrete runway. It seemed to gain speed as it chased the jet.

Crocker was trying to take out the soldier firing the .50 cal when his weapon went dry. Instead of searching his vest for another mag, he tossed the MP7 aside and picked up the M870, which was preloaded with an M1030 cartridge.

The pickup raced past, forty feet away, machine gun rounds careening off the runway. The jet started to lift off the ground.

Crocker, utilizing some Kentucky windage skills he'd picked up, fired at the truck as the jet roared into the sky. The cartridge slammed into the truck's side. A second later the gas tank exploded and the machine gun stopped firing. The pickup veered off the concrete strip, hit the ground in front of it, and turned over onto its back.

"Good shot," Mancini groaned from the ground.

"You okay?"

In muted light Crocker saw that Mancini was in the process of ripping his pants leg, which exposed a bloody area under his knee.

"I got nicked. Must've hit a nerve, because my leg went numb," Manny said.

"You need me to carry you?"

"No. Leave me here."

"Fuck that."

CHAPTER SIXTEEN

Intelligence is the ability to adapt to change.
—Stephen Hawking

THEY WERE on their own with little ammunition, Mancini's bum knee, and several truckloads of angry Federales closing in on them. Crocker made a beeline for the hangar, where he found the Ford Explorer. Thankfully, Gomez had left the keys in the ignition.

Sweating from every pore in his body and breathing hard, he fired up the ignition, spun the vehicle around, drove to where Mancini was waiting, helped him aboard, and exited through the side gate in a cloud of dust.

Bullets ripped into the back of the SUV, shattering the rear window. Crocker operated completely on instinct, driving hard with the headlights off and turning right, down a dirt path that led in the direction of the river.

"I don't think this is a road," Mancini said as he wrapped the wound under his knee and covered it with a white bandage.

"It is now. How's the leg?"

"I'll manage."

In the rearview mirror he saw the headlights of the Federales' vehicles less than ten yards behind them. A helicopter banked overhead, its searchlight sweeping the canopy of trees.

The vehicle bounced hard down the pitted path. Branches scraped the sides, producing a horrible screeching sound. After several hundred yards, the narrow path ended with concrete steps and a broken concrete embankment that angled down sharply to the wide gravel bed and then the river.

"I got half a mag left," Mancini said, holding his MP7 and turning to look behind.

"Hold on."

Crocker braked first, then eased the Explorer down the steps to the embankment at a forty-five-degree angle. The vehicle jolted violently from side to side, scraping bottom over sections of concrete that had risen due to changes in the topography of the river. Several times it was in danger of flipping onto its hood or turning over sideways.

"How's your knee now?" Crocker asked.

"Hurts like a motherfucker."

A Vietnam-era UH-1 Iroquois helicopter swooped low in front of them and unleashed a stream of bullets that tore into the hood. A hot piece of metal grazed Crocker's cheek, but he kept pushing the SUV forward and found gravel. Engine growling, the Explorer lurched forward and entered the river with a splash.

"Get ready to swim."

Water rose past the wheels to the hood. Crocker gunned the accelerator, and the tires spun over wet gravel and rock.

"The engine's gonna flood," Mancini warned.

The tires spun and gradually gained traction, causing the vehicle to plow through the ten-foot-wide ribbon of water to the other side.

"Frisky mofo."

"We're in Guatemala now," Crocker announced, steering the smoking Explorer up a sandy embankment into some low trees.

"Is that good or bad?" Mancini asked.

The helicopter swooped in low over the river again.

"Watch out!"

They ducked behind the dash together, but the helo didn't fire. In the rearview mirror Crocker saw the two Federale pickups stop on the other side of the river. Armed men jumped out with automatic weapons ready. But instead of taking aim, they spat on the ground.

"Looks like they're gonna respect Guat sovereignty," Mancini announced.

"They're probably notifying their counterparts in the Guatemala police right now."

Their next challenge was getting past the Guatemalan border guards, who Crocker didn't feel like wrangling with. He took what he hoped was a detour through back dirt roads that wound up into low hills dotted with little coffee and marijuana farms. As he tooled down a narrow country road, windows open, the engine coughed and the SUV lurched and sputtered to a stop.

"What happened?" groaned Mancini.

"I think we ran out of gas."

"Fuck."

Crocker had three hundred dollars in cash in the heel of his boot in case of emergency. This certainly qualified, so he got out and walked ahead toward some dim yellow lights. He made out an old man sitting on the front porch of a dilapidated house smoking a pipe.

"*Buenas noches, Señor,*" Crocker said.

The old man pointed at the moon and said, "*La luna se lloro esta noche.*" ("The moon cries tonight.")

Crocker nodded but didn't understand. "*Tengo…mi auto, ahi,*" he said, trying to recall his meager Spanish. "*Muy grande problema. No más gasolina.*"

"*¿Necesita gasolina?*" the old man asked, rising slowly and looking deeply into Crocker's eyes. He didn't seem to mind the fact that Crocker's face, neck, and arms were covered with cuts and abrasions. Instead, he nodded and pointed to a twenty-year-old faded-red Datsun 510 sedan parked under some banana trees by the side of the shack next door.

"*¿Este tiene gasolina?*" Crocker asked.

"*Viene aqui.*" The man escorted Crocker to the shack next door, talking in Spanish the whole way. He knocked on the door and entered. A chubby young woman sat in a T-shirt and shorts embroidering a blouse as incense burned on a table covered with statues of saints in the corner.

The old man spoke to her in a language Crocker didn't understand, then pulled Crocker outside. The woman followed on bare feet.

"*¿Que pasa?*" Crocker asked.

"*Ella quiere ver a su auto.*" ("She wants to see your car.")

"*¿Mi auto? ¿Porque?*"

The woman carefully inspected the dirty, bullet-scarred Explorer inside and out, studied Mancini's biceps and tattoos, which seemed to interest her, then proposed a trade: the twenty-year-old Datsun for the new but damaged and out-of-gas Explorer.

"*¿El Datsun tiene gasolina? ¿Anda bien?*" Crocker asked.

"*Si, claro.*"

Crocker considered for a few moments, then returned to the Datsun to make sure it ran and did have a half tank of gas. It did, so he accepted.

He and the woman shook hands and exchanged keys.

Equally important was the map the old man drew on the side of a shopping bag that showed the route to the Pan-American Highway.

"*Gracias, Señor,*" said Crocker, squeezing the man's callused little hand. And to the woman: "*Gracias, Señorita.*"

"Some lousy deal maker you turned out to be," Mancini complained as Crocker helped him into the front seat of the Datsun.

"She wanted me to trade you for a box of mangos. I seriously considered it."

"Very funny."

After forty minutes of bouncing over rough, dark roads, they reach the paved highway. Then it was easy winding through the dark, verdant hills of the Mayan highlands, the half-moon lighting the thin ribbon of asphalt. The surface was so smooth and the route so back and forth that it rocked Mancini to sleep.

233

He snored in the passenger seat as Crocker pulled into a gas station outside Quetzaltenango to refuel and buy a prepaid Nokia 1616 for fifty dollars. Outside, standing in the cool night air with marimba music playing from a radio nearby, Crocker dialed the number he had committed to memory.

"ID yourself," said the female duty officer who answered in Langley.

"I'm BC292. BC295 is with me."

"Are either of you in need of immediate medical help?"

"My partner has a wounded leg, but it's not life threatening."

"Where are you, and how can I help you?"

"We're on the Pan-American Highway on our way to Guatemala City, escaping from a mission in Mexico."

"Hold on."

Three minutes later she returned to the line. "Are you in a vehicle?"

"Yes, we are."

"Proceed to La Aurora International Airport in Guatemala City. Drive directly to the north terminal. In front of the TACA Airlines departure area, you'll find a silver Toyota Tundra with a dark-haired woman at the wheel. Her name is Danila. Park directly behind her, identify yourself as hikers from Montreal, and get in."

"Thank you."

Three and a half hours later, they arrived at La Aurora International Airport and found Danila, a tall, no-nonsense Hispanic woman with a high forehead, wearing large hoop earrings. Without saying a word, she drove them past the main terminal to an Interjet hangar and stopped alongside a white BE20 Super King turboprop plane.

"There's your ride," she said.

"Thanks. Where's it taking us?"

"Panama City."

"Florida?" Mancini asked.

"No, Panama City, Panama. Enjoy."

Fifteen hours later Crocker stood looking out a fifth-floor window at the sky turning orange, amber, and gold as the sun set over the Bay of Panama. Eighteen years earlier, before he became a SEAL, he'd served as a young navy corpsman assigned to Rodman Naval Station half a mile away from where he was standing now.

In March 1999, the six-hundred-acre base, which once housed the naval component of the U.S. Southern Command (SOUTHCOM), was turned over to the Panamanian government. So were a number of other U.S. military bases, including Forts Gulick, Davis, and Sherman on the Caribbean side of the isthmus, and Howard Air Force Base, Fort Amador, and Fort Kobbe on the Pacific or southern side. All of them had once formed a powerful air, land, and sea defense perimeter around the strategically important Panama Canal.

When U.S. control of the Panama Canal formally transferred to the Panamanian government on December 31, 1999, the bases were closed and most U.S. military personnel left. Rodman Naval Station was now a tank farm run by Mobil Oil. Howard Air Force Base was being developed into an international business park called Panama Pacifico.

It was strange being back in what was once called the Gorgas Army Hospital. Eighteen years ago when part of the facility housed a U.S. Navy clinic, Crocker had been operated on here for a ruptured appendix. It happened a day after he competed in a cross-isthmus marathon that originated at the Vasco Núñez de Balboa Park, which was only a couple of blocks away.

The light-green walls and the antiseptic smell were the same, reminding him of sickness and his own mortality, which he didn't feel ready to deal with yet. He thought back to the ranch in Tapachula and the old man he had met in the Mayan hills.

Life followed a mysterious path and offered unexpected challenges, disappointments, and pleasures. They hadn't found the Clarks' daughter, which meant there was still more to accomplish, and more enemies to defeat.

Ambition burned white-hot at the base of his spine, goading him forward, compelling him to work harder and perform at an even higher level than he had before.

Somewhere he had once read: If you only do what you think you can, you never do much.

A young Hispanic woman in a light-blue uniform walked in and asked him in heavily accented English why he wasn't in bed. Her short hair had been bleached blond, but the dark roots showed.

"I feel like looking out the window," Crocker answered.

"You not ready," she said, taking him by the forearm and leading him back to bed. She tucked the sheets around him and recorded his temperature and blood pressure on a chart that she then replaced in a plastic sleeve and tucked under her arm.

"What's wrong with me?" Crocker asked.

"Many things."

"Like what?"

"I call the doctor."

"How long have I been here?"

She left without answering, the backs of her too-big yellow Crocs slapping against the blue linoleum floor.

He remembered the Super King turboprop landing in Panama City, red-and-blue flashing lights, Lisa Clark waving as she was wheeled to the back of an ambulance, and Max Jenson introducing him to the CIA station chief in Panama—a friendly dark-haired man who said he had met Crocker briefly when he was stationed in Afghanistan.

The nurse reentered, accompanied by a tall doctor with a large watermelon-shaped head. His name tag read DR. DANNY RAMOS.

"How are you feeling?" Dr. Ramos asked in a Texas accent as he pressed a stethoscope to Crocker's chest.

"Better than I did last night."

"Breathe deeper."

Waves of pain rose from his abdomen and ribs.

"Turn over."

Dr. Ramos pulled up the back of the light-green hospital gown and pressed the middle of Crocker's back. "Any pain?"

"Nothing I can't deal with."

"What does that mean?"

"Pain is just weakness leaving the body."

The doctor chuckled. "That's an interesting concept that's not backed up by science."

Dr. Ramos marked something on the chart and replaced it

in the plastic sleeve at the end of the bed. "The skin around your eyes and eyelids is still swollen. But that will go down. I'll have the nurse re-dress the bandages in the morning, then I'll examine you again to see if you're okay to go," he said, waving his big hand at the thirty or so little white bandages on Crocker's forehead, cheeks, neck, arms, shoulders, and chest.

"What was I admitted for?"

"Chlorine poisoning, smoke inhalation, and multiple bruises, cuts, and abrasions."

"What about the woman I was admitted with? Mrs. Clark?"

"Her poisoning was more serious. But she's stabilized now."

"Where is she?"

"Down the hall."

"Can I visit her?"

"You stay here. I'll inquire."

Fifteen minutes later, Crocker was sitting up in bed watching an NBA playoff game on the TV bolted to the ceiling when Akil and Mancini walked in carrying a Burger King bag and a big plastic cup that featured a likeness of the Starship *Enterprise*.

"You owe me ten balboas," Akil said, setting the cup and greasy bag on the table beside Crocker's bed.

"What for?"

"Two Whoppers with *queso*, *papas fritas*, and a *grande* Coca-Cola in a collector's cup."

"You look like Jabba the Hutt," Mancini said, remarking on Crocker's swollen cheeks. "What happened to your face?"

"The aftereffects of chlorine poisoning," Crocker answered. "How's your knee?"

"Some minor damage to the superficial fibular nerve. But aside from that, all good."

"Where's Suárez?"

"He's at church praying that he gets assigned to another team," Akil cracked.

"He did good work," Crocker said as he bit into the burger, which tasted good but overcooked. "How was your flight?"

"I slept through it, so I guess it was fine," Akil answered as Mancini checked Crocker's medical chart.

"What's it say?" Crocker asked.

"Severely diminished brain activity due to repeated and prolonged blows to the head," Mancini answered, pretending to read from the chart. "Delusions, slight dementia, an asymmetrical mustache. Other than that, you're fine."

"Nice."

"He never used that organ anyway," joked Akil.

"Where are you gorillas staying?" Crocker asked, stuffing fries into his mouth and chewing.

"Something called the Balboa Palace, otherwise known as the Roach Motel. About a half-mile south along the bay," Akil answered, sitting with his feet up on the frame of the bed.

"Why don't you make yourself comfortable."

"The happiest people don't necessarily have the best, but they make the most of things," Akil replied.

"Where did you come up with that?"

"It's my life philosophy."

"Any news about the younger hostage?" Crocker asked.

Akil looked at Mancini by the window, who shrugged back and answered, "Only that the senator is arriving soon and will be meeting with Jenson and Arno."

"Who's Arno?"

"John Arno's the local station chief—we met him last night."

Crocker looked confused.

"See, his brain was damaged," Akil said. "By the way, the senator wants to know why you were showering with his wife."

"That's not funny."

"You're right. Sorry."

The same nurse bustled in, saw Crocker sitting up in bed finishing off the burger, and snapped, "You no can eat."

"Why not?"

"No food without doctor permission."

Mancini grinned. "I don't know if that qualifies as food."

"Bery bad," the nurse scolded.

"Turn him over and spank him," Akil suggested.

"Maybe I do," the nurse said, wagging her finger. "Maybe I spank you, too."

Akil grabbed her by the wrist and pulled her onto his lap. "Only if I get to spank you first."

She giggled and tried to slap him. Akil spun her over. Just as he raised his hand to spank her, Captain Sutter walked in.

"What the hell is going on here?"

"Sir."

Akil pushed the nurse off his lap and stood at attention as their CO turned to Crocker and said, "Seems like I've walked in on an episode of *The Three Stooges*."

"These men are trying to amuse me, sir."

"Are they succeeding?"

"Not really. No."

"This episode is called 'The Three Stooges Meet the Nurse from Hell,'" Akil announced. Whereupon the nurse slapped him in the face and stormed out.

CHAPTER SEVENTEEN

We will either find a way or make one.

—Hannibal

IVAN JOUMA sat in a wheelchair in a third-floor suite of the Clínica Central Cira García in the Miramar sector of Havana, Cuba, studying a photograph of himself when he was two years old, sitting on his mother's lap, wearing new boots and a straw cowboy hat that matched his father's. Of the three, he was the only one who seemed happy, lost in his boyhood world of dreams and imaginary friends. His father scowled at the camera from behind a thick black Pancho Villa mustache, his eyes burning with anger and defiance. His mother smiled wanly as though she was trying to put a good face on a life of struggle, disappointment, and little hope.

He'd hated his abusive father since he kicked him out of the house at age thirteen but remembered his mother fondly, even though she'd stood by passively when his father drank and burst into wild rages, destroying the little furniture they had and beating his son with a leather belt.

He would never forget how she helped him with little gifts of tortillas, oranges, and money when he was living on the streets and stealing. Both of them were dead now, memories of a past that he hoped to erase.

"La Santísima Muerte," he said. "Look over my mother and tell her that her son is about to redeem himself with the help of a *gringa*."

He'd been a hopeful, joyful kid. The more he learned about the world and its inequalities and crushing poverty, the more furious he became. And the more he thought of the beatings and humiliations he'd endured, the dirt he'd eaten when his stomach ached with hunger, the shit-filled animal pens he'd slept in when there was no place else to escape the cold, the more he wanted to scream out loud and blame the oppressors who had stolen the bounty that God had provided to everyone and claimed it as their own.

His musings were interrupted by three knocks on the door.

"Come in," he barked in Spanish, stuffing the black-and-white photo back into his wallet.

Instead of a nurse or doctor, it was one of the young men who made up his inner circle of aides—Los Lobos, he called them—who entered and stood with his hands behind his back.

"*Señor Jefe.*"

"I can see from your face that you have bad news," the Jackal said. "So tell me."

"*Jefe*, the doctor said that maybe this isn't the best time."

"Then why the hell are you here?"

"To see if you need anything."

Jouma gritted his teeth and looked out the window to the

park across the street. "I don't give a shit what the doctors say. Tell me what happened."

The young man took a deep breath and started, "*Jefe*, there was a raid on Las Lagrimas last night."

Jouma quickly cut him off. "When?"

"Around midnight. The house was burned down, eight guards were killed, and the American woman was taken."

"Dead or alive?" Jouma asked, clenching his fists.

"The *gringa*? Dead, we think, but we don't know for sure."

"I want to know!"

"Yes, *Jefe*. The gas was timed to go off automatically."

Jouma gazed down at his hands, which were small and delicate and had always been a source of embarrassment. The skin over them appeared mottled and gray. He didn't care so much that the house had been destroyed or the woman taken.

"Names?" he asked grimly.

"Which names, *Jefe*?"

"The names of the men who died."

"Alvarez, Tamayo, Elvis, Flaco, Ramirez, Molina, Danny, Sapo."

It pained him, because he thought of the people who worked for him as part of his family. "Sapo, too?"

"Yes, *Jefe*."

Sapo had always been one of his favorites. A short, barrel-chested man from Juárez with no neck and stubby legs, who worked tirelessly, never complained, and played the guitar and sang with the voice of an angel.

"Make sure all the funerals are paid for. First class. Flowers, good caskets, food. And take care of the families in the usual way."

"Yes, *Jefe*."

He'd learned the importance of building loyalty as a young recruit in the army and had always been generous to friends, family, the men and women who worked for him, supporters, and even communities of people in areas under his control. He called it "spreading the wealth." He'd paid for college tuitions, weddings, houses, medical procedures, clinics, schools, homes, farms, cars, motorcycles, horses, birthday parties, and even local beauty pageants.

"Who?"

"*Jefe?*" the aide asked.

"Who betrayed me?" His arms and head started to shake with anger.

"We don't know for sure, but the rumor is that Luis Vargas was paid off by the *gringos*."

"Who the fuck is Luis Vargas?"

"He's a sergeant with the Federales, who comes from Mazatlán."

The Jackal couldn't remember hearing his name before. "If he wanted money, why didn't he come to me?"

"I don't know, *Jefe*."

"Find out. Ask him!"

The aide looked confused. "Yes."

"Where is he now?" Jouma asked.

"No one has seen him, or his wife, or their two sons since the raid."

"Which means the Americans probably gave him a new identity and are hiding him somewhere."

"Yes, *Jefe*."

"Tell Nacho I want him to launch an investigation and do

anything he has to do. We have to find this *hijo de puta* and make an example."

Nacho Gutierrez was his chief of security—a man of legendary brutality who recruited, trained, and managed a group of professional hit men (known as *sicarios*) who operated throughout Mexico, Guatemala, and El Salvador and into the United States. They were sociopaths recruited from the universities, police academies, and army.

"Yes, *Jefe*. I'll inform Nacho immediately."

He glanced at the photo again and the indignity and outrage burning in his father's dark eyes. When he was a boy he earned a dollar fifty a day picking lettuce, chilies, watermelons, and tomatoes in New Mexico and Arizona. Now he had so much money, he couldn't count it.

"Who executed the raid?" he asked.

"*Gringos.*"

"*¿Gringos militares?*"

"They weren't wearing uniforms, *Jefe*. So we don't know for sure."

"Did they use helicopters?"

"No helicopters."

"How many men?"

"Five or six. Maybe more."

He clenched his jaw. "Are these the same *gringos* who attacked the house in Puerto del Hiero?"

The young man shrugged. "Maybe, *Jefe*. We don't know."

"Tell Nacho I want his best *sicarios* on this case. His top men. First, they need to find the identities of these *gringos*. Second, I want them to kill their wives and children. Third, they have to burn down their houses. Finally, I want the *gringos* brought to me so I can watch them being skinned alive."

Captain Sutter wasn't in a playful mood, which became apparent when he sat in a chair alongside the bed and demanded a full accounting of what had happened in Tapachula.

"The whole thing?" Crocker asked, finishing off the soda and wiping his mouth on a thin paper napkin.

"From conception to completion."

He, Mancini, and Akil took turns relating the entire operation—the shootout, the recovery of Mrs. Clark, the burning of the house, the arrival of the firefighters and Federales, and their escape.

Sutter frowned at the end, got up, and walked to the window. "Excellent work rescuing Mrs. Clark," he said somberly.

"Thanks."

"But you left out the most important part," Sutter said. "Who authorized the raid?"

"I did," Crocker answered from the bed, sitting up and adjusting the pillows so his back was more comfortable.

"You alone?" asked Sutter, the veins in his long neck sticking up.

"Jenson was on the phone to someone in Washington waiting for the go-ahead, but the deadline was approaching," Crocker explained. "It was about fifteen minutes away. So it was a judgment call on my part. I knew that none of us would be able to live with ourselves if we did nothing and let those two women die."

"I was afraid of that," groaned Sutter, kicking a chair in the corner.

"Why, sir?" Akil asked. "The mission was a partial success."

"Why? Because you deployed without White House approval, goddammit. And they're demanding heads."

"Tell 'em to chill," Akil groaned. "A woman's life was saved."

"That stupid attitude is not going to help you."

"Sir—" Crocker jumped in but was immediately cut off.

"It wasn't your decision to make!"

"But—"

Sutter's face had turned bright red. "The president was in communication with President Peña Nieto," he explained. "I understand there was some uncertainty about the location of the woman, because intel was sketchy and everything happened quickly. But once the site in Tapachula was confirmed, the Mexican president assured him that his military was in position to execute the raid."

"But they didn't, sir," said Crocker.

"How the fuck do you know that?"

Crocker had never heard Sutter curse this much.

"Because we got to the ranch several minutes before the deadline and the Mexican military was nowhere in sight."

"Had they been there, would you guys have stood down?" asked Sutter.

"Maybe, depending on circumstances."

"Wrong answer!"

"The truth is, they didn't act, sir," explained Mancini. "Not in time."

"If we hadn't found Mrs. Clark when we did, she'd be dead," Akil said. "That's a fact."

"Gentlemen," started Sutter, trying to contain his emotion. "I'm on your side. I'll defend you all the way. But you and I work for the government, led by our commander in chief. What you're telling me is that you launched a major operation on foreign soil without his approval, and without the go-ahead of the leader of that country. Which means we've got a major problem on our hands and need to figure out how the hell we're going to manage it without losing our jobs."

"Fuck 'em all," Akil groaned in disgust.

Mancini: "Akil, don't talk like an idiot."

Crocker cleared his throat. "With all due respect, sir, the problem all of us, including the White House, should be focused on is the location of the Clarks' daughter."

Sutter shook his head. "That's not a problem anymore."

"Why not?" Akil asked aggressively.

"Olivia Clark is dead."

They all turned silent and looked at one another.

"How do you know?" Crocker asked.

"According to reports out of Tapachula, her remains were found in the burned wreckage of the house. The Mexican pathologists are checking her dental records now."

For a second Crocker thought he wasn't hearing right. "They found her remains in the main house?" he asked.

The CO nodded. "They found her. Where exactly, I don't know."

"Sir, we searched the house, and thoroughly," Akil explained.

"The grounds, too," Mancini added.

"Apparently you didn't search it thoroughly enough."

"I strongly doubt that, sir," declared Crocker.

"It doesn't matter, Crocker. The Mexicans claim she's dead."

He dressed in the black pants and polo Mancini had purchased for him and took the sad news with him down the hall. Outside the room ahead, he saw Senator Clark standing with his wide back to him, talking to a shorter, thinner man.

When the senator turned to greet him, Crocker was taken aback by the change in his appearance since the last time he'd seen him on TV. His formerly bold blue eyes had turned several shades darker and had withdrawn into dull orbs of pain. The skin around them hung loose and pale, lending his face a hollowed-out, skull-like grimness that reminded Crocker of the last photographs of Abraham Lincoln.

"I want to thank you, Crocker," the senator said, taking his hand and pulling him into a hug.

Though awkward, the gesture was heartfelt, reminding Crocker of the senator's loss and the unimaginable pain he must be experiencing. Crocker said, "I wish I could have done more."

"Me, too."

There were tears in the senator's eyes. Crocker wanted to say that he and his men weren't finished and wouldn't be until the Jackal was dead, but Senator Clark already had his big hand on Crocker's back and was guiding him into the room.

Clark leaned close to him and whispered, "My wife has asked to talk to you alone."

"Of course."

It was a large corner room. The yellow curtains were pulled shut. A respirator stood on the opposite side of the bed.

Lisa Clark sat up in bed, her hair pulled back and the overhead light shining off her forehead, cheekbones, and lips. Her eyes looked tired and were rimmed with red. A tube in her left wrist fed her a glucose solution through an IV.

Even without makeup and under the stark fluorescent light, she looked poised and beautiful.

"It's good to see you again, Chief Warrant Officer Crocker," she said, smiling weakly.

"Call me Tom. Please."

She offered him a pale, bony hand, which he held for a second. "I want to thank you and your team from the bottom of my heart for your courage and determination. What you did last night was incredible."

"Thank you."

"I pray you're all in good health."

"Yes, ma'am, we are."

"No major injuries?"

"A few scrapes and bruises."

"Would you like something to drink? Coffee, water, a Coke? I'll ring the nurse."

"No thanks." He eased his stiff, sore body into the aluminum chair beside her bed.

"The doctor told me that if you had arrived two minutes later, I would be dead now, or in a coma, or blind."

Crocker pushed his short, thinning hair back and said, "I wish we'd gotten there sooner."

She bit her lip and looked down at the bed like a hurt little girl, which only added to the sense of intimacy between them. Her voice trembling, she said, "I thank God I'm still alive. But…but I'm also…distressed."

"I understand, ma'am. I heard."

She seemed different from the series of emotionally needy women he had dated and tried, unsuccessfully, to save, including his first wife. Mrs. Clark was more like Holly—graceful, self-confident, strong, and smart. Unlike Holly, she was the girl in high school who dated the quarterback of the football team and wouldn't have anything to do with wild, rough-mannered hooligans like him.

Now they were two mature human beings struggling to deal with a difficult situation.

In a small but clear voice she related the entire story of her kidnapping and what she had been through—her fears, impressions, descriptions of rooms, faces, the picture of La Santísima Muerte, the guards, the Jackal, her nightmares and dreams. She even talked about the problems she'd had as a young woman living in D.C.

Looking up at him with eyes pregnant with emotion, she said, "We live in a world of moral puzzles and strange connections. I don't understand them all yet, but I'm determined to keep trying."

He wasn't sure he understood what she meant, but he answered politely, "Yes, ma'am."

"But that's not what I want to talk to you about."

"Ma'am..."

She sighed. "Whatever responsibility I might have in what happened, as a senator's wife, and as someone who has made mistakes myself, my daughter, Olivia, is innocent. She didn't deserve this in any way, shape, or form."

"Of course not."

"She's a good kid, pure-hearted..." Lisa covered her eyes.

"When's the last time you saw her?" Crocker asked gently.

"I'm not sure. I was drugged. The doctors found opiates and benzodiazepines, specifically diazepam, in my system. It was either two or three days ago. I don't know."

Crocker knew that benzodiazepines were the chief ingredients of the most effective sleeping pills, and diazepam was most commonly found in Valium. "Do you remember seeing your daughter in Tapachula?" he asked.

Mrs. Clark nodded. "That's the last time, I believe. Very briefly when we got off the plane."

"That must have been two days ago."

"I think so. Yes."

"You remember the plane you flew in on?"

"Vaguely. Very vaguely."

"She was on it."

"I believe so."

"Was she present when you recorded your statement?" Crocker asked.

"No. I was waiting for her to appear, but she didn't. I didn't hear her there, either."

"What about the Jackal?"

"I had the impression that he would be there, but he wasn't."

"Who was with you at the end?"

"Guards, a video camera operator, and a woman who did my hair and makeup."

"How many guards?"

"The numbers and faces changed all the time. The first house we stayed in was bigger, newer, and more luxurious. Then about two days ago we were moved to the one in Tapachula."

"So the Jackal wasn't with you when you recorded your statement?"

"No, he wasn't."

Crocker rubbed his bandaged chin as he tried to put the pieces together.

"Did you see him leave, or hear a jet take off?"

"Not that I remember," she answered.

He nodded. "Anything else I should know?"

"Yes." She fixed her blue eyes on his and lowered her voice. "I know all about what the Mexican authorities said about the body, and the dental forensics that are taking place now. But I'm her mother, and I know she's still alive and is probably with the Jackal. I think she's in terrible, terrible danger."

He took her hand and held it as she wept, then handed her a Kleenex from the box on the table beside the bed. "If Olivia's alive, we'll find her."

"How?"

"I don't know, but we will."

Two Cuban doctors—one male and one female—sat across from Ivan Jouma and discussed the procedure step by step. They both wore white coats and serious expressions. The man clasped his hands together as he leaned forward and spoke in a deep voice. His beard and mustache were speckled with gray. The woman was younger, in her early forties maybe, with straight hair to her shoulders. They both wore old leather shoes.

As they related the possible complications, which included bleeding, infection, blockage of blood vessels, and leakage of bile, Jouma's mind drifted back to his grandmother and something she had told him as a young boy as they sat in the backyard under a ceiba tree husking corn. "Big fish eat little fish. That's the primary condition of nature. What separates us from savage, unruly animals is the concept of justice."

He didn't understand then, but he did now. *Justice*, he thought, *is what I've demanded since I was a kid living on the streets.* It hadn't been offered to poor *campesinos* like himself by Mexican institutions, courts, or society. So he had fought to achieve it himself, in the only way he knew how, with the resources he'd been given.

Justice, he repeated in his head.

To his mind, his quest to achieve it put him in the company of Gandhi and Che Guevara. All three were liberators and purveyors of people's rights. While Gandhi and Guevara had used the poor's outrage at being exploited, his strategy was different. He fed an insatiable need of the oppressor. The spiritual emptiness of rich people in the United States and Europe resulted in their need for drugs, which provided him a means to accrue money and power, thus tilting the scales of justice to his side of the equation.

Though depleted physically due to his own excesses, he was pleased with himself. Once healed and stronger, he planned to take his cause a step further and tell the Mexican people that it was time to rise up against their inept, corrupt government, which protected the rich from the poor and made them vassals of the United States.

It was his reason for being.

The doctors had stopped talking and were staring at him.

"Yes?" he asked.

"Did you hear us, Señor Jouma?" the male doctor asked

gently. "We asked if you have any questions about the procedure."

He shook his head. "No, not now."

"Then all you need to do is sign this consent form and we'll start early tomorrow, at six a.m. We ask that you don't eat anything after your dinner tonight."

He took the pen the doctor offered and signed the document.

"The surgery will take approximately six hours," the female doctor added. "Possibly longer. Afterward you will be taken to a recovery room, then to the ICU, where you'll be connected to monitors that will display EKG tracing, blood pressure, breathing rate, oxygen level. You can expect to stay in the hospital for two weeks."

"Yes."

"During that time you will likely have a tube inserted through your throat so that your breathing can be assisted by a ventilator. Another thin plastic tube might have to be inserted through your nose into your stomach to remove air that you swallow."

"When will it be removed?" The longer he was incapacitated, the more time rival drug traffickers and ambitious lieutenants had to take advantage.

"It will be removed when your bowels resume their normal function. You won't be able to eat or drink until we remove that tube, and will be fed through an IV."

"Then what happens?" he asked, calculating the timing of his return to Mexico.

"During this whole time, we will continue to monitor all your other body functions and immunosuppression medications. When we feel you are ready, you will be moved to a private room, where you will continue your progress."

"When will I get back to normal?" In this dog-eat-dog world he had to anticipate every danger and challenge.

"Everyone responds differently, so it's hard to pinpoint a specific time. But if there are no major complications, expect it to take twelve weeks."

"Twelve weeks." He thought he could handle that.

CHAPTER EIGHTEEN

A woman's guess is much more accurate than a man's certainty.

—Rudyard Kipling

AS **CROCKER** limped back to his room, his mind sifted through the things Mrs. Clark had just told him and settled on what he considered were two significant points. One, she had not seen either Olivia or the Jackal during the last four or more hours at the ranch. Two, the Jackal appeared to be in failing health.

What the two things meant, and how and if they were related to one another, he didn't know but hoped to find out.

Entering the room, he spotted four familiar faces: Akil's, Mancini's, Captain Sutter's, and Jim Anders's. The last was the one he least expected.

They all seemed to be mentally engaged in the same problem.

"Jim," Crocker said, addressing the deputy director of CIA Operations. "You come to try to help us save our jobs?"

"That's not my agenda. No."

"Then what's going on?"

"We just received a preliminary report from the Mexican minister of the interior," Anders said. "The results of the forensic exam were inconclusive."

Crocker leaned his back against the wall and let the implications of what he'd just heard process through his mind.

"When you say inconclusive, what does that mean exactly?" he asked.

"It means that the remains they recovered were in such a deteriorated condition that a definite conclusion couldn't be reached even with Olivia Clark's dental records."

"I'm not surprised."

"The question is, what if anything can we do now?" Sutter said as he rubbed his chin.

"I for one never thought it was Olivia Clark," Crocker declared.

"Me, neither," added Akil.

"Why not?" Anders asked.

"Because she wasn't at the ranch when we raided it."

Anders: "What are you basing this on?"

"What I just learned from Mrs. Clark and my own observations," Crocker explained. "Mrs. Clark told me that she didn't see either her daughter or the Jackal during the last day she was at the ranch, and according to the satellite photos, the plane they had flown in on had left. Once we secured the ranch, we searched the house and grounds thoroughly. Unless the guards disposed of Olivia's body, or locked her in some hidden underground chamber, she wasn't there."

"I agree," Mancini added. "She wasn't in the house. The Jackal wasn't there, either. I believe he moved her somewhere else."

"Where?" asked Anders.

Crocker shrugged. "Don't know."

As Crocker related what Mrs. Clark had told him about the last hours in the house leading up to the raid, Senator Clark entered silently and sat on the edge of the bed.

When he finished, Anders turned to the senator and asked, "Senator, what's your opinion about this?"

Clark raised his left hand, which held a rolled-up document. He said, "I've had the forensic report translated and read it carefully several times. It states that the fire was so hot and burned for so long that the jawbone the Mexicans recovered had almost completely incinerated and the front teeth were destroyed. All they had to go on were some badly cracked molars."

"That's a professional translation?" Anders asked. "Can I see it?"

"Of course."

As Anders perused it, Crocker asked, "What about DNA?"

"The high heat destroyed any DNA, which means we might never be able to ascertain one way or another," Clark answered. "But I'll tell you something that I believe is just as important: We're almost certain the Jackal escaped alive. And as long as we know that, there's a strong possibility that he took my daughter with him."

"Okay," Anders agreed. "But under what circumstances?"

Senator Clark seemed confused by the question. "I don't know what you mean."

"I'm not sure how to put this delicately," said Anders. "Did she go willingly?"

"Olivia?"

"I mean, are we talking about a possible Stockholm syndrome condition here?"

All eyes turned to Senator Clark, who rubbed his forehead and seemed to struggle to find the right answer. "If you're asking if my daughter has somehow bonded with that criminal and even become his lover, that's a hell of a difficult question for me. My response is, I doubt it, and the prospect frankly sickens me."

"I'm sorry."

"No, don't be sorry. Those are the kind of questions that need to be asked."

"If we're able to ascertain the reason they went off together and under what circumstances, we might begin to narrow in on a destination," Sutter suggested.

"Maybe."

"What do we know about the Jackal's movements since Guadalajara?" asked Sutter as he poured himself a glass of water.

Anders shrugged. "We know from the same source that told us about the ranch that he was with the two women in Tapachula, and we also know that the private jet he flew in on left sometime yesterday afternoon."

"The day of the raid."

"Correct."

"How do you know that?" asked Senator Clark.

"From satellite photos," Crocker answered. "The last one we saw taken at 1600 yesterday afternoon showed no jet on the airstrip."

"Maybe it was hidden in a hangar," suggested Anders.

"There was a hangar on the property, which we checked and found empty. It looked like it hadn't been used in weeks."

"How certain are you of that?"

"Ninety percent."

"Has the Jackal made a statement of any kind?" asked Sutter.

"Since the raid on the ranch?" Anders shook his head.

"So no one's seen hide nor hair of him, or heard from him, since Mrs. Clark spoke to him yesterday morning in Tapachula?"

"Based on the knowledge we have now, that's correct," Anders answered.

"What do we know about the plane?" asked Clark.

"It was a private jet."

"I found this," Crocker answered, opening the door to the closet and reaching into the dirty, blood-stained utility pouch for the documents he had recovered from the hut by the runway. They listed the plane's serial number (N662MS), purchase price ($8,950,000), and seller (Maxfly Aviation).

"Can I have them?' asked Anders.

"Of course."

"I don't know that these will do us any good, but I'll inquire."

Upon receiving the order from the Jackal, Nacho Gutierrez activated three of his best young *sicarios*—Guapo, Osito, and Stallone. Dressed in designer jeans, tight T-shirts, and leather sneakers, they looked like hip young men out for a night of clubbing. But the savage expressions in their eyes spoke to a more serious agenda.

High-level hits like this one were worth lots of *plata*— tens of thousands of dollars each, as well as perks like sports cars, SUVs, expensive watches, and their pick of beautiful girls kidnapped from Mexico, Texas, and California. It was a results-reward, high-stakes business.

Good results, lots of money. Bad results, a kick in the ass, or maybe a bullet in the head.

These three former members of the Mexican Navy boxing team took pride in their speed and cold-blooded efficiency. The first thing they did was locate Bob Marion of Global Banking & Investments, which took a couple of calls and a visit with his secretary as she was getting her nails done in a hair salon across the street from the office.

They caught up with Marion and a female companion two hours later as they were enjoying the salmon tartare *amuse-bouche* with a slightly chilled French rosé in the modern, atmospherically lit dining area of the chichi Lula Bistro in the Jardines de los Arcos area of downtown Guadalajara.

Guapo ("handsome" in English), who had a pleasant, boyish face and looked like a young businessman, waited in a café across Calle San Gabriel until Marion and his date exited arm in arm on their way for a nightcap and dancing at the nearby Ibiza Club, which featured nude dancers covered in gold paint and feathers in cages that hung from the ceiling. The Dutch record producer and DJ Tiësto was performing a set there tonight, and Marion had scored two very expensive and hard-to-get tickets from a friend who worked for the promoter who had booked the DJ into the club.

Outside on the rain-slicked sidewalk, he kissed his Versace-clad companion, then slipped a tab of Ecstasy into her sweet mouth.

"I feel like letting go tonight," he whispered, swallowing one himself.

"We only live once, Bobby."

Her name was Selvina and she was slim and model-tall with a mane of wavy hair and toned arms and shoulders. She was the only child of an Estonian mother and a Mexican father and had recently entered the intern program at the audit and risk review division at Banamex, which was the Mexican affiliate of Citibank.

Guapo put away his iPhone, crossed the street, and called, "*Hola*, Bob. Johnny Valdez."

"Who?" Marion asked.

"Johnny Valdez. We met at a party last month."

Marion, who was terrible at remembering names but good with faces, examined the young man's smooth features, ears that stuck out slightly, and defined jaw against the databank of images in his head. He noticed but wasn't alarmed by the black Cadillac Escalade that slid by and stopped at the curb.

"Don't you remember?" Guapo said, smiling and keeping up the false charm. "Tony Alvarez's house in La Florida?"

At the mention of the coworker who worked the Jackal's account and had recently been roughed up by a group of U.S. intelligence officers, Marion grabbed Selvina's arm and started to pull her across the street. As he maneuvered around the Escalade, the back door opened and Guapo pushed them both inside.

One of Selvina's new Prada high heels fell off in the

process, causing her to release a stream of Russian curse words into the dark interior. She stopped abruptly when a silenced Glock 9mm was pointed at her face.

As the vehicle moved quickly, Marion sat determined not to show any fear. He explained to Guapo that he had nothing to do with Tony Alvarez and demanded to know who the men were and what this was about.

Guapo reached past the girl and slapped the back of Marion's head so hard that it jolted him out of his cocoon of security and privilege. Marion started to worry that maybe he had been arrogant to think that playing both sides of the fence—Ivan Jouma and the FBI—wouldn't catch up with him.

But there was nothing he could do now but wait for an opportunity.

As the vehicle turned into an alley between two office towers, Guapo asked for their phones and Selvina's purse.

She was reluctant to hand it over but relented soon after Stallone grabbed the front of her dress and pulled so hard that the cotton-Spandex-blend shoulder straps snapped.

A very tense six minutes later, the Escalade entered the underground garage of a dark office building and wound down four levels to the bottom, which was being used as a storage area for desks, partitions, chairs, and other furniture and equipment. As he was dragged roughly from the vehicle, Marion said, "El Chacal is a close business associate of mine. He won't like this."

Without saying a word in response, Guapo duct-taped Marion's wrists behind his back, then taped him to an executive chair.

Marion watched dry-mouthed and trembling as Selvina's

dress and bra were ripped off, revealing the tattoo of a dragon on her lower stomach. The three men made a series of lewd comments about the meaning of the tattoo; then Stallone punched it hard, causing her to double over and fall to her knees.

"Tell me about the dragon," he said, grabbing her by the hair. "What's it mean, bitch?"

"Nothing," she whimpered.

"It's silly, like you. Isn't it?"

He grabbed her by the hair, lowered his zipper, and forced her to perform oral sex on him. Guapo snapped pictures with his iPhone, then took a turn. She spoke to herself in Russian and blubbered, causing black mascara to streak down her face.

How far are they going to take this? Marion asked himself as he stared at the ceiling and scolded himself for staying in town.

"Tell me what you want," he said, "and I'll give it to you now!"

Osito, who was the shortest and most muscle-bound of the three, ripped off Selvina's panties, leaned her over a desk, and started to sodomize her, which made Marion throw up over the front of his suit.

He tried to ignore the sound of Osito's pelvis smacking against Selvina's butt and the little squeals of pain that sometimes issued from her mouth. But that was impossible.

By the time Osito was finished, Selvina resembled a rag doll, stripped of will, humanity, and dignity.

Osito pulled out of her, shouting *"¡Olé!"* spun her so that she faced him, and shot her in the head. As Selvina crumpled to the cement floor, Marion lost control of his bladder. He decided he didn't care what came next, he just wanted it to end quickly.

Without asking him a single question, the three *sicarios* took turns beating him with bats and sections of pipe until all his teeth were dislodged or broken, blood dripped down the front of his suit, and his head was a throbbing, swollen mass of pain.

Then Guapo pointed a Glock to his smashed nose and asked him for descriptions of the four *gringos* who had executed the raid on the house in Puerto del Hiero. All Marion could remember was that they were Navy SEALs from a base in Virginia.

Slipping in and out of consciousness, he repeated that information twice and described the four men as best he could.

"Should we do the *guiso?*" Osito asked, pointing to some empty oil drums along the wall. The *guiso* was the practice of putting a victim in a fifty-five-gallon drum, pouring gasoline over him, and setting him on fire.

"Not here," Guapo said. "Too much smoke."

Instead, they stripped him naked, shot him in the groin, carved the word "*rata*" into his stomach, then used rope to string him and Selvina by their ankles from a pipe that ran along the ceiling.

The staff at what was now called the Hospital Santo Tomás needed the room, so Crocker, Sutter, Akil, and Mancini moved to a suite at the nearby Balboa Palace, where Akil and Mancini were staying. Despite its designation, it wasn't luxurious at all. Two and a half stars on Hotels.com with a slew of negative comments about the rudeness of the staff and the filth.

Crocker was too tired and preoccupied to give a shit about the peeling green brocade wallpaper, the stained pewter carpet, or the smell of mildew. It had beds and running water, which was all he wanted. In the shower, he remembered Mrs. Clark and her distress, which made him think of Holly. So he wrapped himself in a towel, closed the door to the bedroom, and called home.

"Holly. It's me."

"Tom?" she asked brightly.

"Yes, sweetheart."

"You here in the States?"

"No. But I've been thinking of you."

"Really? That's nice. You okay?"

"Yeah. I'm just mad at myself for missing your birthday."

"At least you remember that you missed it. That's something."

"You deserve better. I'm sorry. I was tied up."

She sighed. "I'm forty-two, Tom. I feel old."

"You're more beautiful than ever. I'll make it up to you."

"That's so sweet, Tom. How?"

"I'll surprise you."

"I'd like that."

"When I'm finished here, I'm taking two weeks' leave. And once Jenny is out of school, which won't be long, I'm gonna take the two of you to a beach somewhere where we can decompress and relax."

"Sounds great. She still wants to talk to you about colleges."

"Colleges, yes. I didn't forget," he lied.

"What about that place in the Yucatán, near Tulum?" Holly asked.

"Not Mexico this time. Someplace else."

Holly said, "I love the idea, Tom, but your timing stinks."

"Why?"

"I started back at work on Monday."

Crocker had forgotten that the six-month leave of absence she had taken from her job with State Department security after her ordeal in Libya had ended.

"So you decided to return?" he asked.

"Yes."

"And how did that go?"

"It's really good to be back among old friends who know me and appreciate what I went through. And it's nice to feel useful, too."

He had a lot of things he wanted to tell her but for the time being said, "I'm proud of you, sweetheart. I really am."

"Thanks. Tomorrow after work, I'm driving Jenny to a soccer tournament in Charlottesville. Her team made the state finals."

"That's fantastic. Is she there?" Crocker asked. Between recent missions in Venezuela, Israel, Syria, and Mexico, he'd missed every single game of the spring season.

"No, she's at her friend Leslie's working on a biology project, and sleeping over," Holly answered.

"Say hi to Leslie for me and tell Jenny I'm proud of her. I wish them both good luck."

"I will. You hear about the rescue of the senator's wife in Mexico?"

"Not really. No."

"I know you can't tell me where you are, but if you're near a TV, you should turn on CNN."

"I will."

They talked for ten more minutes about the new *Great Gatsby* movie, which she'd liked, and replacing some worn-out screens on the doors to the rear patio, which Crocker promised to take care of as soon as he got back. Feeling as though they were living in different dimensions of the same reality, he told her he loved her and Jenny and hoped to see them soon.

Then he turned on the flat-screen opposite the bed and found CNN International. The banner across the top of the screen read THE RESCUE OF LISA CLARK. As various correspondents spoke excitedly, the TV broadcast helicopter footage of the charred wreckage of the house. Then they interviewed local authorities and various drug cartel experts.

Most of it wasn't useful, but Crocker paid attention when one of the commentators pointed to a chart of the house that showed where Mexican authorities claimed they had found Olivia Clark's remains—near the front door. The theory forwarded by a former FBI cartel expert speaking by video feed from Memphis was that Olivia had attempted to escape when the fire broke out and was overwhelmed by smoke.

"Bullshit," Crocker muttered out loud. "Total crap."

When the expert conjectured that the rescue team had screwed up, because the first step in any rescue operation was to secure the hostages, Crocker shut the TV off.

He pulled on a shirt and a pair of running shorts he had borrowed from Akil and returned to the main room, where

Akil was on the phone ordering a late dinner. "You want a chicken sandwich, a burger, or a chef's salad?"

"What time is it?" Crocker asked.

"It's almost ten p.m."

"I'll take a chicken sandwich and a Diet Coke."

"Mayo, pesto, or BBQ sauce?"

"Just a slice of tomato and some fresh lettuce if they have it."

"At your service."

"You know if this joint has a pool or a fitness room?"

Akil turned to Mancini, who looked up from the magazine he was reading and said, "Boss, you can't go into the pool looking like that."

Crocker had forgotten the bandages that still dotted his torso, arms, and shoulders. "You're right. I think I'll go for a run."

"Now?" Akil asked. "What about your sandwich?"

"Keep your dirty mitts off it. I'll be back."

It took great effort, but Ivan Jouma found the energy to squirm out of the wheelchair, grab on to the windowsill, and, using both arms, pull himself to his knees.

As the muscles in his legs shook, he clasped his hands together and prayed:

"La Santísima Muerte, formed by the powers of the Almighty to be the protector of souls born to this earth. Mistress of the Darkness, I kneel before thee, placing my whole being into your hands, seeking your charity and your aid in the dungeon where I am chained.

"I place my faith and trust in you, Holy Mother of the

Heavens, to be my protector always, restore me and give me the strength to continue to fulfill my mission, which is to spread your magic on this earth, and to liberate my people from the yoke of oppression.

"I kneel before you, as they did in ancient times, seeking your aid and protection. Lift my spirit up, my mother, and lift it to the heavens. Heal my ravaged body with your magic. While I am weak, never let my enemies see me. Never let them hurt me in any way.

"Fill me with your dark, miraculous energy and make me more powerful and feared than ever, most powerful queen, and I pledge to give you everything that is mine in return. I am your child, your servant in darkness. Amen."

He took a moment to listen to the wind swirling outside and birds calling from one of the nearby trees. As he started to pull himself up, he heard a knock at the door.

"*¿Jefe?*" asked the voice on the other side.

"Yes. What do you want?"

"I have good news, *Jefe*," his aide said through the door.

"What?"

"Your nephew Luis called from California. He said that your horse Mr. Piloto won the handicap race at Hollywood Park."

"Señor Piloto?" the Jackal asked, trying to remember if he'd ever heard his nephew talk about that specific horse, or if he'd ever seen it. He'd purchased dozens of quarter horses over the past ten years and housed them in stables in Oklahoma, Texas, and New Mexico.

"He called it Mr. Piloto," the aide continued. "I wanted to tell you the news, *Jefe*, because I think it's a good sign."

"Yes, this is a good omen. Thank you."

"Goodnight, *Jefe*. Sleep well."

As Crocker ran along the bay, he focused on the red-and-yellow lights of boats moored in the water. Disparate images flashed in his head—his distraught father leaning over his kitchen table; Ritchie's bisected body lying on the ground; Holly sitting up in bed in a frilly white nightgown reading, her auburn hair framing her face; Mrs. Clark kneeling in the corner of the shower shivering; the Mayan woman who sold him the Datsun; the Ferris wheel spinning in the amusement park.

The seeming randomness of the images disturbed him, but he couldn't get them to end, even as he pushed himself harder and faster until his lungs burned and his whole body begged him to stop. Eight miles wasn't enough.

By the time he had logged ten miles and the images kept repeating and overlapping, he concluded that his brain had been affected by the chlorine poisoning. But that felt like an excuse, and what he wanted was a direction, or a sense of closure. So he kept pushing himself through the sweet night air.

At the fourteen-mile mark, he arrived at the uneasy feeling that some kind of danger waited somewhere in the dark and was about to strike. But as hard as he ran and concentrated, the why, where, who, and when eluded him.

At eighteen miles, he started to feel light-headed. And at twenty-one, he lost consciousness, stumbled, and fell in some long grass.

When he awoke twenty minutes later, he didn't know where he was, or how he had gotten there. He felt a sharp burning sensation just below his right knee where the flesh had been ripped away. And slowly the unease returned, and the dilemmas involving Captain Sutter and his job, and the situation with Olivia Clark, all came into focus.

As he groped in the dark and pulled himself up, he knew he had to do something to solve them. But he didn't know where to start.

CHAPTER NINETEEN

The only easy day was yesterday.

—A SEAL Team motto

AT SIX-FIFTEEN Friday morning, thirty-eight-year-old Gloria Maldonado stood before the closet in her small two-bedroom Guadalajara apartment, studying her figure in the mirror and trying to decide what to wear to work. She asked herself whether or not she should wake up her thirteen-year-old son, Ernesto, before she jumped in the shower, when she heard the doorbell ring.

"Ernesto, my love," she called, glancing at the clock and wondering who it could be at that early hour. Holding the bodice of her nightgown shut, she had turned and started out when she heard the front door open and her son call, "Mom, it's for you."

"Who?"

"Some colleagues from work."

She didn't know what that meant. Alarmed, she grabbed a

robe from the closet and put it on as she hurried to the front door to see who it was and what they wanted.

The three well-dressed *sicarios* told her that they had been sent by Nacho Gutierrez and needed her help with something immediately. She noticed dried blood on the sleeve of the good-looking one's shirt. Understanding that if Nacho wanted something, you didn't mess around, she threw on a blouse and skirt, combed her hair back, handed her son fifty pesos, and told him how much she loved him and that she wanted him to buy his lunch at school and take the bus.

The *sicarios* walked her to the Escalade, which was parked outside the entrance, and drove her to her office at Inicio, which was a division of Mexican Immigration. As they waited in the lobby, she hurried to her cubicle, turned on her computer, logged in to the system, and pulled up the immigration card that had been filled out by Thomas Mansfield, a Canadian who had arrived in Guadalajara a week ago with three other business associates. She printed out their passport photos and records and gave them to the *sicarios*, who discussed them in hushed tones as they escorted her back to the Escalade.

They didn't seem pleased or angry, so Gloria kept quiet. She didn't know if they were going to shoot her in the head and desecrate her body or shake her hand. After they drove her back to her apartment, they handed her seven thousand Mexican pesos (approximately $544.44) for her time.

She thanked them profusely and got out.

The *sicarios* turned the Escalade around and took off in the direction of a Zetas safe house near the University of Guadalajara campus. There they watched in wonder as a young one-armed computer hacker named Miguel X used various programs to search databases to try to locate someone named Thomas Mansfield who was or had been a Navy SEAL. When Miguel's efforts failed to produce a match, he tried the name of one of the men who had arrived with Mansfield, Manny DaSilva. That didn't work, either.

Miguel X, who tended to get hyper when he got stressed, offered the *sicarios* coffee and told them not to worry. He explained that he was going to load Mansfield's photo into a very advanced facial recognition software program called PicTriev and try to match it with visual images from various large databases on the Web.

The process took time, during which the *sicarios* fidgeted, bit their nails, checked their phones, riffled through Miguel X's collection of comic books and pornography, and smoked.

Twenty minutes later, Miguel X jumped up from his desk, boasting that he had found an 89 percent match with the photo of a U.S. Navy SEAL named Thomas Crocker, whose picture was published four years ago when he placed eighth in an Ironman competition in Lake Placid.

According to PeopleFinders.com, a man named Thomas Crocker, in his early forties, currently resided on Cherry Oak Lane in Virginia Beach, Virginia. Manny DaSilva, whose photo matched that of another Navy SEAL named Joseph Mancini, lived a quarter of a mile away on Palmetto Drive.

The *sicarios* rewarded him with ten thousand pesos and ten grams of high-grade cocaine.

Armed with the information about Crocker and Mancini, Guapo, Osito, and Stallone drove to Don Miguel Hidalgo y Castilla International Airport, where they texted Nacho Gutierrez, then caught a flight to Dallas–Fort Worth. Once they arrived in Dallas, they purchased tickets for a connecting flight to Reagan National Airport in Washington, D.C., then called a Zetas contact in northern Virginia and told him to meet them with an SUV when they arrived at 5:15 p.m. local time.

At eight the same morning, Crocker, Mancini, Akil, and Suárez arrived at Tocumen International Airport, after a short, sleepy ride from Panama City. They had just passed through Security and were buying coffee and sweet rolls from a vendor when they heard a message in Spanish and English over the PA telling a Thomas Mansfield to report to the airport information desk immediately.

"That's you, boss," Akil said.

"I remember my alias. Thanks."

Crocker found a Copa Airlines attendant, who pointed him in the direction of the info desk. There a dark-skinned woman wearing thick glasses examined his passport, then pointed to a green phone at the end of the counter.

"Hi," he said into it. "It's Tom Mansfield."

"Tom, this is Anders," the CIA officer answered. "I need you and your friends to meet me out in front of Terminal Muelle Norte a-sap."

"Some of us checked our bags."

"Forget about your bags. I'll have someone recover them for you."

"Okay. We'll be there in five mikes."

He found Akil chatting up two blondes near the departure gate. Leaning close to him, he whispered, "We're leaving."

Akil put his arm around Crocker's shoulder and winked at the girls. "This is my buddy Tom."

"Hi, Tom."

"Lisa and Tammy are surfers. They just got back from an island on the Caribbean side."

"Isla Bocas del Toro," the taller and blonder of the two girls said. "A real chill spot."

"Why is surfing like sex?" Akil asked.

"Don't know."

"When it's good, it's really, really good. And when it's bad, it's still pretty good."

"Yeah," Crocker said, smiling at the girls. "But you gotta excuse me, because I've got to borrow my friend for a minute."

"No problem."

Crocker pulled Akil ten feet closer to the departure desk and said, "Forget the chicks and the surfing and grab your gear."

"Now?"

"Anders wants us to meet him out front. Something important has come up."

Akil looked back at the two blondes and said, "This better be good."

Outside the most modern of the three terminals, Crocker and his men found Anders standing beside a new black Chevy Suburban. They squeezed in. Before the female driver even pulled away from the curb, Anders started to speak.

"There's been a change of plans," he said. "Based on some of the medical data you seized from the house in Tapachula and phone intercepts from the NSA, we believe that Olivia

Clark is with the Jackal in a nearby country, and about to become an unwitting organ donor."

The information hit Crocker like a slap to the head.

"An organ donor?" he asked.

"Yes."

"Fuck," Akil grunted. "Is that why he kidnapped her in the first place?"

"We believe so. Yes."

"So all that other people's liberation stuff is bullshit?"

"That's our current thinking. Seems like someone hacked into her doctor's medical files two weeks ago, so we believe the whole thing was planned," Anders explained.

"Sick."

"Which organ?" asked Mancini.

"The liver."

Akil: "Makes sense."

"Why?"

"He's a fucking drug dealer. Isn't he?"

"Where's Olivia?" Crocker asked as the vehicle accelerated.

"NSA traced the plane's flight path, then zeroed in on the cell phone of one of his doctors," Anders explained from the passenger seat. "It seems the transplant is scheduled to start tomorrow morning, so we've got to move fast."

"Okay. But where?"

"Havana, Cuba."

Suárez let out a hoot of joy from the backseat.

"Holy shit."

"Yeah, holy shit," Mancini echoed. "This is an interesting turn of events. I thought we were about to get court-martialed."

"You guys are going to have to go in scrubbed clean," Ander continued. "Completely black. No IDs, no phones, no documents or pictures or wallets, no jewelry, no names, nothing."

"I always wanted to go to Havana. How are we gonna get in?" Akil asked.

Anders directed the female driver to cross the Bridge of the Americas to the west side of the Panama Canal and the former U.S. Army base Fort Kobbe, which was now under Panamanian control.

Turning back to Crocker in the middle seat, he said, "We're going to use some assets we have here to drop you off the coast."

"When?"

"As soon as we get you geared up and prepped."

"How will we get out?" Crocker asked, thinking ahead.

"That's more problematic. We're working with some local assets we have in Cuba. It won't be easy. We figure there's about a twenty percent chance of success. Your call."

Crocker took a moment to consider the grisly alternative. When he turned to check with them, all three men nodded.

"We're in," he said.

"Good."

"Has this op been cleared by the White House?"

Anders grinned. "Officially, they know nothing about it. Nobody in the U.S. government knows anything about it. Unofficially, the president finds the organ-harvesting scheme reprehensible and wants us to do anything we can to save the girl."

"Good."

"But if anything goes wrong, he's going to deny he's ever heard of you or the mission."

"Understood."

"You can't be captured. That can't happen. If any or all of you are killed by the Cubans and they're able to ID your bodies, we'll say you went rogue. Won't be too far from the truth, with the way you've been handling ops recently."

Crocker nodded to indicate that he understood. "Where's Captain Sutter? Does he know about this?"

"He just landed in Miami. I spoke to him a few minutes before I contacted you and filled him in. He's okay with it, if you are."

"You said Olivia Clark's in Havana. Do you have a fixed location?"

"Yeah. The Cira García Clinic, which is a private hospital that caters to rich foreigners. It's located on the west side of the city, not far from the coast, a couple blocks from the Almendares River. There's a big park there where you can land. I'll show you a map."

They were passing over the canal now. Crocker had never been to Cuba, but he'd heard a lot about it over the years and had always been intrigued. The prospect of sneaking into Havana and rescuing a hostage right under Fidel and Raúl Castro's noses appealed to the daredevil in him.

"How's this gonna work?" he asked.

"We're planning to drop you in the Straits of Florida and having you swim in, up the Almendares River," answered Anders as the female driver turned off a road on the other side of the bridge and stopped at a gate guarded by Panamanian soldiers.

"According to the latest phone intercept, the transplant's

scheduled to start at 0600," Anders continued. "So we're thinking of launching at around 0200."

A soldier checked the driver's credentials, recorded the number of passengers and the license plate number, then waved to another soldier, who opened the security barrier.

"We're gonna need a jump platform, fixed wing or rotor, parachutes, a Zodiac, Drägers, black skin suits, masks, fins, watertight bags, compasses, and weapons," said Mancini.

"We'll take care of all that now."

Guapo descended the escalator to the baggage claim area at Reagan National Airport with his two compatriots and spotted a stout, no-necked man on the left holding up a sign with his name scrawled on it. He stopped in front of the man and said in English, "I'm Guapo. Who are you?"

"Lionel Mendoza," the man said. "Nacho sent me."

"A pleasure to meet you. You have a vehicle for us?"

"Yes, it's parked outside. You need to pick up your luggage?"

"We don't have luggage," Guapo answered.

"Then I'll show you where it is."

They followed the man's short legs into a parking structure and rode the elevator to Level 4. There he led them to a silver Toyota RAV4, reached into the pocket of his shirt, and handed Guapo the keys.

"Here."

"Equipment?" Guapo asked.

"Three hush puppies"—Smith and Wesson M39s with detachable suppressors—"with ammo, incendiary grenades, gaffer's tape, rope, ski masks, three prepaid cell phones. Programmed into each cell phone is a number. You need any-thing, or when you're finished with the vehicle, call and we'll pick it up. The SUV has a full tank of gas and is equipped with a Garmin GPS. Those were my instructions. Anything else?"

Guapo thought for a moment and said, "I think we're okay."

"Good."

"You want us to drop you off somewhere?" Guapo asked.

"No thanks. I have a ride. Good luck."

Twenty minutes later, they exited the Washington Beltway onto I-95 South. The female voice on the Garmin instructed them to take Exit 84A and merge onto I-295 South.

Approximately three and a half hours after they left D.C., the three *sicarios* arrived in Virginia Beach. It was almost 9 p.m., so Osito used his iPhone to consult Yelp.com and find a place to eat. He chose the Abbey Road Pub on Twenty-Second Street, because his older brother was a Bea-tles fan and *Abbey Road* was one of the CDs that played over and over in the bedroom they shared growing up. The three men ordered shrimp cocktails to start, followed by the prime rib *au jus*.

A quartet of middle-aged *gringos* played Beatles songs on a little stage at the end of the room. Osito thought their rendition of "Blackbird" with mandolin accompaniment was particularly good. He sang along on the final verse, and when they left, tipped the quartet twenty dollars.

An hour later, their bellies full, the Garmin directed them to Tom Crocker's residence on Cherry Oak Lane. They found a dark street with two-story gray clapboard houses spaced at least fifty feet apart, surrounded by tall trees and backed with marshland.

"*Quieto*," Guapo commented.

"*Muy quieto. Sí.*"

Number 2040 was set a hundred yards back from the road behind a patch of oak and poplar trees. As they passed, Guapo glimpsed yellow light glowing on either side of the front door and inside the house on the first floor. He parked farther down the street near some tall trees and got out. He saw no sign of people, just trees swaying in the breeze, and the moon playing hide-and-seek behind high clouds.

A dog barked vigorously from inside Crocker's house when he rang the bell. No one answered. Glancing at the houses to the left and right, he noticed that both were completely dark and there were no cars in either driveway.

Guapo glanced at his watch, which read 10:16, then circled to his left to the garage, which was empty. Continuing to the back of the house, he peered through a glass door and saw a single light on in the kitchen and a German shepherd barking from a doorway behind it.

Returning to the SUV, he said in Spanish, "No one's home."

"We should break in and wait inside," Osito suggested. "That way we can drink his beer."

"*Gringo* beer tastes like piss. We'll wait here."

The copilot of the unmarked C-23 Sherpa turned to Crocker, sitting on a bench along the fuselage, and held up ten fingers. Crocker nodded and looked at his watch. It was 0220 and the altimeter indicated that they were flying at 8,223 feet.

The SEALs had used the thirty-odd minutes of the flight to don their jump gear and conduct riggers' checks on the parachutes to make sure they were folded and packed properly, then inventory their first-, second-, and third-line gear.

Each man carried a watertight weapons bag with Heckler & Koch 45 automatic pistols with Ti-RANT suppressors, MP7A1 submachine guns with extended forty-round magazines, optics, flashlights, and four-inch silencers. Also included in their first-line gear were wet suits, NVGs, pocketknives, Leatherman knives with some 550 cord wrapped around the handles, handheld radios, dummy cord, compasses with self-luminous tritium light sources, Phoenix IR strobe beacons that issued a personal combat identification (CID) that was invisible to the naked eye but could be spotted through NVGs at twenty miles away, Oceanic OC1 Titanium Dive Computer watches, and Rockwell PSN-11 Precision Lightweight GPS receivers.

The secure (Y-code) differentials on the GPS units allowed the users to receive 24/7 2-D and 3-D positioning anywhere on the planet with the help of twenty-two military satellites without giving up the users' location. They were accurate to within less than a yard and weighed a mere 2.7 pounds each with batteries installed.

As the lead swimmer, Akil also wore a special miniature underwater GPS (MUGR) with position and navigational information that would allow the team to enter the Almendares River without coming up to the surface. It was preprogrammed with charts of the river and maps of the city that showed the target location (Clínico Central Cira García) and the exfil point a block and a half away.

Second-line gear carried in their backpacks included re-breathing Drägers, dive masks, fins, six extra magazines for each weapon, grenades (M18s and M67s), strobe lights, blowout patches, MREs, gloves, and water purification tablets.

Each man also carried third-line gear appropriate to his specific role on the team. Crocker, as the corpsman, packed an emergency medical kit, which included multi-trauma dressings and a needle for a possible thoracentesis. Suárez, as the team breacher, had various explosives, timers, detonators, and fuses.

In his pack, Mancini lugged a high-tech pneumatically fired grappling hook called a Rescue Air Initiated Launch (RAIL), which consisted of a black cannon about the size of a man's arm that could launch a metal grappling claw attached to a nylon-jacketed line over 150 feet.

Crocker helped Akil secure the F47OU Combat Rubber Raiding Craft (CRRC or Zodiac) to the wooden platform, which involved inflating the 75-inch-wide by 185-inch-long boat with CO_2 cartridges, then tying the IR chemical light to the bow and stern, fastening three paddles to the side, and stowing the air pump and hose in the pockets in the right front and left rear. Next they placed a thirteen-by-thirty-six-inch piece of honeycomb on the floor of the boat and stowed and secured the engine and fuel tanks. Finally they lashed the CRRC to the platform, secured a G-12 cargo parachute with the rise compartment facing up, then installed a 5,000-pound M-1 release.

Once that was accomplished, Crocker huddled the men together in the rear of the fuselage and went over last-minute details.

"We're gonna deploy our chutes low, at two thousand feet. The CRRC is going down first. Hopefully it makes it intact. If it goes down like a lawn dart and disappears into the water, the aircraft will drop us at an alternative DZ and we'll have to swim in turtle-back."

"Why didn't we bring an extra rubber ducky?" Akil asked.

"Because they didn't have one," Mancini growled.

"Assuming the Zodiac makes it," continued Crocker, "we're gonna ride to within fifteen hundred yards of the coast and swim from there. Akil is carrying the MUGR. He'll lead the way. Once we enter the river, we're gonna swim over two tunnels, then under the Calle Eleven Bridge. The river will bend sharply to our left. That's where we surface, in the vicinity of Parque Almendares."

"Currents and tide could be an issue, so if we reach a second bridge, the Calle Forty-Two Bridge, we know we've gone too far," Akil pointed out.

"Correct," Crocker shouted over the engines. "The clinic is four blocks west of the park on Avenida Forty-One. Akil will be primary point to and from the target."

"What do we do if we're compromised by dogs, guards, or policemen?" Mancini asked.

"We take 'em out. We can't risk capture. Each of us is carrying a couple kill pills. I don't need to tell you what they're for."

"What about civilians?"

"Situation dictates. Use your judgment."

"What are our actions at the objective?" Suárez asked.

"We conduct a thorough search for the hostage. It's a three-story structure. CIA believes that the operating rooms are on the third deck. We find her, secure her, kill the fucking scumbag Jackal if we can find him, and get the fuck out of there. Then we hightail it to the exfil point, which is in front of a small park a block and a half southeast. We're supposed to rendezvous with a guy named Flores, who will be driving a small blue-and-white tourist bus with '*Vizul*' written on it."

"Flores."

"Yeah, Flores. He's gonna put us on a DHL cargo jet that will take us to Miami."

"How come we're not flying FedEx?" Akil asked.

"Because FedEx is an American company, and they don't like Americans. The Cuban authorities fucking hate us. DHL is German owned."

"They gonna seal us in a box?"

"I don't care what they put us in. Neither will you at that point. Get jocked up and ready for the jump."

Guapo, Osito, and Stallone sat in the RAV4 taking turns watching Crocker's driveway. When no one arrived by 2 a.m., they took a vote and decided to try Mancini's house, which was a couple of blocks south. Palmetto Drive was even more desolate—a two-lane country road with modest one-story ranch houses on large plots of land. Number 1005 featured a front lawn half the size of a football field, with an American flag hanging from a pole in the middle next to a family of ornamental deer. To the left of the deer stood a dark blue Real Estate Group FOR SALE sign.

Guapo parked the vehicle in a church parking lot across the street. From that vantage, they saw a late-model blue Mustang resting in front of the two-car garage. Lights shone through the front windows.

The *sicarios* tucked Glocks into the back waistbands of their pants and crossed together. Through sheer white curtains they saw the profile of a man sitting in a brown recliner watching TV. The theme song from *Friends* wafted under the front door.

Guapo indicated to the other two men to hide in the bushes on either side of the door; then he rang the bell. Ten seconds later, a hand pushed aside the curtains, and a bearded face peered out at him. Guapo smiled, waved, and pointed to the door.

Mancini's young brother, Paul, opened it a crack and spoke past the safety chain. "What d'you want?" he asked.

He'd been living there for three weeks now and planned to stay until either the house was sold or he traveled to College Park, Maryland, to start engineering school in the fall. His brother's wife and two young sons had recently moved to a new colonial-style house farther south on Dam Neck Road.

Guapo flashed his friendliest smile. "Sorry to bother you," he said, "but my car broke down, and my cell phone is out of juice."

"You live nearby?" Paul asked.

"I drove down from New Jersey. I'm visiting my cousin."

Twenty-three-year-old Paul, dressed in shorts and a sleeveless Terrapins T-shirt, gave him the once-over. "Wait here," he said, "while I get you the cordless."

"Thanks."

Half a minute later, when Paul reached through the door to hand Guapo the phone, Guapo grabbed him by the wrist and pulled him forward abruptly. Though Paul was strong enough to have won several fights as a UFC light heavyweight before he ripped the rotator cuff in his left shoulder, he was caught off guard, fell forward, and slammed his forehead against the doorframe, which caused him to drop the phone. Guapo aimed the silenced Glock through the crack in the door and shot him once in the side of the head. Paul groaned, "What the fuck did you do that for?"then slumped to the floor.

Guapo instructed Stallone to run back to the Toyota, bring it around to the front of the property, and keep the engine running.

Then he and Osito entered the house and searched the bedrooms. In a closet they found old camouflage boots and uniforms. Aside from clothes, some furniture, and a few items in the kitchen, the house was empty.

Miguel X had told them that the SEAL named Joseph Mancini was married. But the two *sicarios* saw no evidence of a woman or any other person living in the house. So they dragged Paul's big body back to the recliner, sat him in it, wiped the butt of the Glock clean of fingerprints, and placed the pistol in his hand.

They used rolled-up newspaper to set the curtains and rug on fire before they exited.

"One *gringo* down," Guapo announced when he returned to the RAV4 and flames lit up the night sky. "One more to go."

CHAPTER TWENTY

Everyone has a plan until they get punched in the mouth.

—Mike Tyson

AT 7,980 feet the back door of the C-23 Sherpa aircraft swung open and Akil pushed the platform with the Zodiac, forty-horsepower engine, fuel tanks, and paddles out. The SEALs waited until the CRRC landed safely in the water. Once the aircraft circled back over the target, Crocker gave the signal to jump.

He loved to free-fall, even if this was only a hop and pop at two thousand feet. Still, it was exhilarating—diving like an eagle through the fresh ocean air and steering the risers toward the Zodiac with Havana glowing in the distance.

He and his men had trained hundreds of times for infils like this, and they executed this one to perfection, all splashing down within ten yards of the boat.

They slammed into action immediately, cutting the CRRC from the wooden platform, inflating the keel (a fin at the bottom of the boat that helped convert sideways force into forward propulsion), attaching the engine, loading their gear, and assuming their preassigned positions in the boat.

"Ready?" Crocker asked Akil, who sat next to him in the stern.

"Ready, boss."

He fired the engine as Akil fixed the location (approximately 23.10 north/82.22 west) on his digital compass. The boat took off with a low growl.

"¡Cuba libre!" Suárez shouted from the bow.

The temperature hovered at around eighty-two degrees Fahrenheit, and there was a mild nine-mile wind blowing in from the east. The tide had started to recede, and the current in the Straits of Florida wanted to pull them northwest into the Gulf of Mexico.

Crocker and Akil worked in tandem to keep the boat on course. All four SEALs were wearing a combination of Sharkskin with Polartec lining and more lightweight Lycra dive skin, which Crocker preferred.

As the Zodiac climbed up moderate swells and rode down, the men slipped Rocket Fins over their IST Proline 3mm boots and got the LAR V Dräger rebreathers ready to strap to their chests.

Crocker had chosen a DZ west of the commercial shipping lane into the port of Havana. When he saw the lights of a vessel to their left, he instructed Akil to cut the engine. The four men paddled, making little progress against the current.

"We need to pick up the pace," Crocker said as the muscles in his back and shoulders started to burn.

Once the lights faded out of sight, he instructed Akil to restart the engine and checked his watch, which read 0417.

They had to move faster if they were going to reach the target on time.

Crocker visualized the mission in his head—the bridge and tunnels, the bend in the river, Almendares Park on their right. When they got within a mile and a quarter of shore, Mancini spotted another vessel directly ahead through a pair of Night Owl Tactical Series G1 Night Vision binoculars. He couldn't tell if it was a Cuban patrol boat or a fishing vessel puttering along the coast. The SEALs cut the engine again and paddled.

Cuban security forces were no joke. Led by Commander in Chief Raúl Castro, they consisted of a highly trained and largely Soviet-equipped army, navy, and air force. In the past they had foiled a number of CIA plots, including the 1961 U.S.-planned invasion at the Bay of Pigs.

When the boat got within three quarters of a mile of the coast, Crocker saw additional small vessels ahead to their left. He said, "Strap on your Drägers and get in the water. We'll sink the Zodiac here and swim."

First they dropped the engine and fuel tanks into the bay, and then they attacked the rubber vessel with Leatherman knives.

The water they dove into was cool and pitch black. They swam in teams of two, connected by a swimmer's lanyard, with forty-pound packs on their backs and waterproof weapons bags slung across their shoulders, secured with bungee straps. Crocker was paired with Akil; Suárez followed with Mancini.

Akil led, focusing on the luminescent dials of his dive compass and MUGR GPS, while Crocker timed each leg with his watch. Every fifteen minutes of swimming at a particular bearing, he'd squeeze Akil's arm, which signaled him to stop and reset the direction on the compass.

The Drägers recycled the air they were breathing into a closed circuit, where it was filtered of carbon dioxide. As a result, the SEALs were taking in pure oxygen and not producing bubbles, which was ideal for a clandestine mission like this. But there were drawbacks. One, the closed-circuit underwater breathing apparatuses (CCUBA) were only operational at a maximum depth of seventy feet. And two, since the men were breathing pure oxygen, they could only use the Drägers for four hours before the high concentration of CO_2 became toxic.

Each diver constantly monitored the primary and backup gauges, which measured the oxygen pressure in the loop. A low concentration could result in hypoxia, unconsciousness, and eventual death. A dive exceeding O_2 depth-time standards could produce hyperoxia and convulsions, which could cause a diver to lose his mouthpiece and drown. Crocker had seen it happen.

It took them an hour and a half of vigorous swimming to reach the mouth of the Almendares River. Now it was 0458, according to Crocker's watch.

The water was murkier and the current hit them head-on. Crocker squeezed Akil's shoulder, indicating that he wanted him to pick up the pace.

Akil did for a leg and a half, but as they approached the first tunnel, he stopped, looked back at Crocker, squeezed his arm three times, and pointed to the MUGR, which detected the presence of a sonar device to spot intruders and submerged vehicles. Crocker passed the three-squeeze message to the next diver, Mancini, who relayed it to Suárez.

Mancini, who was the only man wearing DVS-110 underwater night-vision goggles, located the square sonar device on a pylon that rose four feet from the top of the tunnel. Akil led the team in formation along the west shore of the river and circled around the back of the pylon. He disabled the sonar device by cutting through the cable with his knife.

Just when Crocker's body begged him to stop, he felt an enormous rush of adrenaline that pushed him past the second tunnel and under the Avenida Septima Bridge. It was another quarter mile to the park. His legs and shoulders burning, he glanced at the luminescent dial on his watch: 0518 hours.

He squeezed Akil's shoulder again, and the two men pushed their bodies harder than they wanted to go.

Crocker was concerned about overswimming the rigs and developing a CO_2 hit, which felt like an ice pick thrust into your brain. Reaching the bend in the river that marked the location of Parque Almendares, Akil stopped, changed bearing, and continued the leg until they neared the shoreline. Even in less than three feet of water, the SEALs were undetectable from the surface.

Akil conducted a slow, quiet recon of the beach, exposing only the top of his hooded head and mask. When he saw that all was clear, he squeezed Crocker's shoulder four times in succession, which was the signal to climb up the rocky slope to shore.

They peeled off the Drägers and masks and replaced their diving boots with black ankle-high trekking shoes that they'd carried in their packs. Then, moving together, they removed their weapons from the watertight bags and slipped the Drägers back into the water, along with the discarded dive boots, fins, weapons bags, and masks, tied to their weight belts so they wouldn't resurface.

Akil, in his role as point man, led the way through the park, which rested deep in shadows with secrets hidden behind Spanish moss. They passed the figure of a life-sized *Tyrannosaurus rex*, then entered a narrow street with large houses behind overgrown walls that ran into one another. Akil indicated "heads down," and they knelt behind an ancient Mercedes sedan as a delivery truck with only one working headlight rumbled past and turned.

The sun was starting to rise past Crocker's right shoulder. His heart leapt when he recognized the Clínica Central Cira García on the corner—an image he had memorized. The white-and-beige three-story layer cake looked like it had been built in the 1950s.

Akil turned right and hugged the wall along the opposite side of the street from the circular drive in front. Then he looked in both directions for oncoming traffic and motioned to the men to cross.

They passed through a modest-sized parking lot that was empty except for an old Toyota van and a newer Russian-built sedan and hid behind thick tropical foliage that covered the end of the building that had no windows. Crocker decided this was a good place for Mancini to launch the cannon-shaped RAIL, which made a loud whistling sound as its titanium claw shot into the air and landed on the roof.

As the lead climber, Crocker tested the sturdy nylon-jacketed line to make sure it was secure to the lip, then proceeded to grapple up the side of the building the way he'd done so many times on oil rigs and ships.

"Show-off," Akil whispered as he joined him on the roof, lugging his pack, ammo, and weapons.

The four SEALs knelt on the flat surface and huddled around Crocker. He used hand signals to remind them that he and Suárez would enter the third deck and clear right while Mancini and Akil cleared left.

Suárez readied an explosive charge to blast through the door. But it wasn't needed, because the door was wired shut. Mancini snipped it open. Heckler & Koch 45 automatic pistols and MP7A1 submachine guns ready, they ran down the concrete steps.

A split second after entering the fluorescent-lit hallway and turning right, Crocker saw a soldier in a blue-and-white uniform hurrying toward him carrying a Soviet-made SKS carbine. The man looked like he couldn't believe what he was seeing. Before he was able to shout a warning, Crocker cut him down with three 4.65x30mm rounds to the chest.

When the guard's SKS banged against the linoleum floor and echoed, the element of surprise was lost.

Olivia Clark lay on something soft. She wanted to focus and see where she was but couldn't lift her head. Nor could she see, because a strong light blinded her.

Her body felt as though it had been inflated with air.

Something brushed across her arm, sending shivers up into her neck and head.

"Miss Clark, can you hear me?" a gentle voice asked in accented English.

She tried to say the word "yes."

"Please squeeze my hand."

As she squeezed, someone pressed a rubber mask over her nose and mouth. She inhaled something with a metallic sweetness, then lost consciousness and drifted across a black sea that seemed to go on forever.

She drifted until light broke through the darkness and she heard the sound of voices whispering in Spanish.

From near the ceiling, she looked down at heads and figures in light blue and white huddled on either side of a long table. Lights, monitors, and little tables were scattered behind them in no order. When they stepped back, she saw a woman lying on her back, with long blond hair. She was naked from her neck to her groin, which was covered with a white sheet, and she had a clear tube in her mouth.

She appraised the young woman's smooth pale skin and the contours of her breasts and stomach, then realized she was looking at herself, or someone who looked just like her.

A male doctor wearing a face mask stood to the right of a table covered with stainless steel instruments. Behind the table hung a thick blue curtain.

The doctor gestured to a female doctor who was looking at a machine with glowing numbers.

Olivia watched as the doctor pressed two fingers into the flesh on the right side of her abdomen, beneath her diaphragm and above her stomach. Then he used a little sponge to paint iodine on her skin. He stopped, placed a hand on her forehead, and grew still, as though he was saying a prayer.

When he finished, he nodded to a female nurse, who grabbed the blue curtain and pulled it aside with a metallic squeal. On the other side sat another long table, occupied by a man with sallow skin, covered with a blue blanket and breathing through a tube.

The doctor turned to him and pulled away the blanket, revealing catheters in the man's neck and groin. Then a nurse placed a scalpel in the doctor's white-gloved hand and he started to cut into the man's flesh.

The blade made a slanting incision just under the ribs on both sides of the abdomen that extended up over the breastbone. It passed through a layer of skin, white muscle, then pink flesh, and deeper through darker stages of red to dark red and almost brown.

The male nurse helped the doctor attach a circular clamp that pulled the man's abdomen wide open and exposed his organs. Then the doctor carefully placed several metal clamps over arteries and veins to stop the blood flow to an organ that had a rough nodular surface.

He handed the scalpel back to the nurse, who set it on the little table and replaced it with a clean one.

The doctor turned, leaned over Olivia, and started to cut.

Sadness came over her as she watched from the ceiling. She wanted to beg him to stop, but the command from her brain didn't seem to reach her body. Or did it? Because suddenly the doctor stopped and looked up as though he was going to address her. Instead, he turned to a woman in a white blouse and black pants standing at the door and shouted something in Spanish.

Crocker had entered eight rooms along the right side of the hallway, most of which held sleeping patients, and reached a double door, which was locked. His heart beating hard, he reared his right foot back and kicked it open. Immediately a woman charged at him, screaming. He shoved her away with his left arm so she fell back and hit the wall.

"Where's the American girl?" he asked, grabbing her roughly by the jaw. "¿Dondé está la niña? ¡La niña Clark!"

"¡No puede entrar!" the woman spat back.

He didn't see the scalpel in her left hand. As he leaned over, she reached up and cut him across the chin.

Crocker elbowed her, causing her head to snap back, and she lost consciousness. Crouched and ready in case someone else entered, he quickly taped her mouth, wrists, and ankles. He rose and checked the double doors to the operating room on his right. They were locked. So he took three steps back, lowered his left shoulder, and crashed through.

Blood spilling from the wound to his face, he confronted five shocked people in surgical masks—two doctors (a man and a woman) and three nurses (one of whom was a man). Seeing that he was armed, several of them raised their hands over their heads, and all of them backed away to the wall.

Breathing hard, he evaluated the situation in an instant: the two patients on separate operating tables—Olivia Clark on the one in front of him and the darker-skinned older man to his left. Both were connected to monitors, breathing through tubes, and had incisions in their abdomens, though the man's was much bigger and wider.

Out of the corner of his eye, he saw the male nurse duck behind a monitor and dash toward a fire alarm switch on the wall.

"¡Pare!" he shouted, training the MP7A1 on the nurse.

The nurse continued, so Crocker squeezed the trigger and cut him down, splattering blood against the wall and over the dark-skinned man on the operating table. One of the women screamed.

"Quiet!" Crocker growled. "Another sound or sudden movement and you'll all be dead! *¡Muerto!*"

The male doctor nodded vigorously; others started to cry and pray out loud.

Crocker removed the handheld from his pants pocket and spoke into it urgently: "I need help at the east end of the hall. I found her."

His mind moved fast, trying to ascertain how to get Olivia out safely and deal with the people in the room.

"Is that Ivan Jouma?" he asked, pointing to the man on the operating table with a clamp holding his abdomen open. "Is that the man known as the Jackal?"

The male doctor shrugged.

"You speak English?"

"A little, yes," the doctor said through the white surgical mask.

Crocker ripped off the mask. "Is it Ivan Jouma, or isn't it?"

"It is," the bearded doctor said. "We had orders to do this. It wasn't a choice."

Crocker crossed to where Jouma was lying, removed the forced-air blanket, and ripped the tubes out of his mouth, stomach, groin, and arm. The female doctor gasped.

"He'll asphyxiate," she said in accented English, shooting him a hateful look. "Because of the anesthetics, he can't breathe on his own."

"Good."

"It's not good. No."

She lunged forward and retrieved the breathing tube.

Crocker stopped her. "You want to die for this criminal?" he asked her.

The woman stared at him through black-rimmed glasses and shook her head vigorously. "No. I have a family."

"Then sew the girl up. Quickly!"

She turned to the male doctor and started to stammer. "He...Dr. Ramos...he only started to make the initial... t-transverse sub-subcostal...incision, but because of the location I don't know if the sutures will hold."

"How deep is it?" Crocker asked.

"How deep is what?"

"The incision, goddammit. How deep?"

"Only as far as the skin and rectus sheath."

"Then staple her together," Crocker ordered. "She's coming with me."

The two doctors moved toward the operating table, mumbling to the nurses in Spanish. Crocker, who didn't trust them, watched carefully as they prepared to close the incision.

Suárez entered, crossed to him, and whispered in his ear, "We've got to go, boss. Two guards are down. Manny and Akil are holding six people in a room at the other end of the hall."

Crocker pointed his elbow at the table where the doctors were working on Olivia. "They're closing her up now."

"Is that the Clark girl?"

"Yeah. And that's the Jackal."

Jouma made a painful choking sound and stopping breathing. His face froze in an awful grimace. Crocker checked his pulse.

"Dead."

"Excellent," Suárez said. "I hope he burns in hell."

"What have you given her in terms of anesthetics?" Crocker asked the female doctor.

"Fentanyl and naropine," she answered.

"I'm gonna need a thick robe to keep her warm, slippers, a cap of some kind, morphine for pain, and antibiotics to guard against infection. I'm also going to need a laryngeal mask so we can remove her breathing tube. Do you have one?"

"I think so." The woman bit her lip nervously. "But they're in another room."

"Close by?" Crocker asked.

"On this floor."

"Okay." Turning to Suárez, he said, "You go with her."

They left together. Crocker watched the male doctor staple the three-inch-long incision shut, spread local tissue glue over it, and cover it with white gauze and tape.

The doctor warned, "You have to keep her dry and avoid sudden movements. Get her to a hospital as soon as possible."

Crocker continued to scan the room with a straight finger over the trigger, measuring each second in his head, expecting Cuban soldiers to burst in any minute. The male doctor smeared antibacterial cream on the cut across his chin and covered it with a gauze bandage. Then Suárez and the female doctor returned with the supplies.

"You found the LMA, good," Crocker said. "Now hand over your cell phones."

Suárez collected them in a plastic bag. Simultaneously, the female doctor removed the breathing tube from Olivia's throat and inserted the laryngeal mask, or LMA, which would allow her to breathe on her own until the anesthetic wore off.

Satisfied that it was working, Crocker spoke into the radio: "Manny, we're moving. Lock the people in, take their phones, warn them not to try to leave for thirty minutes, and meet us at the stairway."

The male nurse helped Suárez transfer the still-unconscious Olivia to a gurney.

Crocker faced the Cuban doctors and nurses and warned, "I have men guarding the building, so stay here and don't move for thirty minutes. If you do, they'll shoot you dead. After thirty minutes, you're free to leave."

He and Suárez wheeled Olivia out, then inserted a metal pole through the door handles to bar it from the outside and met Manny and Akil at the stairway. Because of the gurney, they elected to take the elevator. The ground floor of the clinic was completely quiet and the front door locked.

Crocker grabbed Suárez and pointed to a small park across the street. "Go locate the driver. His name is Flores and he should be driving a blue-and-white van with 'Vizul' painted on it. Tell him to pull into the driveway so we can load the girl."

"Will do."

CHAPTER TWENTY-ONE

*Opportunity does not knock, it presents itself when you
beat down the door.*

—Kyle Chandler

CROCKER WAS standing beside Olivia, monitoring her breathing, when he saw Mancini in his periphery, pointing to the clock on the wall: 0628. He nodded. Precious time was slipping past. He knew that if they didn't get out of there soon, they'd be screwed. Looking through the glass front door, he saw Suárez running back.

"What happened?" he asked.

"The van's not there," Suárez reported, out of breath.

"You sure?"

"I checked all sides of the park. There's nothing there. No vehicles."

Crocker slapped Akil's shoulder and pointed to Olivia. "Watch her."

He dashed out the door into the clinic parking lot and found a faded silver 1992 Toyota Previa van in the corner under a tree. The driver's-side window was broken, so he reached through and let himself in. Using the expertise he'd gained as a wayward teenager, he quickly hot-wired the engine, which clicked in a steady rhythm, indicating that the timing belt needed replacing or the transmission was screwed up.

Crocker put the van in first, spun it around into the circular drive, got out, and helped load Olivia in. Her temperature and pulse felt normal. They carefully laid her across the rear seat. Akil knelt beside her.

"Keep monitoring her vital signs," Crocker instructed. "If anything changes, let me know."

"Roger, boss."

"We going to the airport?" Mancini asked from the middle seat.

Crocker steered the van onto a sleepy residential street green with lawns and palm trees as he considered. "Probably not a good idea, since the local contact didn't show," he said. "The Cuban authorities might be waiting for us. Let's get out of Dodge and head toward the coast."

"East or west?" asked Suárez from the passenger seat. "East will take us over the bridge into old Havana."

"West is closer to Florida, correct?" Crocker asked.

"Yeah. And it's the direction we're headed now."

"West is good."

"Then what?" asked Akil.

"Who the fuck knows? Keep your weapons out of sight and try to look inconspicuous."

"Now that we're here, let's find out where the Castro brothers live and kick their asses," Akil suggested.

Suárez said: "Great idea."

Crocker found Akil's face in the rearview mirror and grunted, "Keep watching the girl and keep your big head down."

The Toyota puttered down a stately avenue with a divider in the center featuring elaborate curved street lamps. Behind walls and gates on either side stood large old houses. Most of them looked like they could use a coat of paint.

"This area is called Miramar," Suárez explained from the passenger seat. "Back in the day, it's where wealthy people lived. Most of these houses were taken over by embassies and Cuban government agencies."

"Won't this shitbox go any faster?" Mancini asked.

"Forty seems to be its max," Crocker groaned back.

Traffic was sparse and most of the cars were old—Chevys, Fords, and Buicks from the 1940s and '50s and several Soviet-era Lada sedans, jeeps, and wagons. When they passed a red-and-white car with elaborate fins, Akil asked, "What's that?"

"That's a fifty-eight Edsel Corsair," Mancini answered. "The first car to come with a rolling dome speedometer, push-button transmission, and warning lights."

Crocker heard a siren approaching and pulled over as two red fire trucks sped by going in the opposite direction.

"Someone at the clinic pulled an alarm," Mancini conjectured.

Crocker: "You're probably right."

When they reached a traffic circle, he took a road that brought them within a block of the coast. The houses and businesses were more spread out and dilapidated and the few people on the sidewalks looked indigent and spaced out on either booze or drugs.

"I see the beach," Akil said, pointing to the right.

"How do you feel about swimming back to Florida?" Mancini cracked.

A white police car with blue-and-red lights flashing turned on the avenue and took off east.

"What do we do if we hit a roadblock?" Suárez asked.

Crocker spotted a sign for the Havana Yacht Club ahead—an elegant building surrounded by lush green grounds. "Check it out."

"My uncle told me about this place," Suárez said. "Back in the fifties, it was the scene of fabulous parties with movie stars like Rita Hayworth and Marlon Brando."

"Looks like a sleepy-ass retirement home now."

Crocker saw three armed guards at the entrance, which caused him to change his mind about entering.

"How's she doing?" he asked Akil in back.

"She's moaning and moving. I think she's about to wake up."

They had left the city and were passing a large mural with Fidel's grinning face on it and a revolutionary slogan painted in red. Traffic was even more sporadic. A glance at Crocker's watch revealed that it was 0713. A white-and-blue helicopter flew past in the opposite direction.

Beyond palm trees on the right, he saw a series of canals with pleasure boats and an entrance.

"What's that?" he asked.

Suárez shrugged.

The sign read MARINA HEMINGWAY.

Crocker drove past the entrance and stopped along the beach. He put the van in neutral, stuck the silenced .45 under the back of his black T-shirt, stuffed the radio in his pocket, and said, "If you don't hear from me in five minutes, keep driving along the coast until you find a boat you can hijack. Key West is about a hundred miles north."

"Where the hell are you going?" Mancini asked.

Crocker was already out and climbing a rusted fence at the edge of the marina. He hurried along the closest parallel canal, which was lined with cruisers and sailboats, looking for an opportunity. As he approached a twenty-seven-foot Carver Santego named *Seas the Day*, he heard a woman's voice speaking English. He jumped aboard, ran down three steps, and entered the door to the galley.

A middle-aged man and woman sat at a table eating scrambled eggs. He said, "Excuse me for barging in. Are you Americans?"

The man looked up warily. He had sharp features and thinning blond hair. "Maybe. Who are you?"

"Me and my associates just rescued a kidnapped girl. We're working with the U.S. government and need assistance."

The man groaned, stuck a forkful of eggs in his mouth, and swallowed. "Look," he said, "my wife and I arrived yesterday to do some marlin fishing. We're on vacation."

His rail-thin wife said, "We're neutral when it comes to governmental matters. You should try someone else."

Crocker wasn't sure what she meant. "I can shoot you both here and take your boat, or you can help me."

The man rose to his feet like he was about to start something. Crocker grabbed him by the front of his T-shirt and pointed the .45 at his chest.

"This isn't up for debate," Crocker said. "A young woman's life is at stake."

"They've got our passports," the man said, pointing outside. "They monitor everything."

"Who?"

"The *guardias* and dockmaster. They're nice guys, but all business."

"Don't worry about your passports. I'll get you new ones," said Crocker. "What's your name?"

"Darrell," the man answered.

"Okay, Darrell," Crocker offered. "You're gonna start the engine and act like you and your wife are taking a little excursion down the coast."

The red light on Crocker's radio flashed. He answered it. "What?"

It was Mancini asking him if he was okay.

Crocker said, "I've got a boat. We're gonna pull out of the marina in a couple minutes and head west. It's a white cabin cruiser named *Seas the Day*."

"What do you want us to do?"

"Follow us along the coast while we look for a place to load you."

Crocker put the radio down and turned to Darrell, whom he was still holding by the shirt. "If we cruise up the coast, will that raise suspicion?"

Darrell looked at his wife, who shook her head. "We've got a fishing permit. Probably not."

"Good," Crocker said. "Let's go."

As he let go of Darrell, his wife said, "I don't like this."

"You'll be doing a good thing."

"Darrell," she started, stepping into the doorway to block him. "Don't."

Her husband pushed by her and climbed the steps to the cockpit, where he started the engine and flicked on the transmitter.

"Tell me what you're doing," Crocker said as he knelt on the steps out of sight.

"I'm going to inform the dockmaster we're leaving. You can listen if you want. He's on channel sixteen."

Turning back to the cabin, Crocker saw the wife reach for something in a drawer by the sink. "You want to die?" he asked, aiming the .45 at her. He pointed to a red-leather-covered bench on the wall opposite him. "Sit over there with your hands on your lap and keep quiet."

She complied. Meanwhile, Darrell had steered the boat into the main channel. As they passed the dockmaster's station, a man emerged waving a red flag.

Crocker asked, "What's he want?"

"He wants me to pull over."

At that same approximate moment, Crocker's handheld flashed. "What?" he asked in a low voice.

"The girl threw up!" Akil exclaimed. "She's choking."

"Reach in her mouth and remove the breathing device. Then sit her up and clear her throat."

Darrell steered the boat alongside the dockmaster's station and idled the engine. A burly mustached man in a white shirt and blue shorts pointed to the ocean and shouted something in Spanish as seagulls circled over his head.

"Okay, boss. She's better," Akil said over the radio. "But she seems disoriented and is asking for her mother."

"Calm her down," Crocker whispered. "Tell her she'll see her mother soon."

Crocker watched from the steps as Darrell shouted back to the dockmaster, waved, and shifted out of idle. The boat puttered out of the channel.

Seeing the bay in front of them, Crocker asked, "What was that all about?"

"He was telling me that fish are biting farther west near Mariel," Darrell answered, donning a pair of sunglasses and a white captain's hat.

"West is good, but hug the coast."

A mile or so later, he spotted a pier at the end of a stretch of beach and instructed Darrell to pull over. The SEALs loaded Olivia Clark aboard as some local fishermen watched. Then Darrell set a course north toward Key West.

Shortly after midnight Sunday morning, the C-12 Huron that Crocker flew on landed in Virginia Beach. Relieved, exhausted, and sunburned, he drove himself home and pulled into the garage. The light in the kitchen, which Holly usually left on at night, was off. He figured that she and Jenny were still in Charlottesville attending the high school state finals soccer tournament and the bulb had burned out.

So he hit the button that activated the device that automatically closed the garage door and climbed the wooden steps to his office. As he entered, he was confronted by a familiar thick, sweet smell, which reminded him of death and caused the little hairs on the back of his neck to stand up.

He had returned the .47 and MP7A1 to the CIA officials who had greeted them in Miami, so he was unarmed except for the Leatherman knife he carried in his bug-out bag. In the dark, he set the bag on the office floor, then crossed to his desk and opened the bottom right-hand drawer, where he kept a 9mm automatic and six-inch suppressor.

Something told him not to open the door to the kitchen. So he quickly screwed on the suppressor and retraced his steps down to the garage and out the side door. The three-quarters moon had turned the sky a dull shade of blue, and frogs croaked from the marsh behind his house.

At the rear left corner, he checked to see if the small back-yard was clear, then peered through the glass patio door. The moon that shone over his shoulder illuminated the gray-tiled kitchen floor. On the right, between the island and the stove, he saw something dark, which he made out to be the head of his dog, Brando.

He tapped the glass, but Brando didn't move, causing Crocker's sense of urgency to rocket from zero to a thousand. He'd been trained and selected for his ability to remain calm in the face of danger, but this was different. It was his dog, his house, and his fucking family!

He couldn't remember when Holly had told him she and Jenny were scheduled to return, or even if she had related that information.

Trying to contain his rage and figure out what was going on, he circled to the other end of the house, then crossed the eight feet of lawn into the woods. He crouched behind a tall oak tree and looked over his shoulder to the other side of the house and the driveway to see if Holly's Subaru was parked there and he had missed it when he drove in. That was when the cell phone in his back pocket sounded, playing the opening of "Sympathy for the Devil" by the Stones.

He quickly pushed the silence button. The call was from Mancini, so he let it go to voice mail.

Instead of wondering why Mancini had called, he was relieved that the Subaru wasn't there, which meant that Holly and Jenny weren't home yet.

He waited a minute and listened, in case someone in the vicinity had heard the phone. But nothing moved or sounded, except for the leaves of the trees gently rattling overhead.

He moved stealthily from tree to tree until he neared Cherry Oak Lane. A silver Toyota SUV sat parked to his left in front of one of the houses being built on the cul-de-sac. He studied it from twenty yards away. Through the windshield he made out the dark shadow of someone in the front seat.

Remembering what Sheriff Higgins had told him in Guadalajara about the viciousness and reach of the Mexican cartel leaders, he thought he knew who it might be. It could also be a cop from Fairfax, or another foreign enemy. That didn't matter now.

Calmly, he circled left through the woods, over an old fence, around the bare wood skeleton of the half-finished house, to a Porta Potti standing near the curb. From that vantage, he was three yards from the back of the SUV.

The man in the driver's seat was smoking a cigarette. Crocker saw white smoke waft out the side window and closed the gap quickly with the pistol ready, safety off. When he was halfway there, headlights climbed the hill at the other end of the lane and lit up the street. He recognized the shape of Holly's Subaru as it braked and turned left into the driveway.

The man in the SUV flicked the cigarette out the window

and opened the door. As sparks skipped off the asphalt, Crocker grabbed him by the back of his collar, spun him around, and squeezed him so tightly around the neck that the young man's eyes started to pop out of his head.

"Who the fuck are you?" Crocker whispered into the man's dark eyes.

The man mouthed the words *Fuck you*.

In the moonlight Crocker saw the black-and-gold Mexican passport in the console between the two seats and thought he had his answer.

He raised the pistol, fired two bullets into the young man's head, watched the life drain out of him, and let him go. As the man slumped to the pavement, Crocker heard Holly telling Jenny to grab the suitcases out of the back of the car, and alarms went off in his head.

He ran as fast as his tired legs would take him through the woods in the direction of the house, screaming, "Holly, hit the ground!"

Crocker knew he was letting emotion determine his behavior, but he couldn't stop himself. Just then someone opened fire from a position to his right. A bullet tore into his left arm just above the elbow, and he stumbled and fell face-first to the hard ground. Still, he had enough presence of mind to roll to his right, into an elderberry bush, as the two shadows moved closer.

He fired into them. A man screamed "*¡Mierda!*" and fell. Then he heard the explosion that lifted his whole body off the ground and knocked him unconscious.

When he came to seconds later, he saw the whole front of his house in flames. He pulled himself up desperately and ran toward it shouting, "Holly! Jenny!"

More shots rang out. A round caught him in the back of the thigh, causing him to stumble and drop the pistol. But he wouldn't let it stop him. Ignoring the bullets whizzing past, he pushed himself forward.

When he reached the Subaru, he saw a bleeding, half-conscious Jenny lying near the rear bumper, trying to pull herself up. And in his left periphery, he saw a man with a pistol charging from the woods.

As the running man aimed the weapon at Jenny, Crocker screamed, "No!" and grabbed the hilt of the knife and threw it—the way he'd practiced hundreds of times as a kid. The knife flipped end over end and embedded itself at the base of the man's neck, causing him to fall backward and fire wildly into the air.

Starting to feel light-headed and trying to stem the blood pouring from the wound to his thigh, he saw Holly lying on the asphalt by the front of the car, holding her leg. Jenny stood beside him, her young face twisted into a mask of horror and desperation.

She pointed to the burning house and choked out the word: "Leslie!"

Crocker tried to find the strength to ask who Leslie was, then remembered that red-haired Leslie Ames was his daughter's best friend and soccer teammate. The last realization he had was that Leslie had entered the house and set off the booby trap the Mexican had fixed to the kitchen door.

He told himself he had to rescue her. He pushed, tried, and cajoled. But his body wouldn't respond and the scene around him wobbled. Then, feeling as though he was sinking to the ground, he passed out.

Five days later, armed navy security officers escorted Crocker and his daughter, Jenny, from the Navy Gateway Inns & Suites, where they were living temporarily, to a black Ford Taurus parked alongside the curb. As the car headed north on semirural Birdneck Road past the Owl's Creek golf course, he sat deep in his own thoughts.

His sense of bereavement was profound. He and his family had lost their home, their dog, a majority of their personal possessions, and most importantly, their sense of security. His teammate Mancini had lost his brother. Holly remained in the hospital, recovering from the shards of wood and glass that had punctured her liver.

There was irony in that, he thought as he gazed out the window. But it gave him no comfort and taught him nothing, except to underline the fact that evil was an active force that had to be guarded against and eradicated.

As much as he thanked God for sparing his wife and daughter and tried to focus on the positive, his sense of violation wouldn't go away. SEALs like him were trained to endure pain and difficult combat, but personal attacks on their families weren't supposed to occur. Certainly, not by foreign criminals operating a few miles from ST-6 headquarters.

Again, he vowed to punish the people responsible and never let anything like that happen again. But the pledge felt hollow this time, and even as he made it, he wondered if he shouldn't consider moving far away from Virginia Beach and find a new line of work.

The car turned right onto Mill Dam Road and slowed in

front of the high school. Feeling a combination of confusion and anger, Crocker turned to Jenny beside him on the back seat and saw that she, too, was deep in thought, probably remembering her late friend.

The strength and dignity Jenny had demonstrated so far had been incredible. Considering her young age and the fact that she had suffered from emotional difficulties in the past, he wondered how much longer it would last.

"You okay, sweetheart?" he asked, taking her hand.

"Yeah, Dad. I'm fine."

He leaned across the seat and kissed her on the cheek.

"I'm proud of you, sweetheart," he said as she opened the door and climbed out.

"Thanks, Dad."

As she stood on the sidewalk and adjusted the straps of her backpack, Crocker saw that she was pausing to look at the flag that flew at half-mast and a large smiling photograph of Leslie Ames printed on a sheet affixed to the brick wall. Written underneath were the words "You'll be in our hearts forever" and the letters "RIP."

He worried that the weight of what had happened would hit Jenny again and she wouldn't be able to continue. Kids milling under the portico and in the entrance became aware of her presence and stopped and turned silent.

As she lowered her head, a boy called out, "Welcome back, Jen!" Other kids started to applaud and the outpouring of emotion spread. Another boy offered to carry her backpack, and kids of various ethnicities and backgrounds gathered around to hug and kiss her and pat her on the back.

Seeing this filled Crocker with unexpected hope. It was difficult at times to understand whom specifically he and his men were fighting for and why they made the sacrifices they did. But when he saw these young people, he knew.

As one of the navy security officers put the Taurus in gear and drove away, Crocker thought of Ritchie. Sometimes the gap between the living and dead seemed vast and incomprehensible, and other times the dead seemed present, as Ritchie did now. Crocker sensed him in the shadows near the opposite window and imagined him saying, *Suck it up, boss, and fight on.*

ACKNOWLEDGMENTS

Don and Ralph would like to thank all the remarkably skilled people at Mulholland Books / Little, Brown who made this book possible—including Wes Miller, Amelia Possanza, Sabrina Callahan, Pamela Brown, Ben Allen, Barbara Perris, and Kapo Ng—and our excellent agent at ICM Partners, Heather Mitchell.

We also want to express our warm appreciation to our loving and supportive families: Don's wife, Dawn, and his daughter, Dawn; and Ralph's wife, Jessica, and his children, John, Michael, Francesca, and Alessandra.

ABOUT THE AUTHORS

DON MANN (CWO3, USN) has for the past thirty years been associated with the U.S. Navy SEALs as a platoon member, assault team member, boat crew leader, and advanced training officer, and more recently as program director preparing civilians to go to BUD/S (SEAL Training). Until 1998 he was on active duty with SEAL Team Six. Since then, he has deployed to the Middle East on numerous occasions in support of the war against terrorism. Many of today's active-duty SEALs on Team Six are the same men he taught how to shoot, conduct ship and aircraft takedowns, and operate in urban, arctic, desert, river, and jungle warfare, as well as close-quarters battle and military operations in urban terrain. He has suffered two cases of high-altitude pulmonary edema, frostbite, a broken back, and multiple other broken bones in training or service. He has been captured twice during operations and lived to talk about it.

RALPH PEZZULLO is a *New York Times* bestselling author and an award-winning playwright and screenwriter. His books include *Jawbreaker* and *The Walk-In* (with former CIA operative Gary Berntsen), *At the Fall of Somoza*, *Plunging into Haiti* (winner of the Douglas Dillon Award for Distinguished Writing on American Diplomacy), *Most Evil* (with Steve Hodel), *Eve Missing*, and *Blood of My Blood*.

If you have enjoyed Hunt the Jackal, why not catch up on Thomas Crocker and SEAL Team Six's earlier adventures?

SEAL Team Six: Hunt the Wolf

When Crocker's team learn that young girls are going missing all over Europe, they are determined to track down the ruthless men behind the kidnappings. But as they follow the trail from Scandinavia to the Middle East, they find themselves facing a web of terrorist cells with more terrifying ambitions than they could have imagined.

SEAL Team Six: Hunt the Scorpion

A series of attacks all over the globe are linked by a single, deadly intent: someone is gathering everything they need to make a dirty bomb. The terrorists behind it are shadows; their targets unknown. Thomas Crocker and his team need answers. They need to go to the source: to find the material the terrorists are searching for, and stop it falling into the wrong hands.

SEAL Team Six: Hunt the Falcon

The team's number one enemy, Iranian terrorist Farhed Alizadeh, codename 'the Falcon', resurfaces as the mastermind behind a series of attacks on American diplomats across the globe. Crocker and his men are ordered to bring him to justice, and their hunt leads from Bangkok to Caracas, and finally to Iran itself, when the team go in 'full black' to take down their mark.

All available in print and eBook from Mulholland Books